LONDON
SPY

Also by Tom Rob Smith

Child 44
The Secret Speech
Agent 6

The Farm

TOM ROB SMITH

THE COMPLETE SCRIPTS

LONDON SPY

SIMON & SCHUSTER

London · New York · Sydney · Toronto · New Delhi

A CBS COMPANY

First published in Great Britain by Simon & Schuster UK Ltd, 2016
A CBS COMPANY

1 3 5 7 9 10 8 6 4 2

Simon & Schuster UK Ltd
1st Floor
222 Gray's Inn Road
London WC1X 8HB

www.simonandschuster.co.uk

Simon & Schuster Australia, Sydney
Simon & Schuster India, New Delhi

A CIP catalogue record for this book
is available from the British Library

Trade Paperback ISBN: 978-1-4711-5943-5
eBook ISBN: 978-1-4711-5944-2

Printed and bound by CPI Group (UK) Ltd, Croydon, CR0 4YY

MIX
Paper from
responsible sources
FSC® C020471

Simon & Schuster UK Ltd are committed to sourcing paper
that is made from wood grown in sustainable forests and support the Forest
Stewardship Council, the leading international forest certification organisation.
Our books displaying the FSC logo are printed on FSC certified paper.

London Spy: The Complete Scripts
By Tom Rob Smith

Introduction

A Note On Lies

The blanket ban on gay men and women working for the intelligence agencies was a statement that gay people couldn't be trusted with the protection and security of their country. They could be tolerated by society, not imprisoned, although some lamented that concession, but under no circumstances were they allowed to offer their lives in service of society. The rationale, if that isn't too lofty a term for bigotry, for this ban can be roughly summarized — gay people spend their life lying, and hiding, and concealing the truth, therefore they're susceptible to blackmail. It was a savage irony that these kinds of laws made it necessary for many to hide their sexuality thus making them open to blackmail in the first place. It was akin to punishing a person and then refusing to employ anyone who has ever been punished.

Growing up with deceit as a necessary means of getting by — in some cases, an act of self-preservation, in others, as a means of protecting their relationships with their families — exacts a price on many people.

We will love you as long as you lie about who you are. With Alan Turing in the back of my mind, it seemed to me that if someone was going to bring all lying to an end, it might be a gay person, a man or woman obsessed with the notion of truth because they're grappling with the question every day. It should be remembered that even today the statement 'I am gay' is not accepted by many as a truth; they dismiss it as words from a mind not functioning correctly, a sickness that can be treated. With the mind 'cured', the person's thoughts would revert to the only truth that they believe exists — 'I am straight'.

While some have disliked the revelation at the centre of *London Spy*, to me, it was never about the real world of espionage, which is largely, today, about preventing terrorism. Terrorism, which is about hatred, has nothing to do with this story, which is about love. For a character who has spent his life lying, including to the only person he has ever loved, I wanted him to create some way of telling him that their love was, at least, true.

A Note On The Scripts

It would be wrong to call these scripts the 'Shooting Scripts'. Instead I've opted for 'The Complete Scripts', which refers not only to the fact that all five episodes are included but also material that wasn't filmed and the longer original ending.

Some of the variations between the script and screen version are small, some are more significant. Most strikingly, I've reinserted the original ending. I never had any desire to extend the story beyond these five episodes. This is a story about Danny growing up. He's naive and innocent in the opening and, by the end, he's found some measure of himself as a man. You can only grow up once.

A Note On Storytelling

One lengthy sequence present in the script but not in the show is located towards the end of episode two. I have a fondness for storytelling as a device. Episode two features two train stories: one is narrated by Scottie, about meeting a mysterious man on a train, and then Danny finds himself plunged into a strange variation of Scottie's story, where he encounters a mysterious man on a train. Throughout these scripts people tell each other stories. Some I've invented, others are out there in the world, in circulation, parables, fables, fairy tales and jokes. In the spy world, telling stories is intriguing because you can tell the same story to different people and it will mean something entirely new; to some it will merely be light-hearted, to Danny, in this instance, it is a threat. Yet as he tries to unlock the nature of that threat, he's grasping at smoke, because the speaker can shrug and say it was a story they heard some place else. I've noticed people do this with jokes, too; they're framed as merely a joke, when they can often be intended to insult, or upset.

A Note On Fear

People have rightly pointed out that there's nothing frightening about having an HIV test, it's necessary, vital, in fact, the facilities in the UK are excellent, and I agree. I had three HIV tests during the writing of these scripts — the writing took place over three years. The health care professionals were always exceptionally kind and supportive. The scene in the episode called 'Blue' was never about a fear of being tested. In the script Danny discovers, while waiting for his test result, that his entire medical history has been altered, he's being set up — his body is being set up, his very biology is being staged. He isn't afraid of the test, he's afraid of the power of his enemies, their ability to go to any length against him.

A Note On Writing Scripts

There's considerable detail in some of these scenes. I'm told it's unusual. Writers are given a number of arbitrary rules about writing screenplays. My sense is that the writer should put down whatever he or she believes to be relevant to the story. Tell it how you see fit. Be sparse, be detailed, be whatever you like. If people are gripped they'll finish the screenplay, if not, they won't, so the risk has always been the writer's to weigh up.

A Note On Love

It has been claimed that writing a show with a gay love story could only be in service of an 'agenda' or a 'quota' or it's a political statement, compared to writing a straight love story, which is about writing a love story. Needless to say, I found the terms of this debate depressing. There are so few gay love stories dramatized that maybe I should have weighed the desire for happiness more carefully. While I can't imagine what a happy ending would have been, in narrative terms, I'm sad that I wasn't able to give those viewers who have written to me the kind of happiness they sought from the show.

   With all that said, it's time to bid these characters a fond farewell. I've lived with them for many years and I'll miss them very much.

Tom Rob Smith, March 2016

EPISODE ONE:

"LULLABY"

EXT. LONDON. VAUXHALL. MI6 HEADQUARTERS. NIGHT

The Headquarters of British Intelligence. An embassy of
secrets. Intense security. Cameras. Bomb proof walls.

A cab parks outside. A young man steps out. Mid-
twenties. Lean and handsome. He's Danny. His clothes
are cool and casual. His hair styled.

Danny turns his back on MI6, crossing the street. We
follow him to the opposite side --

Gay clubs, bars and sex saunas, underneath railway
arches. People queuing to gain entry to the clubs.

With a Saturday-night swagger Danny bypasses the queue,
saying hi to many. Known by most. Danny gives the
bouncer a handshake. And is ushered in. A socialite.

As the door opens we do not follow Danny inside,
catching a fleeting glimpse of intense lighting.

The doors close --

EXT. VAUXHALL. RAILWAY ARCHES. DAWN

The doors are thrown open --

Danny emerges. Pupils huge. Skin sweaty. Re-presented
with the world, he seems cowed by it.

His swagger gone, Danny appears gaunt rather than lean.
His clothes are club-grimed. His hair dishevelled.

The 'gay strip' is quiet. A few hardened souls. A few
taxi drivers hawking trade.

To the side of the club there's no queue, no people, just
the fencing & the hoarding, flat on the ground.

The area is deserted. The buzz is gone.

Danny tries to swallow: it's painful. We hear the sound
of his throat, the movements, dry slow swallow of spit.

He takes from his pocket the pack of cigarettes. It's now
utterly crumpled and smashed. He opens it.

Inside is an empty drug bag. And a single crushed
cigarette, broken in half.

Danny tries to light the broken half but the lighter
pathetically sparks with no flame.

His hands are trembling.

He gives up.

He walks forward, looming over him is MI6: the building means nothing to Danny. His eyes slide across it without catching on it.

He takes out his phone. He dials. His voice is broken. Fragmented. Slow.

> DANNY (ON PHONE)
> Hey guys... if you get this
> message... I wanted to know... if
> you were still... up... I don't
> feel like... being alone... if
> you're still up... ring me...

He hangs up. He shuffles off.

EXT. VAUXHALL. CENTRAL ROAD JUNCTION. DAWN

The enormous road junction at the heart of Vauxhall. Normally full of traffic. Now eerie-empty.

Danny crosses into the central pedestrian reservation, automatically trudging towards the passage under the train tracks, on auto-pilot, heading home.

But he stops, staring at the tunnel, a route he's taken many times. He looks in the opposite direction, towards the bridge & the morning sky.

Danny - surrounded and dwarfed by the huge empty roads - lingering and deciding.

And, finally, he changes direction, walking towards the river. Passing MI6, he doesn't even glance at it.

EXT. LAMBETH BRIDGE. DAWN

In the middle of the deserted bridge Danny looks out over London, The Thames & Parliament.

His beautiful-saucer-eyes dart about, perplexed by this world. Drugs push his thoughts close to the surface.

He takes out his phone. And considers. We can see he knows, on every level, that this is a terrible idea. Except he does it anyway.

He dials.

The phone rings. Danny prepares what to say. The phone is answered. Danny about to speak but he's abruptly cut off. We don't hear what is said, if anything.

Danny's stunned. Offended. Finally, he's hurt.

In an act of frustration Danny leans back, arm behind him, ready to throw the 'fucking-phone' into the river but he stops, frozen in this javelinesque position.

His eyes switch from the river to the phone. From sadness and anger to pragmatic. He changes his mind.

At this point Danny realizes he's being watched.

An early morning runner, standing some five or so metres away. Dressed in sleek pro gear. Athletic. Handsome. Roughly the same age as Danny.

He seems to be assessing Danny as though he were a peculiar but not uninteresting phenomenon.

We have no idea how long he's been there.

Danny is struck by how handsome this man is. And straightens up, trying to return to normal society mode, and not entirely succeeding.

He wags the phone, explaining why he didn't throw it.

> DANNY
> It would've been satisfying...

As he wags it the phone slips out of his sweaty fingers and hits the pavement, smashing.

The runner and Danny stare at broken fragments. Danny smiles, a smile becoming a laugh, a laugh becoming a world weary sigh. The runner simply observes.

Danny crouches down and starts to pick up the pieces.

To his amazement the runner joins him. Even though it's pointless, and the phone can't possibly be fixed.

With his hand full of fragments the runner carefully - slowly - tips his small collection into Danny's palm.

We hear the faint sound of the metallic and glass tinkle, as though there were no other competing city sounds.

Eye to eye with this man, Danny knows not what to say. That flint-spark of an inexplicable connection.

The runner's voice is educated, gentle, the emphasis and rhythm of his words unusual.

> MYSTERIOUS RUNNER
> Are you okay?

> DANNY
> Me? I'm fine. You don't know me
> but if you did you'd know that I'm
> always fine.

The runner observes Danny's pupils, without judgement, and offers a sports drink affixed to his arm.

The runner spots a bead of sweat pooling on Danny's face, rolling towards his eye. Instinctively his hand flicks out, catching it.

Danny observes this. The runner is embarrassed, as if he's gone too far. He abruptly leaves.

> DANNY
> What about your drink?

Several strides away, the runner glances over his shoulder, bashful and apologetic.

> MYSTERIOUS RUNNER
> You can keep it.

With those words he's off. Danny's left alone.

INT. WAREHOUSE. DAY

A huge warehouse. A maze of tall steel shelves full of goods. Danny's collecting orders, holding a computer device that maps the shortest route between items.

Danny isn't come-down sad. Distracted. Daydreaming.

And then the device bleeps angrily: "Increase speed".

INT. WAREHOUSE. TOILET CUBICLE. DAY

Danny stands in one of the cubicles trying to urinate. Sweating. Straining. A tiny amount of gloppy orange.

INT. WAREHOUSE. TOILET. DAY

Danny running his face under the flow of cold water at the sink. He takes small sips.

INT/EXT. TRAIN CARRIAGE. VAUXHALL STATION. EVENING

Danny slumped against the window, returning to the centre of London, the MI6 building, just another building.

His eyes on the London view; his thoughts are not.

EXT. DANNY'S APARTMENT. VAUXHALL. EVENING

Danny unlocks the door. A low rise block of apartments adjacent to the railway, the clubs and MI6.

INT. DANNY'S APARTMENT. CORRIDOR. EVENING

Danny enters. He shares a small, beat-up apartment.

INT. DANNY'S APARTMENT. KITCHEN. EVENING

Danny enters a bustling kitchen. A foreign language
chatter. His flat-mate Pavel is eating pre-night shift
dinner with friends dressed for construction work.

Danny peers into the fridge. Decaying scraps.

INT. DANNY'S APARTMENT. BATHROOM. NIGHT

A handwritten sign warns people to use the hot water
for no more than sixty seconds. A feeble dribble
flattens Danny's hair. And he does not mind.

INT. DANNY'S APARTMENT. BEDROOM. NIGHT

A tiny, narrow, chaotic bedroom, with a clothes hanger,
packed with second hand clothes. On the floor protein
powder jars intermingle with cheap sneakers.

Danny flops onto the bed, eyes on the bedside cabinet,
atop of which sits the sports drink.

EXT. RIVERBANK. MORNING

Danny running, wearing mismatched T-shirt and Bermuda
shorts. The sports drink stuffed into a pocket.

The river embankment is popular with joggers. While
everyone else runs in neat straight lines, Danny runs
with no strict route, turning round, eagerly checking
who they are, looking back & across the river.

Not the mysterious runner. Danny isn't dismayed, he's
having fun, certain he'll find this guy.

INT. DANNY'S APARTMENT. LIVING ROOM. EVENING

A jovial but tatty living room. An old television. A
games console. Bashed up furniture.

An attractive, off beat woman in her twenties is
sprawled on the sofa - Sara. Danny is lying beside her.

Sara's on her phone perusing an internet dating site.
She moves through the men with breath-taking speed.

> SARA
> (with variation)
> No. No. No. No. No. No. No.

To dismiss a profile you flick the screen with your
finger, an act that Sara performs with relish.

> DANNY
> I'm going to stay in tonight.

> SARA
> (concerned)
> You don't feel so good?

> DANNY
> I feel fine.

INT. DANNY'S APARTMENT. HALLWAY. NIGHT

Pavel and Sara dressed up for the night, leaving the
apartment. Danny remains inside, shutting the door.

INT. DANNY'S APARTMENT. LIVING ROOM. NIGHT

Alone, Danny turns on the TV. Saturday night variety
shows. Loud. Bright. Noisy --

THIS SCENE IS CUT

INT. DANNY'S APARTMENT. BATHROOM. NIGHT

Danny smoking out the window. Looking at the view of
the internal courtyard --

EXT. DANNY'S APARTMENT COURTYARD. NIGHT

As in 'Rear Window' Danny can see into lots of flats.

We see a couple arguing. A family eating dinner. And an
old man in front of the television, alone.

INT. DANNY'S APARTMENT. KITCHEN. NIGHT

On the table is a garish flyer to a club night.
Underneath is a line of crystalline drug. A cropped
plastic straw. Mischievous temptation.

Danny studies the flyer. He picks up the straw but
doesn't snort the line. Instead, he wipes it away.

INT. DANNY'S APARTMENT. BEDROOM. NIGHT

Danny sets his alarm. Five AM --

INT. DANNY'S APARTMENT. BEDROOM. DAWN.

Five AM -- the alarm rings.

Danny wakes. Dark outside. Tempted to go back to sleep, he almost does. But then, *remembers,* and leaps up.

EXT. VAUXHALL. 'FIRE' NIGHT CLUB. DAWN

Danny passes a club. Still open. He's beckoned in by a bouncer. Danny politely declines.

EXT. LAMBETH BRIDGE. DAWN

Danny stands on the bridge with the sports drink. Watching the north/south riverbank paths. Sunrise.

EXT. LAMBETH BRIDGE / RIVERBANK. MORNING

Unable to wait, indefinitely, on the bridge, Danny's seated, cold, on a riverbank bench near the bridge.

His patience is rewarded: he sees the mysterious runner along the riverbank path.

Danny, apprehensive, walks forward, into the path of the runner, and waits, holding the sports drink, trying to find a natural pose - an impossible task.

The runner sees Danny. And slows to a stop, catching his breath. Perplexed, again. Not unpleasantly so.

Flustered, Danny offers the runner his drink container back. It's cute. And ridiculous.

The runner doesn't accept. He just stares, assessing, neither hostile, nor affectionate - baffled.

The silence becomes too long, even for Danny. Progressively sadder with each beat --

> DANNY
> I wanted to say thank you. Which
> I didn't say. Last time.
>> (beat)
> It was just a hunch. Sometimes you
> have to take a chance, right?
>> (beat)
> Otherwise, how do you know...

> DANNY (CONT'D)
>   (beat)
> Obviously I got this wrong.

Danny puts the drink down on the ground.

Still no reply. Danny walks away. Humiliated. None-the-less, he braves one last glance back. Only to see --

The runner holding the drink container, contemplating it, as though trying to solve a puzzle.

He looks at Danny, the other half of this puzzle.

Danny doesn't quite know what to do. He stops. And they stand facing each other for the second time.

A greater distance between them. And yet, somehow, this time they feel closer.

EXT. RIVERBANK. MORNING

Danny and the runner walking, slowly, side by side.

>   DANNY
> My name's Danny.

>   MYSTERIOUS RUNNER
>   (unusual emphasis)
> My name is Joe.

He can't even answer a simple question with ordinary cadence. These nothing words feel like more.

EXT. RIVERBANK. MORNING

The riverbank walk continues, the pace notably more assured, Danny and Joe side by side.

>   DANNY
> Joe, are you...

Danny pulls back on the question. Joe observes. Danny cleverly, lightly, turns it into a joke.

>   DANNY
> Are you...?
>   (smiles)
> I ran out of questions.

>   JOE
> Ask me. Please.

A crucial line, pulling Danny closer.

>   DANNY
> Are you out?

Understandably the question seems enormous to Joe.

>   JOE
>   No.
>   (as if it were a more
>   nuanced variation)
>   No.

Danny assesses. Joe assesses.

>   JOE
>   If you want to go - I can
>   understand, that reaction.

>   DANNY
>   I don't want to go.

Relief on Joe's face. First emotion we've seen from him. He tries to hide it. But Danny's caught it.

EXT. ALEX'S APARTMENT BUILDING. CHELSEA. MORNING

A square. A grand house. Expensive. Impressive. A security camera. Three locks before the door opens.

Joe observes Danny observing the level of security.

>   JOE
>   I work for an investment bank.
>   (beat)
>   It's their apartment.
>   (beat)
>   Security is a concern.

Danny nods - okay, whatever. They enter.

INT. ALEX'S APARTMENT. LIVING ROOM. MORNING

The apartment is spectacular. Modern. Immaculately clean. No personal touches. No photographs.

Danny's amazed. A grown-up life. Adulthood. He studies this other world of success while Joe studies him.

>   JOE
>   There's a terrace.

A jarring estate-agent-like boast? Actually it's Joe trying to be nice.

>   JOE
>   If you want to smoke, I mean.

Joe disappears into the bathroom.

EXT. ALEX'S APARTMENT. TERRACE. MORNING

Danny stands, smoking, on the terrace looking out over
the city and square. It's incredible.

He turns to the bedroom.

INT. ALEX'S APARTMENT. BEDROOM. MORNING

Danny peeks inside the wardrobe. The clothes are
expensive. Tailored. Elegant. Meticulously organized.

Danny catches himself in the mirror. His own clothes have
ragged style, skilful purchases from second hand shops.

Then, on the surface of a cabinet, an odd looking device.
Danny examines it. A personal panic alarm.

Danny puts it down just in time --

Joe enters from the shower, a towel around his waist. A
great body. Not an invite. Yet not entirely naive.

We're on the borderline: a casual sex pick up, or
something more. Danny must decide.

                    DANNY
          I'll let you get dressed.

Danny passes Joe on his way out.

They're close - that flint-spark pull between them.

INT. ALEX'S APARTMENT. LIVING ROOM. MORNING

The bedroom door closes with no particular haste.

Danny's about to open the door but recovers his senses
and backs off. Muttering disapproval.

Flustered, he accidentally touches the laptop on the
table. It's expensive. The screen comes alive --

Complex computer code. A hypnotic kind of beauty: the
soft glow of unfathomable numbers and equations.

Bedazzled, Danny briefly forgets himself and scrolls
down, revealing more of this strange magic.

INT. CHELSEA. FASHIONABLE RESTAURANT. MORNING

A corner table. A swanky restaurant.

Joe's immaculately dressed. He wears his clothes well.
Cuts a dashing, if austere, figure. Danny admires.

Danny and Joe at breakfast. Danny eyes the prices,
daunted by them. Joe observes.

                    JOE
          I can pay.

                    DANNY
          No, it's fine...
               (beat)
          I must be easy to read.

                    JOE
          You are.

                    DANNY
          Is that bad?

                    JOE
          It makes a change. The people I
          work with are inscrutable.

                    DANNY
          I can be inscrutable.

                    JOE
          Did you look through my clothes?

Danny hesitates, caught, and then laughs. Joe smiles.
For the first time since we've encountered him.

EXT. ALEX'S APARTMENT BUILDING. CHELSEA. MORNING

At the doorstep. A goodbye.

Joe raises a hand for Danny to shake. A stilted
formality. Yet it isn't disappointing or anti-climactic.
Danny finds it cute and happily shakes his hand.

EXT. ALEX'S APARTMENT BUILDING. STREET. MORNING

Danny walking away, with a spring in his step, as though
the date couldn't feasibly have gone better.

He passes various expensive-flash cars, with no interest
in them, glancing back at the terrace. Joe isn't on it.

Danny crosses the road, passing a parked white van. The
inside is thick with cigarette smoke. But no driver.

Again, of no interest to Danny, a background detail.

Danny glances back for a second time. Joe is at the
window - looking at him.

Danny's thrilled. He raises a hand. Joe waves back.

The white van blurred behind.

INT. DANNY'S APARTMENT. LIVING ROOM. DAY

Danny stands, recounting his date with great gusto.

Sara and Pavel are seated on the sofa, back from the
clubs, worse for wear. Sara smoking a joint, laconic.
Pavel is gnashing his jaw, bug eyed.

An empty space on the sofa where Danny would normally
have sat.

> DANNY
> We shook hands.

A love struck Danny checks on his wasted audience.

Sara inhales, unmoved. Pavel turns to Sara, baffled as to
why Danny is so happy when he didn't even get laid.

> PAVEL
> I don't understand.

> SARA
> They shook hands.

Pavel still doesn't understand. And Danny's exceptionally
pleased with their reaction.

EXT. WHITEHALL. EVENING

Danny waits outside one of the ministries. In the hub
of political power.

We see Scottie. Early sixties. Emerging from the grand
entrance of a ministry: a civil servant figure from a
bygone era. Immaculate Jermyn Street tailoring.

We presume this man can't be who Danny is waiting for.
Yet it is. A kiss as a greeting.

EXT. WHITEHALL STREETS. EVENING

Scottie and Danny walking. An excitable energy in Danny
movements, compared to Scottie's steady steps.

> SCOTTIE
> Has he rung?

> DANNY
> He will.

Danny adamantly unconcerned.

                              SCOTTIE
                        (gentle)
                  A week..?

                              DANNY
                  I've never been more certain of
                  anything in my life.

                              SCOTTIE
                  Why?

                              DANNY
                  Because --
                        (thinks)
                  That can't be it.
                        (thinks)
                  There's more. There has to be.

                              SCOTTIE
                  You love falling in love. The
                  moment when it's all possibilities
                  and dreams.

Danny misses Scottie's point.

                              DANNY
                  You think he's out of my league?

                              SCOTTIE
                  The thought never crossed my
                  mind.

Danny's caught. Changes subject. He's breezy.

                              DANNY
                  Where are we drinking tonight?

                              SCOTTIE
                        (without much hope)
                  Somewhere dimly lit and terribly
                  old fashioned.

Danny locks an arm through Scottie's.

EXT. HAMPSTEAD. DAY

After meeting in Whitehall Danny and Scottie have
travelled and are walking.

Danny recounting his date with great gusto. But we're
primarily interested in Scottie's reaction.

                    DANNY
          We're at the doorstep, saying
          goodbye, I'm trying to give him my
          flat mate's number because I don't
          have a phone, except he doesn't
          write it down. And I'm like, *"if
          you don't want to see me again"*
          and he says:
                    (acting)
          *"Numbers, Danny, I have no problem
          with."* Like he could remember
          every phone number in the world.
          And then - we shook hands.
                    (beat, fondly)
          If you'd told me a week ago I
          would've been this happy with a
          handshake at the end of date...

Scottie has been patiently listening. Tolerant of his
friend's indulgent recounting.

                    DANNY (CONT'D)
          I'm sorry. I'll stop talking about
          him.

                    SCOTTIE
          No, it's okay, you're (excited --)

                    DANNY
                    (interrupting)
          It's just... that feeling... You
          know? Not being able to think
          about anyone else?

                    SCOTTIE
          Yes. I know the feeling.

Because he has felt and still feels that way about Danny.

                    DANNY
          Right - of course. With... that
          guy...

Danny doesn't understand Scottie feels that way about him
and presumes he's referring to a past lover.

Scottie watches his friend, waiting for some spark of
recognition that never comes.

Danny's mind has already fluttered back to Alex.

Scottie understands that he will never have Danny. It
will always be so. And he turns his gaze elsewhere,
accepting.

INT. DANNY'S APARTMENT. KITCHEN. NIGHT

Danny enters. Sara's smoking a spliff. Danny's eyes are
full of hope. Sara shakes her head. Offers her phone.
Danny checks, stoically - no messages.

Sara offers the spliff. Danny accepts, smokes and smiles,
defiantly. As if to say: "he's going to call".

INT. DANNY'S APARTMENT. BEDROOM. DAWN.

Danny wakes. Someone knocking on the front door. He
looks at the alarm. Early in the morning.

INT. DANNY'S APARTMENT. HALLWAY. DAWN

Danny staggers out in boxers. And messed up hair. He
opens the door. Standing before him is Joe. Pristine.

However, this time he's nervous. In his own peculiar
speech pattern. An echo of Danny's line.

> JOE
> Otherwise, how do you know?

Danny nods, happy - he knew it.

INT/EXT. JOE'S CAR / VAUXHALL. DAWN

Joe's driving. The car is expensive. In perfect
condition. Danny in the passenger seat.

Danny playfully admires the car. The leather trim. Not
beguiled by wealth, soaking details as character.

The car's music library: Bach. Nothing else. Joe waits
for some comment. But Danny doesn't remark.

INT/EXT. JOE'S CAR / MOTORWAY. MORNING

Joe and Danny in the car.

> DANNY
> At some point you're going to talk
> about yourself, right? Not your
> work, I understand. That's
> 'secret'. But the other stuff?

> JOE
> Why?

> DANNY
> Isn't that what you do when you
> meet someone? I tell you stuff.
> You tell me stuff.

Joe ponders.

> JOE
> Like facts?

> DANNY
> (amused)
> Facts. Sure.

Joe ponders some more. But does not offer any facts.

INT/EXT. JOE'S CAR / COUNTRYSIDE. ESTUARY. MORNING

The countryside. The car's parked. There's nothing
around. Joe steps out. Danny follows.

EXT. COUNTRYSIDE. ESTUARY. MORNING

Picturesque landscape. Bleak. Steel edged. Unusual.

Joe's at the back of the car. Danny walks towards him.

INT/EXT. JOE'S CAR BOOT / COUNTRYSIDE. MORNING

An antique boarding school trunk in the boot. Cracked
leather trim. Rusted metal locks. Seventy years old.

Joe rummages through. A pair of hiking boots. There are
numerous Ordnance Survey maps - at least fifty.

Danny's intrigued by this many maps.

> DANNY
> You've walked all these?

Joe's nervous it implies he's weird. Danny reassures him.

> DANNY
> A lot of...
> (struggling to know
> what to say)
> ...miles.

Joe calculates the exact amount but catches himself.
Instead, he takes out the relevant map for their walk.

> JOE
> This is us.

They sit side by side, map open, each holding half.

EXT. COUNTRYSIDE. ESTUARY. DAY

Danny and Joe walking. Not typical English countryside.
Nothing quaint. Odd. Powerful.

Though Danny might not be expertly dressed, he's fit
and enjoying the walk.

EXT. COUNTRYSIDE. ESTUARY. DAY

Danny and Joe at the water's edge. The mud flats. The
water's ebb. A kind of magic here.

Danny turns, looking at Joe as he observes the view. Joe
turns to Danny. Both looking at each other, not the view.

Danny wants to thank Joe for taking him here but doesn't
quite have the words.

EXT. COUNTRYSIDE. ESTUARY. DAY

Huddled behind the remains of an old fishing boat. Joe
has a backpack. Takes out an elegant thermos. Danny
watches him fuss with the picnic apparatus.

EXT. COUNTRYSIDE. ESTUARY. DAY

They're eating a handmade sandwich. Not thin processed
bread. Wedges from a nice loaf. They sip tea.

                    DANNY
              (through a mouthful)
          You're so grown up. You drink tea.
          Out of a thermos. You go on
          country walks. I must seem young?
          Compared to the people you work
          with?

                    JOE
          You do.

There's an autistic yet ever gentle directness about Joe.
Danny - far from being offended - seems to enjoy it.

                    DANNY
          Why are you so grown up?

                    JOE
          I skipped childhood.

                    DANNY
          You're not joking, are you?

                    JOE
          A joke? No. I started university
          when I was fifteen.

                    DANNY
          You've never... messed around?

                    JOE
          In what sense?

                    DANNY
          Any sense.

                    JOE
          I've been serious. For a long
          time.

                    DANNY
          Why did you change your mind?

                    JOE
          About?

                    DANNY
          Me.

                    JOE
          I wondered what it would be like
          to do one of these walks with
          someone.

                    DANNY
          For a moment I was worried you
          were going to say it was because I
          made you laugh.

Joe considers this seriously. And literally.

                    JOE
          I don't think you've ever made me
          laugh.

Mathematically correct. Danny smiles. Joe worries.

                    JOE
          I'm not saying you won't --

                    DANNY
          I understand.

                    JOE
          I'm sure you will --

                    DANNY
              (amused)
          I understand.

Joe accepts that Danny isn't upset. And that's new.

EXT. COUNTRYSIDE. ESTUARY. DAY

Danny and Joe returning to the car. Danny's increasingly
excited with how the date's going. Not fatigued by walk,
his pace and energy increasing, orbiting Joe.

> DANNY
> (playful - mid-flow)
> -- you show up, on my doorstep -
> which is wonderful - except I
> never told you where I lived - so
> I'm wondering - and just to be
> clear, in advance, I don't mind -
> but did you carry out some kind of
> 'background check' on me?

Joe seems unsure how to respond.

> JOE
> The way we met was unusual.

> DANNY
> (playful)
> Right. I get it. You thought -
> stranger, seduction - not that
> I'm presuming you're seduced by
> me - process ongoing - and...
> what was I saying...? Okay, you
> thought, what? Our meeting was
> part of, like, a 'set up'?

Danny spots Joe's anxiety.

> DANNY
> It's fine. It's fun. I just
> thought you said I was easy to
> read?

Joe slowly understanding that Danny doesn't care one bit
about the oddness. He begins to play along.

> JOE
> That would've been the reason
> you were selected. The
> appearance of innocence.

> DANNY
> Oh. I'm not innocent.

> JOE
> You might be the only innocent
> person I know.

Danny's stumped.

> DANNY
> Can you tell me what your real
> name is now?

Joe looks at him - bewildered and impressed. Danny has no empirical evidence, he just sensed 'Joe' was a lie.

                    JOE / ALEX
          My name's Alex.

From now on JOE is referred to by his real name ALEX.

                    DANNY
          Nice to meet you, Alex.

EXT. COUNTRYSIDE CAR PARK. EVENING

Sitting at the back of the car, taking off their muddy shoes. Danny has no spare set.

Alex gives Danny a fresh of pair of lush, thick hiking socks, to replace his flimsy destroyed trainers.

                    DANNY
          They're better than my shoes.

                    ALEX
          You can keep them.

                    DANNY
          That's the second gift you've
          given me and I've given you
          nothing.

It's clearly a line, Danny's about to kiss him.

Alex fathoms this. Wants it. And panics.

He breaks the moment, standing up, his mind on the kiss that didn't just happen, stuttering --

                    ALEX
          For a gift to truly be a gift
          there should be no expectation of
          it being reciprocated.

Danny amused. Mostly. But he did really want to kiss him.

                    DANNY
          Right.

INT/EXT. ALEX'S CAR / MOTORWAY. EVENING

Danny and Alex in the car.

London ahead, lights glittering in the distance.

The energy of this journey is different to the energy of the journey up. Danny's excited, apprehensive too, clearly mulling sex. He glances at Alex, unsure.

Alex catches his glance.

EXT. DANNY'S APARTMENT. NIGHT

Danny and Alex standing outside the apartment. An
awkward pause turns into a silence.

> DANNY
> I'd like you to come up. If you
> want. Obviously. If you don't want
> – that's cool. I didn't mean to
> say 'cool'. I meant to say 'fine'.
> Can I try that again? It's fine if
> you don't want to come up.

> ALEX
> I want to...

> DANNY
> But?

> ALEX
> It's a little fast.

We can see Danny thinking it's not fast at all. And
actually Alex doesn't either. He panicked.

> DANNY
> Next time, maybe.

He goes to give Alex a hug. A kiss maybe. At the same
time Alex goes to shake his hand.

Suddenly Danny loses his patience.

> DANNY
> You've got to stop shaking my
> hand.

> ALEX
> I'm sorry.
>> (a more nuanced
>> variation)
> I am sorry.

Alex heads off.

Danny watches him go, kicking himself. He considers
running after Alex. Stops himself. Goes inside.

INT. DANNY'S APARTMENT. KITCHEN. NIGHT

Sara's cooking and smoking at the same time. Danny
enters in a fury. Notices she's smoking and angrily
plucks the cigarette from her lips. And stubs it out.

She looks at him. Placid.

                    DANNY
          Fuck.

He runs out.

EXT. DANNY'S APARTMENT BUILDING. VAUXHALL. NIGHT

Danny runs outside intending to catch Alex before he
drives off. Only to discover that Alex hasn't left.

Alex is leaning against a railing, his body knotted with
anxiety. He's desperate to go back to Danny, to try
again, but he's certain that he's messed everything up.

He's certain that once again he's on his own.

In a reverse of the first meeting on the bridge -
carefully and clearly echoing that opening - Danny now
watches Alex and Alex, now the troubled one, is unaware
of being watched, staring into the street as Danny stared
into the Thames.

Alex exposed. Nervous. Unsure. Confused. Upset. Not okay.

We hold this moment. Danny is not in a rush to end it,
observing, understanding. Finally he moves closer.

Alex realizes that he's being watched. He turns to Danny.
All Alex's barriers are down. It looks like he might cry.

Danny sees Alex - *he really sees him* - for the first
time. A man who, for all his success, might just be as
lost as Danny.

And Alex, more than anything, wants to be seen.

INT. DANNY'S APARTMENT. BEDROOM. NIGHT

Alex examines the tiny bedroom. The jumble of clothes.
Danny's self-conscious. He hastily tidies.

                    DANNY
          It's normally tidier than this.
               (beat)
          It's never tidier than this.

The room's so small they're close together. Danny takes
Alex's hand. He's trembling. It surprises Danny.

INT. DANNY'S APARTMENT. BATHROOM. NIGHT

Alex is in the bath. A seated position. Chin resting on
his knees. Thoughtful & sad. The atmosphere is subdued.

Danny's seated on the side of the tub. Not wearing the same clothes as previously - tracksuit bottoms and a T-shirt. No socks. Thoughtful but not sad.

Two electric kettles come to the boil beside him. Danny stands, lifting a kettle.

DANNY

> Careful.

He gently nudges Alex forward as he pours the hot water into the far end.

INT. DANNY'S APARTMENT. BATHROOM. NIGHT

Danny filling the kettles at the sink. He puts them on the boil. When he looks at the tub Alex can't be seen.

Danny walks over, perching on the side of the bath, looking down to see --

Alex sunk under the water, head submerged, but his eyes wide open, looking up through the water at Danny.

Danny's hand breaks the water's surface touching Alex's face, as if calling him back from his hiding place.

INT. DANNY'S APARTMENT. BATHROOM. NIGHT

Alex still in the bath. Danny perched on the edge.

ALEX

> Had you guessed?

DANNY

> I'd guessed you hadn't slept
> with guys. I'd thought maybe
> you'd slept with a few women.

Alex shakes his head.

DANNY

> Can I ask a question? I don't want
> you to feel under pressure. I'm
> trying to understand. Can you
> trust me on that?

Alex nods.

DANNY

> What's stopped you?

Alex entering completely new territory.

DANNY

> You don't have to answer --

                    ALEX
          I want to.

Alex considers. In the end, he settles for:

                    ALEX
          When people tried to kiss me I
          said things like: "For a gift to
          truly be a gift".

But Danny doesn't smile. Or laugh. He waits, patiently,
his fingers in the water. He wants to know. For real.

No more hiding. Alex goes deeper.

                    ALEX
          At school I was old. At university
          I was young. I've always been out
          of step with the people around me.
          In the end, I left it so late, I
          gave up.
                    (with sadness)
          I gave up.

                    DANNY
          Did you imagine you'd spend the
          rest of your life alone?

                    ALEX
          I did.

                    DANNY
          I can't begin to understand what
          that must feel like.

                    ALEX
          You were always sure you'd find
          someone?

                    DANNY
          Always.

Alex can't imagine what that feels like.

                    ALEX
          Being alone has a rhythm, like
          running. It's when you stop that
          you realize how tired you are.

Alex not just saying this for the first time, he
understands this for the first time, in this moment.

                    ALEX
          How do you admit you've never had
          a relationship? Who wants to hear?
          When they do, who wants to stay?

                    DANNY
          I do.

A rare and precious flash of emotion from Alex.

INT. DANNY'S APARTMENT. BATHROOM. NIGHT

Danny by the door. Alex wrapped in towels. They're close.

                    ALEX
          I'd like to try again.

                    DANNY
          We don't have to.

                    ALEX
          You don't want to?

                    DANNY
          We can wait.

                    ALEX
          I've waited long enough.

INT. DANNY'S APARTMENT. KITCHEN. NIGHT

Danny rummages through the alcohol stash. He finds a
brightly coloured spirit in a preposterous glass bottle.

INT. DANNY'S APARTMENT. BEDROOM. NIGHT

Alex, wrapped in towels, on the bed. Condoms and lube on
the side. Danny enters with the bottle. And glasses.

They each have a shot. Evidently revolting.

                    DANNY
          Again?

Alex nods. They take a second shot.

INT. DANNY'S APARTMENT. BEDROOM. NIGHT

Danny and Alex are both tipsy. The bottle half empty.
Alex is no longer protectively wrapped up in towels. The
mood is mellowing, intimacy intensifying.

                    ALEX
          Drugs?

                    DANNY
          I've been using them to make me
          believe that the sex was
          special.

>   DANNY (CONT'D)
> That the person I was with was
> special. But I'd love to know
> what that feels like for real.
> Because I bet it's the best
> feeling in the world.

They're nudging closer.

Alex's peculiar sense of humour is also returning.

>   ALEX
> Can we pretend that alcohol
> isn't a drug?

Danny pours them both another shot.

>   DANNY
> Absolutely.

INT. DANNY'S APARTMENT. BEDROOM. NIGHT

They're standing. Close. Not touching. Apart.

>   DANNY
>   (gentle)
> Will you stop worrying about me?

INT. DANNY'S APARTMENT. BEDROOM. NIGHT

Danny & Alex. A sex scene.

INT. DANNY'S APARTMENT. BEDROOM. NIGHT

Playing with chronology, before the scene sex, Alex and
Danny standing, not touching, apart. Alex echoes --

>   ALEX
>   (gentle)
> Will you stop worrying about me?

INT. DANNY'S APARTMENT. BEDROOM. NIGHT

Danny & Alex - the sex scene continued.

INT. DANNY'S APARTMENT. BEDROM. NIGHT

Back before the sex scene, Alex & Danny standing apart.
Their hands tentatively break the gap between them.

As if this was their first touch. And, in a way, it is.

>   TO BLACK:

EXT. LONDON. VAUXHALL. EMBANKMENT RIVERSIDE. DAY

Close on Danny. Seated on a bench. Looking at camera.
Handsome and happy. With tenderness he addresses 'us'.

>   DANNY (TO CAMERA)
>   You saw me.
>   (beat)
>   What I mean is... You... saw...

Danny struggles to express himself, trying to say 'we saw
him, the real him, not the facade'.

Unable to put that idea into words Danny touches his
chest.

>   DANNY (TO CAMERA) (CONT'D)
>   You saw me.

And Danny can see that the person he's talking to - who
we have not seen, this unseen person - 'we' understand.

>   DANNY (TO CAMERA) (CONT'D)
>   And you asked if I was okay. Not
>   like most people ask it, like
>   they've asked it a hundred times
>   that day already. You asked it
>   like nothing else mattered to you.
>   And I thought: How does this...
>   stranger... this person I've never
>   seen before... how are they the
>   only person in the whole world who
>   *knows*...
>   (sad)
>   That I'm not okay.
>   (beat, then happy)
>   But I was sure if I could just
>   find out your name - if I could
>   just find out who you were -
>   everything would be okay.

Danny sure that everything is now okay. But 'we', the
audience, should feel unease, that last line resonates
off kilter, it doesn't land as sentimental, it lands as
Not True.

Everything is not going to be okay.

Just as Danny is about to smile we --

We flip around to reveal that he's been talking to Alex.

Clearly we're much further along in their relationship.
They're completely at ease with each other.

Danny is expecting his words to provoke a sentimental and
warm moment. But Alex's reaction is troubled.

Alex considers carefully. Unsure if he should say
something. Finally, softly, it slips out --

                    ALEX
          What if everything isn't okay?

Danny's expression alters. As far as he's aware
everything is perfect. With sophistication, he proceeds
carefully.

                    DANNY
          Then we tell each other. And we
          deal with... whatever it is. We
          deal with it. Together.

Alex looks at Danny and nods.

                    DANNY (CONT'D)
          Is there something you want to
          tell me?

With MI6 in the background.

                    ALEX
          No.

EXT. LONDON. VAUXHALL. EMBANKMENT. NIGHT

The exact same location. The same set up from the last
frame of the previous scene. Except the bench where Danny
and Alex were seated is now desolate and empty.

It's a bleak winter night. A light snow falls.

MI6 glows in the darkness.

We pan across - drifting towards a door - as we get
closer we hear the faint sound of Japanese music.

We drift towards this nondescript door, closer and
closer, passing through it into the strange underground
club --

*Over the darkness we hear singing, by the sound, a
woman's voice, tremendous depth of heartbreak and hurt.*

                                        FADE IN:

INT. BALLROOM GAY CLUB. STAGE. NIGHT

Reveal a drag act - *not comedic* - singing a powerful
song. A fragile, sorrowful, Japanese man, dressed as a
geisha. Singing a Japanese lullaby.

The voice is brittle and female: probably lip sync.

A bright spotlight on the mournful singer. Make-up beginning to melt in the heat.

INT. BALLROOM GAY CLUB. BOOTH. NIGHT

The club is old and frayed, a neglected relic, popular forty years ago, now unsettling.

Danny's seated in a shadowy booth upholstered in worn fabric. Opposite him is Scottie in crushed velvet. Attire contrasting with civil service persona.

Their body language is strained. Scottie's watching the act on stage. Danny's watching Scottie.

                    DANNY
          I'm excited you two are going to
          meet.
                  (no reply)
          I should've organized it sooner.

Scottie belatedly nods, emptily.

                    SCOTTIE
          A month or two, I could
          understand, I'm not so old I can't
          remember what it's like to be
          smitten. But eight months of
          listening to you declare how
          wonderful he is while failing to
          introduce us. Eight months feels
          wilful.

                    DANNY
          I'm sorry.

Scottie's eyes remain on the stage and the singer.

Danny's troubled. Watching the depth of Scottie's hurt.

INT. BALLROOM GAY CLUB. STAGE. NIGHT

The fragile, sorrowful, geisha. Hurt and pain. A bright spotlight. The make-up continues to melt.

INT. BALLROOM GAY CLUB. BAR. NIGHT

Danny at the busy bar. The lullaby continues on stage. He turns to see Alex enter.

Alex stands, smartly dressed, formal, straight from work, a little out of place.

He searches the crowd --

Danny doesn't wave, or signal, he waits. Sure enough, Alex and Danny's eyes connect.

With that connection, Alex seems to relax. No longer out of place. But then Danny checks on Scottie.

Scottie's been watching him. Caught, he turns his attention back to the stage --

INT. BALLROOM GAY CLUB. STAGE. NIGHT

The Japanese drag act, at the most intense peak of the song, more and more make-up melting with sweat.

INT. BALLROOM GAY CLUB. BOOTH. NIGHT

Alex and Danny at the table where Scottie is sitting. Scottie pays no attention to Alex, intent on the drag act. She's coming to the end of the song.

> DANNY
> Scottie, this is Alex.

Scottie raises a hand, asking for silence, as the lullaby finishes.

Danny and Alex wait.

The lullaby comes to an end. Scottie rises to his feet - emphatic applause, lasting far longer than anyone else. With this done, the three sit.

Scottie turns to Alex. A dim spark of recognition. As if they know each other but can't remember from where.

> SCOTTIE
> Alex, tell me...

Scottie lets the question hang, we have no idea what he's going to ask. He gestures at the stage.

> SCOTTIE
> What did you make of her?

Alex doesn't have an opinion either way.

> SCOTTIE
> Too much? That doesn't surprise
> me. Danny has always preferred
> his men to be as 'straight' as
> possible. A tedious form of self-
> loathing that I've tried,
> unsuccessfully, to wean him off.

Alex is silent. Danny's furious. Rather than articulate his anger, he tries to change the subject.

DANNY
Scottie, I was telling Alex --

SCOTTIE
I hope you told him that this is
where we first met?
(To Alex)
You must be wondering how an old
queer like me ended up friends
with a handsome young man like
Danny?

Danny seems alarmed at this topic of conversation.
Scottie notices but advances with the subject.

SCOTTIE
Nineteen years old, he walked
through that door, as lost as a
person can be. But this is an
excellent place to come if
you're lost, someone will always
find you, although not always
with the best of intentions. I
saw him in his tatty jeans, with
his cropped hair and his puppy
dog eyes. I could guess his sad
story without hearing a word. I
presumed, if I bought him a
drink, that there wouldn't be a
single second when he wasn't
waiting for someone better to
come along. What can I say? I'm
a soft touch so I bought him
that drink and to my surprise
Danny talked to me the whole
night. He didn't leave even when
others stalked him. A small
gesture, but it meant a great
deal. We've been friends ever
since. I'm the person he comes
to when times are tough. And
they often are. Poor Danny has a
terrible track record of picking
the wrong man. I'm sure he told
you about --

DANNY
I did.

SCOTTIE
And yet Danny stayed with him,
believing love meant sticking by
your man even when they split
your lip. And bruise your eye.
He's an insufferable romantic.
One of the last. When I asked
him, once, what he wanted to do
with his life...

> SCOTTIE (CONT'D)
> (To Danny)
> Do you mind?

Danny does mind.

> DANNY
> Go ahead.

> SCOTTIE
> He said: 'I always dreamed of
> being a better dad than my dad'.

> DANNY
> That wouldn't be hard.

> SCOTTIE
> So what are my duties tonight?
> Does it fall upon me to say –
> 'Don't break his heart'.

> ALEX
> I could never hurt Danny.

> SCOTTIE
> May I ask, as someone who has
> witnessed the breaking of many a
> heart, how you can be so sure?

> ALEX
> Because he's the only friend I
> have.

An exceptionally open remark. The force of it takes
Danny by surprise as it does Scottie, who is struck
full of wonder at this statement.

The wind goes out of Scottie's rhetorical sails.

Scottie raises his glass. His tone changes. His toast
is affectionate. Melancholy. And genuine.

> SCOTTIE
> I'm pleased for you. I'm pleased
> for both of you.

EXT. BALLROOM GAY CLUB. NIGHT

Danny and Alex exit into a bitter winter night.

> DANNY
> Had you two met before?

> ALEX
> No.

Danny's about to say something but Alex moves off.
Danny, troubled, lights up a cigarette.

INT. DANNY'S APARTMENT. BATHROOM. NIGHT

Danny smoking, still troubled. Looks out of window --

EXT. DANNY'S APARTMENT BUILDING. COURTYARD. NIGHT

We see all the flats as before. Except one change:

The old man's flat is empty. All furniture gone. On the
floor is a polystyrene cup of steaming coffee, beside a
glass ash-tray, smoke rising from a cigarette.

INT. DANNY'S APARTMENT. BATHROOM. NIGHT

Danny stares for a moment, thinking nothing of it.

At the sink he uses mouthwash. Looks at his reflection -
clearly weighing something up.

INT. DANNY'S APARTMENT. BEDROOM. NIGHT

Danny enters. The room has been transformed. Organized.
Cleaner, less student-like.

Alex is already in bed, his body language communicates
that he wants to sleep.

Danny shuts the door. He sits on the bed. Alex's back
is turned to him. Danny puts a hand on him.

> DANNY
>
> Scottie asked if you knew how I
> became his friend.

Alex turns and sits up. He judges Danny's expression.

> ALEX
>
> Danny, you don't need to tell me
> anything --

> DANNY
>
> I need to tell you this.

> ALEX
>
> I love you.

The words strike Danny. His reaction suggests it's the
first time Alex has said them.

> ALEX
>
> And I don't need to know.

> DANNY
>
> I love you. And I need you to
> know.

Danny takes a moment. Then speaks calmly, softly, his
control faltering only slightly.

>   DANNY
>   I was nineteen, like he said. A
>   bad time. I'd left home. I was
>   doing a lot of drugs. One night
>   I was wired. Not happy, not high
>   - numb. I posted an ad online
>   saying anyone could come round.
>   I mean - anyone. I'd be waiting.
>   My only condition was that they
>   didn't speak.
>   (beat)
>   And people showed up... I don't
>   remember much about them...
>   there were two older guys. They
>   arrived together. I didn't turn
>   them away. I didn't ask anything
>   of them. I just reminded them of
>   my rule. Not to speak. And they
>   must have thought their luck was
>   in... Because they didn't make a
>   sound.
>   (beat)
>   The next day I couldn't stop
>   crying. I went to see Scottie.
>   I'd only met him a few times.
>   But he was the only person I
>   could trust. He took me straight
>   to the hospital. They put me on
>   a course of PEP --

Danny checks to see if Alex knows what PEP is.

>   DANNY
>   Emergency medication. In case you
>   might have been exposed to HIV. I
>   was on the drugs for twenty eight
>   days. There were... side effects.

Terrible ones, we sense, but no detail.

>   DANNY
>   I took so much time off work they
>   fired me. Because I couldn't
>   explain why... Scottie looked
>   after me. Sixteen weeks later I
>   had an HIV test. I was clear.
>   (beat)
>   And we were friends.
>   (beat)
>   I've never done anything like that
>   again. I swear. I was out of my
>   mind. I'm always safe. Always. I
>   don't know what happened to me
>   that night. I look back and I
>   don't recognise that person.

36

                        DANNY (CONT'D)
                    (new thought)
            And I've never cheated on you.
            Never. I don't want to have any
            secrets from you. I never want to
            have any secrets ever again.

A brief moment of relief for Danny, a burden being
lifted. An echo of Alex's relief.

But then Danny becomes apprehensive he's said too much.

Alex is inscrutable. Indecipherable silence.

And then, slowly, he raises his hand - outstretched, in a
gesture that seems new and exploratory.

Danny, mirroring the new movement, raises his own hand,
placing it against Alex's, palms touching.

As if Alex has said something profound, Danny, nods.
Their fingers inter-lock.

                        ALEX
            That's all we need to know.

*That line lands awkwardly, like we sense it's just an
idea, an idea that can't hold. And they sense it too.*

INT. DANNY'S APARTMENT. KITCHEN. MORNING

Danny bustling. Alex is seated. Danny serves breakfast.

                        DANNY
            Let's go away for the weekend.

Alex considers. Danny's nervous. It's a test.

                        ALEX
            Sure.

Danny's relieved. About to say more when --

Alex turns the radio on, turning it up loud.

                        ALEX
            I have to buy a battery for my
            laptop.

The observation seems strangely irrelevant.

                        ALEX
            I can't go without replacing it.

                        DANNY
            If you need to work that's fine.

>   ALEX
>   As long as you understand.

Oddly emphatic. Oddly mundane. Oddly unnecessary.

>   DANNY
>   I understand.

INT. WAREHOUSE. DAY

Danny's working. But his eye is on the clock. As soon
as it hits six he hurries out.

INT. DANNY'S APARTMENT. BEDROOM. EVENING

Danny packs his bag. For long walks. We see that he's
bought proper hiking shoes.

EXT. ALEX'S APARTMENT BUILDING. EVENING

Bag by his side, Danny rings the doorbell. The security
camera a bulbous black spot. No reply. He waits.

Danny rings the bell again. Checks his watch. He takes
out his phone. Dials Alex. Goes straight to voicemail.

Mild anxiety creeps over Danny. He dials again --

EXT. ALEX'S APARTMENT BUILDING. NIGHT

Danny seated on the steps. Grim-faced. The house is
dark. He looks at his phone. No calls.

Leaving his bag on the steps he walks into the street
and looks up at the flat window.

The terrace. The bedroom. No lights. No sign of life.

EXT. ALEX'S APARTMENT BUILDING. NIGHT

Danny still seated. Upset. Cold. He dials again. But a
sense of futility prevails. No reply.

Suddenly it beeps - it's painful how excited Danny is.
But the phone has a low battery. There are no messages.

INT. DANNY'S APARTMENT. LIVING ROOM. NIGHT

Danny enters. Sara and Pavel and a group of friends are
wasted, drunk, high, seated in a circle, chatting.

                    DANNY
          Has anyone called for me?

But his voice is lost among the noise. No one hears
him. There's laughter. Danny raises his voice:

                    DANNY
          Has anyone called!

Shocked silence.

INT. DANNY'S APARTMENT. BEDROOM. DAWN

Danny seated on the bed. His phone beside him. He
hasn't undressed. He hasn't slept.

EXT. CHELSEA. NIGHT

Heavy rain, Danny walking towards Alex's apartment.

EXT/INT. ALEX'S APARTMENT BUILDING / HALLWAY. NIGHT

Dripping wet, Danny posts a letter written to 'Alex'.
As he's posting he sees a silhouette in the hallway.

Excited, Danny raps on the glass. The silhouette
disappears into the darkness.

INT. DANNY'S APARTMENT. KITCHEN. NIGHT

Danny still hasn't slept. Sara and Pavel are opposite
him. Concerned, Sara places a pill in front of him.

                    PAVEL
          You need to sleep.

Sara reaches out, touches Danny's arm. He looks up,
putting on a weak imitation of his usual self.

                    DANNY
          You never sleep.

                    PAVEL
               (kind)
          No. But you used to.

To appease them, Danny accepts the pill.

INT. DANNY'S APARTMENT. BATHROOM. NIGHT

Danny drops the pill down the sink. Washes it away. Takes
out his cigarettes instead.

He sits at the window. About to smoke.

We see the view --

EXT. DANNY'S APARTMENT BUILDING. COURTYARD. NIGHT

The room that previously belonged to the old man. A
fleeting glimpse of a figure, and then the shutters
slam shut, leaving only cigarette smoke.

EXT. DANNY'S APARTMENT BUILDING. COURTYARD. NIGHT

A ragged-sleep-deprived Danny, uncertain as to what he
is doing, or why, enters the courtyard.

He lights his cigarette, smoking outside, eyes on the
apartment with the shutters.

On the ground: a great many discarded cigarette butts.

He moves forward, without a rational explanation of why,
about to tap on the window of the shuttered apartment,
but he stops, ready to knock, but not doing so --

EXT. SCOTTIE'S HOUSE. HAMPSTEAD. DAY

Danny's hand knocking on Scottie's front door.

It opens.

A bedraggled Danny outside Scottie's home. Scottie
looks him up and down.

There's concern. But also weariness.

INT. SCOTTIE'S HOUSE. LIVING ROOM. DAY

Scottie's home is filled with antiques, books, art - a
collector but the feel is never stuffy. Danny's pacing.

                    SCOTTIE
          How long?

                    DANNY
          Eleven days.

                    SCOTTIE
          What happened?

                    DANNY
          I told him.

With delicate cruelty.

> SCOTTIE
> That you loved him?

> DANNY
> How you and I became friends.

Scottie considers. He gets it.

> SCOTTIE
> That was a mistake.

Danny's winded by the verification of his fears.

> DANNY
> Why didn't I shut my mouth?

> SCOTTIE
> Because you needed to know - could
> he still love you?

> DANNY
> I've fucked it up. I'd fucked it
> up before I'd even met him.

> SCOTTIE
> You've tried everything?

Danny nods.

> SCOTTIE
> There's only one thing left to do.
> Accept that it's over.

> DANNY
> I can't.

> SCOTTIE
> What other choice do you have?

Danny sits, head in his hands.

> SCOTTIE
> You'll get over it, Danny. Not
> quickly. Not completely. But
> enough to carry on. Trust me on
> that. Now, I'm afraid you'll have
> to excuse me. I have work to do.

> DANNY
> You want me to leave?

> SCOTTIE
> I'd never ask you to leave. Rest
> here. Sleep, eat. But today I
> cannot play assistant to your
> personal life.

Scottie moves to the door. But he pauses, looks back:

> SCOTTIE
> Out of curiosity, did you ever
> wonder... what I might want...

Danny processes this information. Puzzled at first.

> DANNY
> What you want?
> (beat)
> What do you want?

Scottie regrets saying anything.

> DANNY
> You want this?

Danny starts taking off his clothes.

> DANNY
> Is this what you want?

He continues to strip. Not erotic. Pitiful. His shirt
gets stuck over his head. He rips it free.

He stands, top off, jeans unbuttoned, in the middle of
the flat. He's angry.

> DANNY
> What do I owe you? Five nights?
> Ten nights? Tell me!

The reference to escorts hurts. As it was intended. A
flash of shame. Danny sees that he's upset his friend.

> DANNY
> I'm sorry.

Scottie slowly picks up the dropped clothes.

> DANNY
> Scottie, I'm sorry.

Scottie folds them neatly and hands them to Danny.

His pain is clear. Not unrequited sexual desire. But of
unrequited love. Danny's ashamed.

INT. DANNY'S APARTMENT BUILDING. COMMUNAL HALLWAY. DAY

In his ripped shirt Danny climbs the stairs towards the
front door, taking out his key --

Only to see it's been smashed open.

INT. DANNY'S APARTMENT. HALLWAY. DAY

The flat is in disarray.

INT. DANNY'S APARTMENT. BEDROOM. DAY

Danny enters his room to find it turned over. The
mattress ripped open.

He stands - numb, believing it to be misfortune.

INT. DANNY'S APARTMENT. KITCHEN. DAY

Danny, Pavel and Sara are seated around the table. We
play this scene on Danny, barely listening. His friends
chat and banter in the background. He's not part.

> PAVEL
> We should call the police.

> SARA
> Nothing was taken. We couldn't
> give our stuff away.

INT. WAREHOUSE. ADMINISTRATOR'S OFFICE. DAY

Danny seated opposite his boss. Danny looks dreadful.
His boss eyes him with genuine concern.

> DANNY
> I'm fine. You know me: I'm always
> fine.

EXT. WAREHOUSE. YARD. NIGHT

Very few people around.

Danny sips an energy drink. And smokes.

INT. WAREHOUSE. NIGHT

A graveyard shift.

Danny is leadenly following instructions on his
handheld computer. Collecting orders.

On screen we see a route mapped through the maze.

Suddenly the computer screen goes blank. It reboots.

Danny stops walking. Waits.

On screen we see a different route mapped to a different location on the warehouse floor.

Danny changes direction, heading towards the gloomy far corner of the warehouse.

He arrives at the only aisle in shadow.

On screen the computer tells him to walk forward.

Danny steps into the darkness, nearing his destination. Straining his eyes in the gloom.

On screen the computer bleeps loudly. He's at the destination. He stops.

He looks about, unsure. Until he spots a small package. Incongruous with the normal items.

Gift wrapped, perhaps.

Puzzled, Danny reaches forward. He takes the small box and examines it. Checks around. No one about.

He opens the box --

Inside are a set of four unmarked keys.

EXT. ALEX'S APARTMENT BUILDING. NIGHT

Danny stands, unsure, keys in hands. He looks at the camera - the black eyeball staring at him.

He tries the first lock. The key doesn't fit. He switches. Second doesn't fit. Switches again --

It fits. The key turns.

INT. ALEX'S APARTMENT BUILDING. COMMUNAL HALLWAY. NIGHT

Danny enters. And examines the tray that collects the post. His letter to Alex isn't there.

Danny turns to the dark stairs leading up.

INT. ALEX'S APARTMENT BUILDING. STAIRWAY. NIGHT

Danny climbs the stairs, tentative, passing the doors to several apartments on the way up to --

The top floor. He knocks. No answer. He waits.

Danny uses the final key. And opens the door.

INT. ALEX'S APARTMENT. LIVING ROOM. NIGHT

Danny enters. The apartment is dark. And spotlessly
clean. Nothing seems disturbed.

                    DANNY
          Hello?

Silence.

Danny tries the lights. They don't work. The room is in
shadow. No laptop on the table.

Danny walks to the bedroom. Door shut.

He reaches for the handle --

INT. ALEX'S APARTMENT. BEDROOM. NIGHT

Danny enters. The bed is made. Untouched. Clean.

Danny notices the cupboard door is ajar. He opens it --

All Alex's clothes are there. Perfectly organized.
Nothing has been taken. No bags packed.

INT. ALEX'S APARTMENT. LIVING ROOM. NIGHT

Danny stares at the bathroom door. It's closed. He
takes the handle.

He opens the door --

INT. ALEX'S APARTMENT. BATHROOM. NIGHT

Danny enters. The bathroom is spotless.

The bath is empty.

Danny opens the vanity closet. Everything there.
Toothbrush included.

Confused, Danny perches on the edge of the bath.
Staring at the keys which are in his hand.

Then he notices on the glistening white tiles: his shoe
has left damp footprints.

Danny crouches, examining the marks.

Not from the bathroom.

He stands and follows the footprints out --

INT. ALEX'S APARTMENT. LIVING ROOM. NIGHT

Danny traces his own footprints. They lead back to --

INT. ALEX'S APARTMENT. BEDROOM. NIGHT

A spot in front of the wardrobe. There's a damp patch on the floor. A small puddle.

Danny looks up at the ceiling and sees a corresponding damp stain on the white ceiling.

He steps onto the bed, examining the ceiling more carefully. It's soaked. Something leaking through.

INT. ALEX'S APARTMENT. HALLWAY. NIGHT

Danny staring at a small steel handle in the ceiling. An access panel. Concealed. Hard to spot.

INT. ALEX'S APARTMENT. HALLWAY. NIGHT

Danny stands on a chair. He grips the handle and pulls. With a jolt down come a flight of stairs.

Evidently, from his reaction, Danny has never seen this before. He looks up.

A faint flickering light beckons him.

                    DANNY
          Alex?

He climbs the steps.

INT. ALEX'S APARTMENT. ATTIC. NIGHT

Danny climbs up through a narrow portal-like gap, entering a dark & unsettling space.

Imagine climbing into the inside of a hollow timber brain, sloping shallow lobes at the front, high in the middle, shallow at the back.

This is a raw attic space. Exposed beams. There are no windows. Not continuous with the apartment.

And yet...

In the very centre, the hub of this space, is a mattress. A bed. Disturbed sheets. But not set up like a domestic bed.

It's a Japanese style low bed. With no headboard. There are lights underneath creating a pool of soft light around the bed. Noirish & enticing.

Opposite the bed is a wardrobe. Much like the wardrobe we saw in Alex's bedroom. Except instead of white this one is black.

Hanging from the ceiling, creating a clearly defined zone, is a circle of soft glow exposed filament bulbs.

Each beautiful bulb hangs from an individual wire. Each beautiful bulb is a slightly different height creating the effect of a halo around the bed, the shape of which mirrors the pool of light on the floor.

This is someone's special space.

The whole set up fits into a single frame - a single image.

Someone has taken time and care to create this place.

Danny is amazed. What-the-fuck-is-this? It's odd and intriguing and beautiful all at the same time.

Danny is drawn forward.

In order to reach the bed he must pass through the cordon of orange bulbs, he brushes them aside and they swing back and forth behind him, like wind charms.

Danny looks down at the bed. The sheets are expensive. Crumpled. Used.

The pillows are arranged, but not for sleeping.

On one side of the bed is a cabinet. And on it is an antique Victorian box. Danny opens it. A music box. A ballet figure turns. A song plays slowly, warped and distorted.

Danny explores this box further. He lifts up the ballet figure. Underneath her we discover --

Set up like a Victorian chemist, exquisite glass jars. Inside the jars are powders, liquids, pills.

Poppers in a glass bottle. Danny sniffs. Powders in glass bottles. Of different kinds. Some crystals. Some chalk fine.

There's a silver straw. A mirror.

Danny empties some of the white powder onto the mirror. He touches it, leaving a clearly defined white finger print.

He tastes the powder. He recognizes the drug.

And now he notices above the bed: a series of mirrors. Not just one, but several rectangular mirrors arranged in a lattice shape. Danny stares up at his multiple reflections.

And beyond the mirror, on the ceiling is sound proof foam.

The entire attic has been insulated. Danny stands on the bed and squeezes it, as though trying to understand it.

He looks down, seeing Alex's specialist laptop on the other side of the bed, on the floor.

Danny sits on the edge of the bed, beside the laptop.

He touches the strange metal keypad.

The screen comes to life. The laptop has been connected to a bank of screens. They all come to life. Bright light.

Grainy footage begins playing on the screens - hard to distinguish. Sexual in nature. Pleasure that sounds like pain. A man. Gay porn.

Danny shuts the laptop, turning the screens off, plunging the attic back into the previously soft orange light.

And now Danny turns his attention to the wardrobe.

In a direct parallel of the apartment sequence Danny opens the doors --

Instead of Burberry suits there are sex suits, carefully hung up, glossy black leather. Perfectly smooth. A discrete zip down the back. Beautiful stitching and expert craftsmanship.

One after the other.

They're works of great skill. Expensive.

Danny looks down. There are boxes underneath the suits.

He opens one, coming face to face with a mask, mounted on a plastic head, black plastic eyes staring at him.

A zipper for a mouth.

Now Danny crouches down, opening the drawers under the wardrobe doors.

Again we parallel the apartment footage.

Instead of ties, in the first drawer, we find ropes, carefully arranged, in neat knots, some fine, some coarse.

Neatly arranged, from the thickest to the finest.

In the drawer below we discover sex toys - dildos, butt plugs. Not cheap, expensive, each in a special case.

Everything perfect. Everything beautiful.

Danny stands. Confused. He shuts the wardrobe door and as he does he sees something behind the wardrobe.

Beside the glow of a heater is the boarding school trunk we saw earlier on the walk.

On its side, upright, like an obelisk.

There are clear damp marks around the base. The timbers it rests upon are soaked.

For the first time Danny becomes scared.

He takes a step towards it, pushing his way out of the ring of bulbs which sway back and forth behind him.

Danny looks down, noticing the scratch marks on the floor.

He crouches, running his finger over the timber scratch marks, as though they told the story of what happened here.

And they do...

The scratch marks lead from the bed to the trunk.

This trunk has moved from its original position.

Danny walks forward, for the first time reacting to the smell.

He examines the liquid coming out of the lip. Not water. Thicker. Glop. Translucent.

He reaches out, touching the top of the trunk, testing its weight - very heavy...

Danny covers his nose. The smell is overwhelming.

The trunk has two combination locks, one on each side.

Forcing himself, Danny presses on the top rusted steel lock. It springs up with a loud click.

Danny presses on the second.

It clicks open, and as soon as it does, a hiss of noxious air and the trunk is forced open, thick ooze flows from the gap all over his hand.

A rush of body matter.

Shocked, Danny lets go.

He sits on the floor, staring.

In the crack that has opened up in the trunk we see the shadowy shape of a man. Horrifically decomposed.

But in the darkness we see an eye.

Danny stares at this eye.

We hold this moment. Eye to eye.

And then Danny scrambles back, running to the stairs.

Stumbling as fast as he can towards the vertical shaft of light, the outside world, the portal, the steps --

INT. ALEX'S APARTMENT HALLWAY. NIGHT

Danny takes the first few steps at speed and loses his footing, tumbling down and landing hard on his back.

His breathing is panicked.

On his back, terrified, he stares up at the attic. He takes a moment. Then slowly stands.

He reaches for the telephone. A portable phone. He picks it up. But then sees on the back of his hand --

A small clump of skin. Human hair visible.

He drops the phone. It smashes on the floor.

Danny runs to the bathroom.

INT. ALEX'S APARTMENT. BATHROOM. NIGHT

Danny is sick in the toilet.

Finished, he scrubs his hands obsessively, using a nail brush, until the skin begins to bleed.

He continues. The sink turning red.

Slowly he calms down. He stops washing his hands.

He takes out his mobile and dials 999.

INT. ALEX'S APARTMENT. LIVING ROOM. NIGHT

Danny waits. He sits. Breathing deeply.

His eyes come to rest on the smashed home phone - the bits spread across the floor.

Including the battery.

Danny picks up the battery and stares at it.

INT. ALEX'S APARTMENT. HALLWAY. NIGHT

Danny at the bottom of the stairs, looking up to the attic. Struggling with an idea. He holds a hand towel which he twists into an improvised mask for his mouth.

Danny climbs the stairs.

INT. ALEX'S APARTMENT. ATTIC. NIGHT

Danny tentatively enters the attic. The trunk has largely emptied.

Danny has no option but to look in its direction.

It's a struggle. The smell: he gags.

But he remains focused. His attention is on the laptop.

Danny walks towards it.

His actions are uncertain, acting on instinct, not knowledge. He takes hold of the laptop, flipping it over and opening the battery case.

Danny takes out the battery and peers at it. Something wrong. A crack down the side. He breaks it open --

The battery case is hollow.

Inside is a small cylindrical object, taped in place.

Danny pulls it free, examining it. We can't identify what it might be. Wrapped tight in plastic tape.

We hear the sound of police sirens.

Danny hurries to the stairs. About to go down.

But then a thought occurs to him. He returns to the laptop and hastily reassembles the hollow battery. And puts it back in place. He wipes his prints off.

The police sirens are getting louder.

Danny hurries to the stairs.

EXT. ALEX'S APARTMENT. TERRACE. NIGHT

Danny opens the terrace doors, looking out.

Seven police cars have pulled up outside.

The officers are in a hurry.

Danny looks at the cylinder.

He hides it in his pocket.

The intercom system rings loudly.

INT. ALEX'S APARTMENT. HALLWAY. NIGHT

Danny at the intercom.

On screen we see the police officers.

Danny buzzes them in.

He looks down at his pocket. The cylinder is clearly visible. He takes it out. And stuffs it in his sock.

There's a loud knock on the door.

Danny is about to open it when he has second thoughts about the cylinder in his sock --

Leaving the door shut, he runs to the kitchen.

INT. ALEX'S APARTMENT. KITCHEN. NIGHT

Danny opens the fridge door, grabbing a bottle of water. He takes the cylinder and puts it in his mouth.

The knocking on the door is urgent and angry.

> POLICE (OFF SCREEN)
> Open up!

Danny gulps the water, swallowing the cylinder. We should see it forced down his neck.

> POLICE (OFF SCREEN)
> Open the door!

The knocking is now so loud it feels like they're going to smash the door down.

Danny is red faced. We think he's going to choke. But it goes down. With excruciating difficulty.

He hurries to the door.

INT. ALEX'S APARTMENT. HALLWAY. NIGHT

Danny opens the door.

A wall of police officers flow into the apartment.

THIS SCENE IS CUT

INT. POLICE STATION. INTERROGATION ROOM. NIGHT

Stark white. The room is strange, disorienting and
bizarre. Proportions odd. Abattoir-like.

Danny is seated. No lawyer present.

The Detective opposite him is in her forties: Detective
Taylor. Her hair is cropped short, not as a style, but
having returned to work after chemotherapy.

She makes no reference to this, a silent fact, imbuing
her character with a sense of experience, wisdom, and
world weariness. Sagacity & lassitude.

There's a second officer present but we're not
interested in them. This is between Danny and Taylor.

Danny is emotional. Confused. When he sips a coffee his
hand trembles. All of which is noticed by Taylor.

>   DANNY
>   His name is Alex.
>   (beat)
>   He's my partner.
>   (beat)
>   It's his apartment.
>   (beat)
>   He disappeared two weeks ago.

Danny is puzzled by her implacable silence.

>   DANNY
>   (hopeful)
>   You think it might not be him?

>   DETECTIVE TAYLOR
>   Tell me what you know about
>   'Alex'.

Danny thinks the question absurdly broad.

>   DANNY
>   What I know?
>   (struggling)
>   He's a genius...
>   (beat)

                    DANNY (CONT'D)
          He went to university at the age
          of fifteen...
                    (beat)
          No family...
                    (beat)
          His parents are dead...
                    (beat)
          Works at an investment bank...
                    (upset)
          What else do you want?

Detective Taylor reaches into a folder taking out a
photograph of Alex and placing it in front of Danny.

He picks it up.

                    DETECTIVE TAYLOR
          Do you know this man?

Danny is thrown.

                    DANNY
          This is Alex.

                    DETECTIVE TAYLOR
          Your partner?

                    DANNY
          Yes.

                    DETECTIVE TAYLOR
          What kind of relationship did you
          have with him?

Suddenly Danny is wary of her. Of this room.

                    DETECTIVE TAYLOR
          Did it involve sadism? Drugs?

Not moralistic. She's matter of fact.

                    DANNY
          No.

                    DETECTIVE TAYLOR
          You see - it's hard for me to
          believe you were in a serious
          relationship, when you don't
          even know his name.

Danny in disbelief. Taylor watches his reaction closely.
Danny's instinct is to protest but he loses his nerve.

Taylor takes the photograph, holding it up.

                    DETECTIVE TAYLOR
          This man is called Alistair.
                    (beat)

                              DETECTIVE TAYLOR (CONT'D)
          His parents are alive.
               (beat)
          He did not work for a bank.

Silence. Danny is bewildered.

                              DETECTIVE TAYLOR
          Is it possible that you enjoyed
          extreme sexual encounters with
          someone who didn't want you to
          know their name? With someone who
          wanted that side of themselves a
          secret?

Danny bewildered as this alternate history of their love
story is mapped out, with evidence and facts.

She puts down photographs of the extreme and
provocative sex instruments found in the attic.

                              DETECTIVE TAYLOR
          Is it possible?

Photographs of the drugs. Of the video footage.

                              DETECTIVE TAYLOR
          Is it possible?

More and more photographs. A layer of them over the image
of Alex/Alistair until he can't be seen.

Danny is utterly defeated. Sure of nothing.

Suddenly the door opens.

An officer walks in and whispers something in Taylor's
ear. She seems surprised.

She leaves the room.

Danny gently sweeps away the crime scene photos,
revealing the photo of Alex/Alistair.

He stares at him.

Detective Taylor re-enters. She seems concerned.

                              DETECTIVE TAYLOR
          Would you agree to being searched?

INT. POLICE STATION. SEARCH ROOM. NIGHT

The room is similarly bizarre. Abattoir white.

Danny stripping down. Clothes in a tray.

The officer carrying out the search leans close and whispers in Danny's ear.

> OFFICER
> If I reckon you're enjoying it
> I'll break your fucking jaw.

The officer's eyes are full of hate. Danny too baffled to make a response.

The door opens.

A well dressed lawyer enters. With Taylor just behind.

> EXPENSIVE LAWYER
> This will stop. Right now.

Danny stares at this unknown man.

INT/EXT. BLACK CAB / LONDON. DAWN

Danny and Scottie are on the back seat.

> DANNY
> He lied. About everything.

> SCOTTIE
> When we met --

> DANNY
> You knew?

> SCOTTIE
> Not exactly. Our paths had never
> crossed. But I recognized the
> type of person he was. I see
> them in the corridors of
> Whitehall. People with power.
> And secrets. Their importance
> emanates from them. I felt it
> strongly in his presence.

Danny doesn't follow. He doesn't understand.

Scottie looks at him with affection. He's an innocent.

> SCOTTIE
> Danny, he was a spy.

The age of innocence comes to an end.

EXT. DANNY'S APARTMENT BUILDING. DAWN

The taxi has parked. Waiting. Door open. Danny is on the street. Scottie beside him.

                    DANNY
          I'm not sure how I'll ever be
          able to repay you.

They embrace.

Scottie moves to the cab but as if struck by an
afterthought, he stops and turns.

                    SCOTTIE
          Danny, the police are concerned
          you might have taken something
          from the crime scene. Some
          personal item. Something of
          sentimental value. But you
          wouldn't have done that, would
          you?

Danny looks at his brilliant friend. And for the first
time doesn't quite trust him.

                    DANNY
          Of course not.

Scottie holds the look, wondering.

                    SCOTTIE
          No. Of course not.

Scottie gets into the cab and shuts the door.

Danny waits, watching him go. Scottie looks at him
through the window at the cab pulls off.

Once the cab is gone Danny turns to look at the street.
At the cars parked. At the windows overlooking him. At
the strangers passing. At the traffic.

And then, in the distance, over the railway - MI6
headquarters. Looming in the skyline.

Danny stares, as if seeing it for the first time.

INT. DANNY'S APARTMENT. FRONT DOOR. DAWN

Danny stands in front of the door to his apartment. His
finger on the scars from the break-in.

INT. DANNY'S APARTMENT. BEDROOM. DAWN

Danny looks at the room with new eyes. The smashed
drawers. The ripped mattress.

INT. DANNY'S APARTMENT. BATHROOM. DAWN

Danny sits on the window ledge - looking out.

We see the view --

EXT. DANNY'S APARTMENT BUILDING. COURTYARD. DAWN

The window of the apartment where the old man used to live. The shutters are down.

INT. DANNY'S APARTMENT. BATHROOM. DAWN

Danny begins checking the bathroom. Every inch. For recording devices. Meticulous & thorough.

He takes the mirror off. Runs a bath.

INT. DANNY'S APARTMENT. BATHROOM. DAWN

Danny plugs the radio in. Turns it to the news.

INT. DANNY'S APARTMENT. BATHROOM. MORNING

The radio continues to sound out loudly.

Danny is standing over the toilet. He's wearing a rubber glove on his right hand.

He gets onto his knees and inserts his hand into the toilet, fishing something out.

INT. DANNY'S APARTMENT. BATHROOM. MORNING

Danny is scrubbing the small metallic cylinder. There's a knock on the door. He jumps. He's jittery.

> SARA (V.O.)
> Danny?

> DANNY
> I'm almost done.

Danny raises the wrapped cylinder to eye level.

He cuts the edge of the plastic with nail scissors and begins to unwind it.

Slowly revealing --

END OF EPISODE

EPISODE TWO:

"STRANGERS"

INT. DANNY'S APARTMENT. BEDROOM. NIGHT

Danny staring at his closed fist. Bloodshot eyes
contemplate the object hidden within his palm.

INT. DANNY'S APARTMENT. NIGHT

Danny peering into every room, checking that he's
alone. Fist tight by his side.

Checks complete, he secures the front door.

INT. DANNY'S APARTMENT. BATHROOM. NIGHT

Danny furtively glances out of the window --

EXT. DANNY'S APARTMENT BUILDING. COURTYARD. NIGHT

The apartment with the closed shutters.

INT. DANNY'S APARTMENT. KITCHEN. NIGHT

Danny closes the blinds. Lights the gas. Boils water.
An arbitrary manufacturing of kitchen noise.

He takes a tatty white table cloth and spreads it over
the table so that it hangs down to the floor. Done, he
turns the kitchen lights off.

Finally he sits *under* the table, on the bubbled linoleum
floor, like a child sheltering from angry parents. He
lights the squat stub of a candle.

Only once protected, within the soft glow of this space,
does he feel secure enough to reveal --

The item he swallowed: a titanium cylinder with a row
of seven numbered rotating dials. Slender. Impregnable.

INT. DANNY'S APARTMENT. KITCHEN. NIGHT

Danny unbuttons his shirt, picks up a roll of duct tape
and fixes the cylinder snug against his sternum.

EXT. DANNY'S APARTMENT BUILDING. NIGHT

Danny exits the building wearing anonymous colors - a
hooded top. Skittish, he scrutinizes passers-by, the
windows overlooking the street & parked cars.

EXT. VAUXHALL UNDERPASS. NIGHT

A line of traffic held at a red light. Danny uses the
side mirrors of stationary cars to check who's behind
him. Various, including a man.

Danny turns to the underground station.

INT. UNDERGROUND STATION. ESCALATOR. NIGHT

Danny on the escalator. He looks back at the people
behind. The man from the underpass tunnel.

Danny sidesteps out of line and descends at pace. At
the bottom he glances back to see the tunnel man has
also stepped out of the line, also descending.

INT. UNDERGROUND STATION. PLATFORM. NIGHT

Danny walks down the platform, almost all the way, then
abruptly turns, walking back up the platform --

The tunnel man is coming straight towards him. Their
eyes meet. The train rushes into the station. Danny and
the man pass. People surge to the edge.

Danny and the tunnel man board adjacent carriages.

INT. UNDERGROUND CARRIAGE. NIGHT

Danny looks through the window to the adjacent carriage.
He sees the tunnel man, standing sideways to him.

Danny studies the other passengers. An older handsome
Asian man in an expensive suit.

A woman seated nearby, reading one of the free London
newspapers. Front Page headed - "Spy Sex Attic".

Danny peers over her shoulder to see a tabloid-style
article. A photograph of the gas mask outfit.
Juxtaposed with a photograph of Alex.

INT. UNDERGROUND STATION. PLATFORM. NIGHT

Danny steps onto the platform amidst the crowd. In the
reflection of a glossy advertisement he glimpses the
tunnel man only a few paces behind.

Danny weaves through the crowd but as the doors to the
tube begin to close Danny sharply alters course and
runs back towards the carriage.

INT. UNDERGROUND CARRIAGE / PLATFORM. NIGHT

Danny lurches inside. Doors shut. Breathless, he peers
out at the tunnel man on the platform. But the man is
seemingly unperturbed by Danny's departure.

As the train disappears into the darkness Danny notices
the woman, previously seated and reading the paper is
now standing and reading. An odd change.

And behind her, the older handsome Asian man in the
sharp suit regards Danny with cool detachment.

EXT. EAST LONDON TUBE STATION & STREET. NIGHT

Danny exits into a rough area. He walks with certainty
and purpose - this area is evidently known to him.

A row of pawnbrokers, loan shops, pound stores. Danny
heads towards a busy fast-food restaurant.

INT. FAST FOOD JOINT RESTAURANT. NIGHT

Crowded. Dirty. Cheap.

Danny goes straight through to the back - the toilets.

INT. FAST FOOD JOINT RESTAURANT. TOILET. NIGHT

Danny takes off his hooded top, reversing it, now a
different color. He puts on a hat. Then climbs through
the small back window, dropping down onto --

EXT. EAST LONDON SIDE STREET. NIGHT

A dark side street. No cameras. Danny swings towards
the shadows away from the main road.

EXT. EAST LONDON SCRUBLAND. NIGHT

Danny climbs over a fence and into scrubland. Abandoned
washing machines. Burnt mattresses. He arrives at --

The skeleton of a former factory. Late 19th century. A
dramatic ruin, towering into the night sky.

From the shadows, Danny surveys the approach - no one
following. Once he's sure, he enters the ruins.

INT. DERELICT INDUSTRIAL WAREHOUSE. NIGHT

Danny passes a wall covered in graffiti, pausing,
locating his own name, amateurishly painted. No
nostalgia: a touch of sadness and regret.

INT. DERELICT INDUSTRIAL WAREHOUSE. MACHINE ROOM. NIGHT

Danny nimbly clambers up the shell of a long-dead
furnace towards the ceiling. Up high, rusted pipes
crisscross in all directions.

Danny finds a section of the pipe and removes the
bolts. It comes free. Inside is a teenage hiding place.

Soft drug paraphernalia. Faded gay porn & poppers.

And a diary wrapped in plastic. Danny flicks through.
Sketches. Lyrics. Aimless teenage creativity.

Danny checks he's alone. From under his shirt he
removes the cylinder. He finds it hard to let go.

Finally Danny hides it inside the spine of the diary,
wraps it in plastic, secretes it away.

He puts the pipe back. Secures the bolts.

To the naked eye there are no clues as to where it
might be. Just a labyrinth of pipes.

EXT. DERELICT INDUSTRIAL WAREHOUSE. ROOFTOP. NIGHT

On the rooftop, like a feral cat, Danny perches on the
edge guarding his secret. All around poverty.

And in the distance the twinkling lights of the city.

INT. DANNY'S APARTMENT. BEDROOM. DAY

Danny standing close to the mirror about to knot his tie.
He's wearing a smartly ironed shirt.

He attempts a knot. It's too small. It looks awful. With
some irritation he unties it. Too much irritation, he's
brittle emotionally. A great deal at stake in his
appearance.

And he's about to try again. When he stops, pausing...

FLASH BACK TO:

INT. DANNY'S APARTMENT. BEDROOM. DAY (PAST)

Danny & Alex getting ready to go out. A smart event,
something celebratory. They're both in good moods.

Alex is immaculately dressed. Shirt, tie, jacket. Danny
struggling with his tie. Alex steps close to him --

But Alex waits a beat in case Danny is offended by the
notion of being helped.

Danny, however, gladly allows Alex to tie the knot.

Which Alex does. The movements are assured. Precise. Alex
glancing from the knot to Danny. From the knot to Danny.

Finished, Alex neatens it. His fingers linger on Danny's
shirt collar. Careful. Meticulous. The moment is
intimate.

                                              BACK TO:

INT. DANNY'S APARTMENT. BEDROOM. DAY (PRESENT)

Danny caught by a wave of emotion. Upset, with tears in
his eyes he ties his own knot, capturing some of Alex's
rhythm. Precise. Meticulous.

Danny ties it well. He neatens the knot, alone.

Finished, Danny's eyes move to the side of the mirror --

Now see that the wall is covered with pages from various
newspapers. Tabloid & Broadsheet.

The pages are all about Alex's death. Without exception
every paper claims it was a sex game gone wrong.

All the pages are carefully annotated by Danny. In red
ink. Underlined. By the headlines and by individual
points:

THIS IS A LIE.

A LIE.

THIS IS A LIE.

Danny's eye move over all the pages. Finished, his eyes
return to his reflection.

                    DANNY (TO HIMSELF)
                (practising)
            Your newspaper has printed a
            series of lies...
                (too negative)

Your newspaper needs to print the
truth about...
          (too baggy)
Your newspaper needs to know the
truth...
          (wrong again)
The public need to know the truth.
          (too saintly)
I'm here - today - to tell you the
truth.
          (too soft)
I'm here to tell you the truth.
          (more blunt)
I'm here to tell you the truth.
          (he likes it)
I'm here to tell you the truth.
          (faster)
I'm here to tell you the truth.
          (final)
I'm here to tell you the truth.

We can bleed these final attempts over Danny's entrance
into the newspaper office.

Building and building, a crescendo, faster and faster,
more and more determined, more and more absolute.

Convincing. Powerful. Angry.

Who couldn't believe him?

What couldn't go wrong?

EXT. NEWSPAPER OFFICE. DAY

Danny wearing a shirt, not a suit, as formal as he can
manage. Tie knotted so-so.

Danny stands outside a glass and steel office. The new
industrial heartland of London.

INT. NEWSPAPER OFFICE. LOBBY. DAY

An impressive atrium. Busy with journalists.

Danny waits, observing office life - the security fob,
chic shoes, strong coffees and smart phones.

He glances up, at the many windows, and spies a man in a
suit, high up, staring down at him.

An assistant arrives and makes a snap evaluation of
Danny: her eyes flick up from his shoes to his hair.

INT. NEWSPAPER OFFICE. ELEVATOR. DAY

Danny and assistant in the elevator.

Jarring silence.

INT. NEWSPAPER OFFICES. CONFERENCE ROOM. DAY

Danny seated on one side of a vast glossy table.

On the other side: a woman in her fifties - a senior
news editor. Dressed sharp. Stern. Cross-trainer thin.

A woman in her late twenties - a journalist. Around
Danny's age, dressed less angularly.

A sturdy old-fashioned lawyer. Tortoiseshell glasses.

A recording device in the centre of the table.

                    EDITOR
          In your phone call you asked --
               (from transcript)
          "How it all works?". We took
          that as negotiating payment.

Danny's taken aback.

                    DANNY
          No. I've never spoken to a
          journalist before...
               (no one believes him)
          I don't want any money.

The lawyer whispers to the editor. She nods.

                    EDITOR
          You used the word "partners" to
          describe your relationship?

                    DANNY
          We were partners.

                    EDITOR
          What do you mean by that?

He struggles and stumbles.

                    DANNY
          I mean...

Against a wall of scepticism, Danny rallies.

                    DANNY (CONT'D)
          I wanted to spend the rest of my
          life with him.

He's never articulated that before. It catches him emotionally. But cuts no ice with his audience.

                    EDITOR
          You'd been together eight months.

                    DANNY
          Yes.

                    EDITOR
          During those eight months how many
          times had you visited the attic?

                    DANNY
          I'd never visited the attic.
               (correcting)
          Except when I discovered...
               (beat)
          That was the first time.

                    EDITOR
          But you must have known about it?

                    DANNY
          No.

                    EDITOR
          The activities that went on up
          there?

                    DANNY
          That's what I'm trying to say. I
          don't know if anything went on. I
          never saw him use those items. I
          never heard him talk about them.

                    EDITOR
          You were his sexual partner. For
          eight months. He never mentioned
          sadism? Never asked you to
          participate? Never discussed his
          predilections? You know nothing.
          That's what you've come here today
          to tell us?

                    DANNY
          I've come here to tell you...

Danny's eye turns to the swirling grey sky over London.

                                        FLASH TO:

EXT. COUNTRYSIDE. ESTUARY. DAY (PAST)

Danny and Alex's first walk together at this melancholy and magic landscape. The water laps about their feet.

Danny looking at Alex. And Alex turns to look at him.

                                        BACK TO:

INT. NEWSPAPER OFFICES. CONFERENCE ROOM. DAY (PRESENT)

The newspaper team waiting for Danny to answer.

Danny, lost in the memory, we're not sure how he'll
react. Frustration is replaced by grief.

                    DANNY
          Why won't you ask what I think
          happened to him?

                    EDITOR
          What do you think happened to
          him?

                    DANNY
          He was murdered.

                    EDITOR
          Who murdered him?

                    DANNY
          I don't know.

                    EDITOR
          Why did they murder him?

                    DANNY
          I don't know.

Silence.

The lawyer cleans his spectacles.

EXT. NEWSPAPER OFFICES. DAY

Danny exits the building, removing his tie.

Away from the immediate proximity of the offices he's
surprised by the younger journalist. She must have used
a different exit. She seems nervous.

                    JOURNALIST
          Not here.

INT. CASUAL RESTAURANT. DAY

The restaurant is casual and scruffy. Danny and the
journalist in a corner. No recording device.

                  JOURNALIST
My brother was an addict.
Cocaine, for seven years, and I
didn't know. Until he was in
hospital, telling me he used to
do it on Christmas Day --

Danny shakes his head.

                  JOURNALIST (CONT'D)
How can you be sure?

                  DANNY
I've done drugs. And if you've
done them you can tell.

                  JOURNALIST
People lie, Danny. And they lie
well.

                  DANNY
Guys who own rooms like that
attic, when it comes to sex they
know what they want. How they want
it. The sex is professional. He
didn't know what he enjoyed. He'd
never found out.

                  JOURNALIST
You don't use his name? Is it true
you didn't even know it?

                  DANNY
He told me his name was Alex.

                  JOURNALIST
I get it. He's a spy. He needed to
be careful. You met by chance.
First date he lied. But eight
months later, you want to spend
the rest of your life together,
but you're still using the wrong
name to say how much you love him?

The pain of the lie is raw. Danny doesn't understand it.

                  DANNY
I can't explain.

                  JOURNALIST
Did he tell you he was in danger?

                  DANNY
No.

                  JOURNALIST
Are you afraid?

The idea takes Danny by surprise.

EXT. CASUAL RESTAURANT. DAY

Outside the entrance a neon sign flashes the name of the
diner. Danny shakes the journalist's hand.

                    DANNY
          Do you believe me?

The question is wonderfully naive. She says, sincerely --

                    JOURNALIST
          It doesn't matter what I
          believe.
               (to Danny it does)
          But yes, I do.

Danny watches her go, a little more hopeful.

EXT. HAMPSTEAD. STREETS. DAY

Scottie and Danny walking towards a pub or a restaurant.
Their pace is slow. Leaden. Danny seems solemn, guarded,
hanging back a little from Scottie. Their energy is off.

                    SCOTTIE
          Journalists make difficult
          bedfellows. You can't just tell
          them what to print.
               (Danny doesn't
                respond)
          You didn't want to discuss it with
          me first?

                    DANNY
          I was sure you'd talk me out of
          it. Make me realize what a dumb
          idea it was.

Danny sharp. Scottie stops walking. He studies Danny.

                    SCOTTIE
          What is this?
               (beat)
          Mistrust?
               (beat)
          It is.
               (beat)
          I see...

Scottie struggles to process it. He's hurt.

                    SCOTTIE (CONT'D)
          You've trusted me with your life.
          But not now? Not with this?

                    DANNY
          My life is small. This is...
          organizations... Institutions...

                    SCOTTIE
          You see me as 'one of them', don't
          you? The suit. The education. The
          job. I'm part of the
          establishment?

                    DANNY
          Aren't you?

                    SCOTTIE
          How dare you - young man. How dare
          you presume to know me. I know you
          because I've heard every secret
          you have to tell. But what do you
          know about me? Answer me!

Scottie's angry seems to come from nowhere. And it takes
Danny by surprise. He can't process it.

                    DANNY
          I know...

                    SCOTTIE
          Where I live? What films I like?
          What music I listen to?
                    (beat)
          Did you know I suffer from
          depression?
                    (Danny didn't)
          Did you know that in the past I
          drank. Every night. Every day.
          Every morning. I drank. Until a
          stranger could smell it on me --
                    (he didn't)
          And do you know - young man - how
          fucking far I am from being part
          of the establishment?
                    (he doesn't)
          How dare you. Mistrust me. When
          you don't know.

It's the first, and only time, we'll hear Scottie swear.
It's the first, and only time, we'll see Scottie lose his
temper.

It surprises Scottie as much as it does Danny.

Danny is taken aback by this anger. He's never seen it
before. But he isn't swayed, either.

Scottie walks away from him, trying to calm down. His
attention turning to the heath. At the end of the street.

An idea strikes Scottie. His anger turns into solemn contemplation.

The heath....

> SCOTTIE (CONT'D)
> You want to know who I am? Who I
> really am? I'll show you.

Scottie sets off toward the heath. Danny remains where he is. Scottie looks back. He's firm.

> SCOTTIE (CONT'D)
> Come on! Then you can decide if
> you trust me or not.

Danny follows. Just behind. They enter the heath.

EXT. HAMPSTEAD HEATH. FOREST. DAY

Scottie leads Danny towards a magnificent oak tree.
They pause, admiring its awesome size and shape.

EXT. HAMPSTEAD HEATH. FOREST. SADNESS TREE. DAY

Up close Scottie presses a hand against its trunk as if reunited with an old friend. Danny observes.

Scottie looks into the branches above.

> SCOTTIE
> We are at the spot my career as
> a spy came to an end.

For Danny, it's a revelation.

> SCOTTIE (CONT'D)
> I was a spy, once.

Scottie's mood turns sombre.

> SCOTTIE (CONT'D)
> A long time ago. In a world very
> different to this one.

EXT. HAMPSTEAD HEATH. FOREST. SADNESS TREE. DAY

Scottie and Danny seated, side by side, on a dead, moss-spotted trunk, staring at the 'sadness tree'.

                    SCOTTIE
        I was recruited at Cambridge. I
        said yes partly because it
        wouldn't be a normal life, with
        regular hours, and I was desperate
        to avoid a five o'clock home time,
        while not being bohemian enough to
        imagine life without a proper
        profession. Not very patriotic
        motives, I suppose. They rather
        liked that about me. An utter lack
        of idealism. Romantics make
        unreliable spies.

Danny reacts to that idea.

                    SCOTTIE (CONT'D)
        It was my third year with MI6. I
        was travelling back to London by
        night train. A handsome man joined
        my carriage. He sat close to me.
        The tips of our shoes touched. Our
        eyes chanced. He asked the most
        mundane questions in the most
        exciting way. When we arrived at
        Paddington I went to the
        'Gentlemen's', waiting in a
        cubicle, door ajar, hoping...
                (beat)
        I cannot express how happy I was
        to see him. It meant I hadn't been
        wrong. And for the next fifteen
        minutes, or so, I wouldn't be
        alone.
                (embarrassed)
        After all these years –
        prudishness runs deep. The next
        day I was approached by a Soviet
        operative. He described how the
        Soviet Union welcomed 'men like
        me'. Under Communism we were all
        equals. Once I'd completed my
        mission here, in a country that
        would always hate my kind, I could
        make a home in Moscow and be free.

Scottie's hands shake. Despite his measured account this
is upsetting. Unspoken about. He glances at Danny.

                    SCOTTIE (CONT'D)
        Some 'men like us' actually
        believed that lie. But I wasn't
        one of them. So all that remained
        was the blackmail. I'd be exposed.
        Arrested. Disgraced. That night I
        bought a rope. And walked here.

Scottie's eyes move to a specific branch.

SCOTTIE (CONT'D)
But sitting on that branch, noose
ready, I thought to myself - there
is another way.

DANNY
You told your bosses that you were
gay?

SCOTTIE
That's a wonderful wrong answer.
However, the option did not yet
exist. No, I explained to my
section head that I'd been
approached by a Soviet operative
and detailed the nature of the
blackmail. He asked if the
allegations were true. I admitted
that I'd made a mistake. With a
man. And that the operative might
have evidence. Of that mistake.
But it was only once. An act of
madness. An act of disgusting
madness --
        (re-enacts)
'I am not a homosexual!'
        (beat)
And I am not a traitor.
        (beat)
Hard to believe the second
statement when the first is a lie.
So I proposed, preposterously,
that they employ someone to follow
me for the rest of my life.
Photograph my every move. I'd
never touch a man. I didn't
discover until later that it
hadn't been a Soviet operative. It
had been an internal
investigation. You've heard of a
mole hunt? This was a fag hunt.
Which they saw as more or less the
same thing. Her Majesty's Secret
Service had its fingers burnt by
one too many queer spies. My
prompt confession saved my life. I
was moved out of MI6 and into, as
it was then called, The Ministry
for Transport, where I became
little more than a bookkeeper,
whispered about by those in the
know. Out of gratitude, and fear,
I kept my end of the bargain. And
for eleven years I did not touch
another man.

Silence.

Danny reaches out and takes hold of Scottie's hand. The gesture catches Scottie off guard.

He looks down at Danny's hand around his - the different skins, one marked with age, one glossy with youth.

Cementing their rapprochement, Scottie clasps his other hand around Danny's.

INT. SCOTTIE'S HOUSE. KITCHEN. NIGHT

Scottie has made fresh soup. Danny and Scottie eat.

> SCOTTIE
> Will you sleep?

Danny shakes his head.

> SCOTTIE (CONT'D)
> Then I propose we stay up all night and wait for the morning papers together.

Danny nods - accepting the proposal.

INT. SCOTTIE'S HOUSE. LIVING ROOM. NIGHT

Shelves of books, antiques, not fusty but cosy. Like a gentleman's club. Without the formality.

Scottie in a leather chair, reading Berg's biography of Woodrow Wilson.

Danny lying in the sofa. Not reading. He peers over at Scottie's book. Scottie catches his glance.

We think, for a second, that he's going to read some aloud. And Danny wants him to. But Scottie isn't sure whether to suggest it. Danny isn't sure whether to ask.

The moment passes.

INT. SCOTTIE'S HOUSE. LIVING ROOM. DAWN

Danny at the window as day breaks. He turns to Scottie. Scottie puts the book down. It's time.

EXT. HAMPSTEAD VILLAGE. DAWN

Danny and Scottie walk to the newsagents. Nervousness from both. The streets are deserted.

They stop at the stack of various papers being delivered. The truck still there.

Danny breaks the plastic and takes out a classy looking broadsheet. Scans the front. Not on the cover.

Danny turns the pages, slowly at first, then faster.

There's nothing.

About to check from the beginning for a second time Danny sees, to the side, the front page of a tabloid --

Danny's face is on the front.

The photo was taken outside the diner. By a photographer that Danny never saw or knew was there.

Even though it was daytime the photo appears dark, as if it were nighttime. A fragment of the neon sign in the frame. But it's a blur. Unable to identify the letters the overall effect is strip-club-soho-sleazy.

The headline: "Attic Spy Sex Partner Secrets".

Danny opens the paper to reveal a double page spread --

"I took drugs." "I never knew his name."

There's a lurid graphic illustrating the attic - the sex toys, the video, the drugs, and trunk.

Danny's admission that he'd been with guys who had rooms "just like this one" before.

Danny's expression falters as he realizes the depth of his miscalculation.

INT. HAMPSTEAD. CAFE. MORNING

Scottie and Danny sit at a table. Danny seems dazed. Vacant. Unable to believe his own stupidity.

Scottie is concerned. But unable to do anything, unable to say anything, he merely pours a tea for Danny.

Unable to say anything, or do anything, Danny stares at the tea, until finally he takes a small sip.

EXT. WAREHOUSE. DAY

Danny arriving for work. Other members of staff glance at him. Not hostile. They're curious. He's news.

INT. WAREHOUSE. LOCKER ROOM. DAY

Danny's getting changed into work clothes. He stops as a man in a suit enters.

INT. WAREHOUSE. BOSS'S OFFICE. DAY

Danny seated opposite his boss. Newspaper on table.

                    DANNY
          Drug test me.
                (beat)
          I need this.

But we know the answer is no.

INT. DANNY'S APARTMENT. BEDROOM. DAY

Danny, despondent, slumped on the bed.

Sara brings in a letter. She sits on his bed. Danny
doesn't stir. She shows him the letter. Handwritten.

                    SARA
          I'm going to open it, okay?

Sara opens it. She finds, inside, a pair of train
tickets. And reads the accompanying letter.

                    SARA (CONT'D)
          It's from his parents.

Danny moves like a bullet, taking the letter, devouring
the words. He turns his attention to the train tickets --

INT/EXT. INTERCITY TRAIN / COUNTRYSIDE. DAY

Danny seated in a packed standard class carriage.
Racing through English countryside.

At first glance it looks like Danny is doing the jumbo
crossword. In fact he's writing the name "Alistair" in
the across grid and "Alex" in the down grid.

EXT. STATION PLATFORM. REMOTE VILLAGE. NIGHT

Danny waiting alone. An old station building.
Countryside. Could be in an England from sixty years ago.

Danny has completely filled the jumbo crossword with Alex
/ Alistair, and continues writing over the letters.

A couple in their early sixties appear at the far end of
the platform. Standing under a moody lamppost.

Danny spots them. He stands, picks up his bag, and walks
towards the couple. They come plainly into view --

The mother, Mrs. Turner, is imperious. Dressed in
vintage black designer.

The father, Mr. Turner, appears in excellent shape.
Physically strong. Country manor tweed.

>   DANNY
>   Mr. and Mrs. Turner?

Mr. Turner gives a nod and offers his hand. Danny
shakes it. The man seems cold, not hostile - neutral.

Mrs. Turner puts on an affected air of aloofness, but
Danny can tell that she's curious & warmer.

No polite questions. No mention of their being late.

>   DANNY (CONT'D)
>   Thank you for sending the tickets.
>   I'm happy to pay for them myself.

Danny reaches for his wallet. The parents watch as Danny
takes out an envelope. Mr. Turner accepts the envelope.
Checks the money. And then offers it back to Danny.

>   MR. TURNER
>   There's no need.

Mr. Turner holds the money outstretched towards Danny.

>   DANNY
>   It wouldn't feel right.

>   MRS. TURNER
>   You're our guest.

>   DANNY
>   (uncertain)
>   If you're sure...

>   MR. TURNER
>   We're sure.

It feels like a test. Danny calculates it's ruder to
refuse. He gives in. Accepts the money back.

Mr. Turner looks at his wife, as if he just won a bet.

Mr. Turner picks up Danny's bag, walking off. Danny's
embarrassed but is unable to extricate it.

Mrs. Turner walks by Danny's side, looking him up and
down. Danny catches her glances. He smiles at her.

She seems flustered by the smile.

EXT. TRAIN STATION. REMOTE VILLAGE. NIGHT

A vintage car. Impressive but not well preserved.

Mr. Turner deposits the bag in the back. There are walking boots, maps, various other outdoor items.

INT/EXT. VINTAGE CAR / COUNTRYSIDE. NIGHT

Danny in the backseat. Alex's parents in the front.

Danny's eyes pick up on every detail.

The view outside is darkness and gloomy forest.

Mr. Turner looks at Danny in the rear view mirror.

INT/EXT. VINTAGE CAR / TURNERS' HOUSE. NIGHT

The car turns off the road onto a narrow drive.

An old stone house embedded in a forest. No neighbours. Modest in size. And run down.

Danny fascinated with his first view of the property.

EXT. TURNERS' HOUSE. NIGHT

Danny gets out of the car. He stands before the house. Eyeing it up and down. As if it were a character.

>   DANNY
>   How long have you lived here?

>   MR. TURNER
>   Alistair didn't tell you?

>   DANNY
>   No.

His parents look at each other.

>   MRS. TURNER
>   What did he tell you about us?

>   DANNY
>   He told me you were dead.

With ice-cold British understatement --

>   MR. TURNER
>   We weren't close.

The Turners head in.

Danny takes a moment to walk to the edge of the wintery forest - menace and beauty in equal measure.

He's about to go inside when he sees a distant light in the depths of the trees -- *the flicker of a flashlight.*

And then it's gone. Danny waits. Nothing more. He heads back to the house, glancing over his shoulder.

INT. TURNERS' HOUSE. HALLWAY & STAIRS. NIGHT

Danny enters, shutting the front door. The interior is angular and unsettling. Not homely.

Mrs. Turner is halfway up the stairs. Waiting. Like a statue. It's weird.

INT. TURNERS' HOUSE. UPSTAIRS HALLWAY. NIGHT

The corridor is long and narrow with eight identical doors, creating a cramped and claustrophobic feeling.

Mrs. Turner opens a door for him. In the harsh light Danny regards her peculiar heightened anxiety.

He enters the bedroom.

INT. TURNERS' HOUSE. GUEST BEDROOM. NIGHT

A single bed. A side cabinet. A wardrobe. Lace curtains. A towel and hand-towel neatly folded on the bed. Along with a small square of pale soap.

A bedroom from fifty years ago.

She enters the room, as if she were intending to stay and talk. Danny can sense she wants to.

                    MRS. TURNER
          Bathroom's opposite. It's all
          yours. Is one towel enough?

                    DANNY
          Plenty.

                    MRS. TURNER
          You'll want some time. Before
          dinner. Is one hour enough?

She seems unaware of the repeated phrase. Danny fights the urge to say 'plenty'.

                    DANNY
          More than enough.

She still doesn't want to leave, stealing glances at Danny, pretending to check the room is in order.

Danny watches her. In the end, as if caught by a sudden thought, she hurries out, shutting the door.

A small crucifix on the wall. Danny takes it off the hook. Wallpaper faded underneath.

INT. TURNERS' HOUSE. GUEST BATHROOM. NIGHT

Awkward jarring cut as Danny opens the vanity cabinet in the bathroom. On one shelf there is a laminated sign. "For Guest Use". The other shelves are empty.

INT. TURNERS' HOUSE. GUEST BEDROOM. NIGHT

Danny has showered. He takes out of his bag a dry-cleaned white shirt. And unwraps it.

INT. TURNERS' HOUSE. UPSTAIRS HALLWAY. NIGHT

Danny smart in a crisp white shirt. The house is silent. He studies the various closed doors. His hand rests on a handle, tempted to explore. But he doesn't.

INT. TURNERS' HOUSE. KITCHEN. NIGHT

Danny enters. Alex's mum and dad are waiting. Silent.

The table's laid for one. Danny stares at it.

> MR. TURNER
> We've already eaten.

Danny's deflated. The clock on the wall says it's nine.

Mrs. Turner is embarrassed by their rudeness. Mr. Turner is not. She tries to compensate.

> MR. TURNER (CONT'D)
> We won't stand here and watch.

> MRS. TURNER
> If you need anything else we'll be
> next door.

They exit into the living room, closing the door.

Danny's abruptly left alone, in his smart shirt.

He peers down --

A cold plate of food under cling-film - a rectangle of anaemic cheese, a hardboiled egg, a half tomato, iceberg lettuce, gelatinous ham. A single white roll.

Two glasses of foil covered wine. One red. One white.

Danny walks to the door, about to open it, and ask why they can't talk, but he decides against it.

INT. TURNERS' HOUSE. KITCHEN. NIGHT

Danny has finished the food. He washes up the plate, dries it, puts it by the sink. Wipes down the table.

Now half past nine. No sign of Alex's parents. He walks to the door. No sound. Danny opens it.

INT. TURNERS' HOUSE. LIVING ROOM. NIGHT

Alex's parents are reading. They look up at Danny.

> MRS. TURNER
> How was dinner?

Danny sounds less effusive than before.

> DANNY
> It was fine.

The Turners nod and return to their books. Danny stands, a little lost. And upset.

INT. TURNERS' HOUSE. LIVING ROOM. NIGHT

Danny sits with Alex's parents. But he's not reading - observing them. They read. Steadily. Heads down. No hint of conversation. Danny refuses to accept this.

> DANNY
> Alistair - tell me about him.

Both parents put down their books and look at him.

Mr. Turner abruptly stands up.

> MR. TURNER
> Tomorrow morning. When you're
> rested.

Mr. Turner leaves. Danny is worried that he's offended him. Mrs. Turner seems torn between various responses.

> MRS. TURNER
> Will you be able to sleep?

> DANNY
> Probably not.

INT. TURNERS' HOUSE. KITCHEN. NIGHT

Mrs.Turner is making hot milk, full cream, spicing it
with fresh ground cinnamon. Danny observes --

Her hands are unkempt. Strong. Sturdy. Working hands.

Her shoes are plain, stout. And do not match the vintage
clothes. In fact, the vintage clothes are not a good fit.

With subtle guile, Danny observes.

                    DANNY
      Alistair suffered from insomnia.

She pours the milk, lovingly handing it to Danny.

                 MRS. TURNER
         (natural)
      That's why he liked running so
      much. To exhaust him. His mind was
      so busy. He ran so he could sleep.

A hint of an accent when she's more relaxed. Suddenly
she's nervous, intimacy too far.

                    DANNY
      Why can't you talk to me?

                 MRS. TURNER
      In the morning, you'll understand.

INT. TURNERS' HOUSE. GUEST BEDROOM. NIGHT

Danny in bed. Lights off. Can't sleep, staring at the
crucifix. He sits up, gets out of bed.

INT. TURNERS' HOUSE. UPSTAIRS HALLWAY / ROOMS. NIGHT

Danny enters the hallway of eight identical doors. He
quietly walks towards one. Opens the door: a cupboard. He
continues his search. Trying not to make a noise.

Finally he discovers a bedroom --

INT. TURNERS' HOUSE. ALEX'S BEDROOM. NIGHT

Danny enters. Shuts the door behind him. Quietly. And
turns to examine the room --

A desk against the window. View out into the forest.
Bookshelves. And many books. The spines are broken. Dense
academic volumes. Mathematical equations.

There are annotations. From the way Danny touches them, we guess that he recognizes the handwriting.

Danny walks to the wardrobe. Opens it. A few clothes. Colour-coordinated. Searches their pockets. Finds nothing.

Danny to the writing desk. Opens the drawers. Nothing.

Danny to the bed. Looks under it. Nothing. Then stands, stares down at it, hand on top of the sheets.

No emotion. No reaction.

INT. TURNERS' HOUSE. HALLWAY. NIGHT

Danny exits, startled to discover Mrs. Turner in the hallway. He doesn't know what to say: caught red handed.

But she's not angry. She seems as lost as he is. About to speak but says nothing, turns and goes back to her room.

Danny watches as she shuts the door.

INT. TURNERS' HOUSE. GUEST BEDROOM. MORNING

Danny woken by a sharp knock. The door opens. Mr. Turner looms in the doorway.

                    MR. TURNER
          Time to talk.

The door's shut.

Danny checks his phone. It's six AM.

INT. TURNERS' HOUSE. KITCHEN. MORNING

Danny enters. Unlike last night the table is laid for three. A hearty communal breakfast. Danny's relieved.

He takes his seat. Alex's mum pours Danny a cup of tea.

                    DANNY
          Thank you.

Danny checks to see if she's annoyed.

Mr. Turner seems oblivious. Apparently she didn't tell him. A secret. A curious one.

Danny waits for them to take the lead.

                    MR. TURNER
          We'd prefer it if there was no
          fuss.

He looks to his wife. She confirms, less convincingly.

>   MRS. TURNER
>   We'd both prefer it.

>   MR. TURNER
>   If there was no fuss.

>   DANNY
>   You read the article?

>   MRS. TURNER
>   We're not making any judgements.

>   MR. TURNER
>   You see the life we lead. We're
>   private people. We don't want
>   attention. The past is the past.
>   What Alistair did in London was up
>   to him. He was an adult. Can't
>   bring him back. We'd just prefer
>   it if there was no fuss.

Mr. Turner places a hand on his wife's hand. She doesn't seem comfortable. But doesn't pull away.

>   DANNY
>   I won't speak to the press again.

>   MR. TURNER
>   That's good.

Danny can't let it stand at that --

>   DANNY
>   But no one was saying it. So I
>   said it. Your son was murdered.

Mr. Turner looks up sharply.

>   MR. TURNER
>   After breakfast, how about a walk?
>   Just the two of us?

EXT. FOREST. DAY

Danny and Mr. Turner walking. Danny's behind him. The forest is dense & dark.

>   DANNY
>   Your son was murdered.

Mr. Turner stops walking. But doesn't turn. Danny arrives at his side, looking at his expression.

                        MR. TURNER
        My son's dead. My wife's sick.
                (beat)
        Her nerves...

                        DANNY
        I'm sorry.

                        MR. TURNER
        Enough.

Holding each other's eye. Danny doesn't push.

The father turns, and walks on, offering no more
explanation. Danny watches him go.

INT. TURNERS' HOUSE. GUEST BEDROOM. DAY

Danny packing to leave, folding his white shirt. He
stops, troubled and unsure.

INT. TURNERS' HOUSE. ALEX'S ROOM. DAY

Danny stands in the room, deep in thought.

INT. TURNERS' HOUSE. KITCHEN. DAY

Danny enters without his bags. And stands opposite
Alex's parents - his energies strangely elevated.

Alex's parents notice the lack of a bag. They've made a
packed lunch for him. In a plastic bag.

A pork pie. An apple. A juice carton.

                        MR. TURNER
        We need to leave soon if we're
        to make your train.

Danny doesn't reply. He stares at Alex's parents - not
a polite, inquisitive glance - he really *stares*.

                        DANNY
         What is this?

They look at Danny. They look at each other.

                        DANNY (CONT'D)
        Who are you?
                (beat)
        That --
                (points upstairs)
        Is not his bedroom.
                (beat)
        This is not his home.

>   (points at them)
>   You are not his parents.

Danny is only seventy percent sure.

Mr. Turner's expression darkens.

>   MR. TURNER
>   Have you lost your mind?

Mrs. Turner, however, says nothing. Danny's attention
concentrates on her.

Mr. Turner looks at his wife - an instruction to her to
echo his comment. She does not.

>   DANNY
>   Who are you?

The couple simply stand. Impassive.

Now certain, Danny loses his temper.

>   DANNY (CONT'D)
>   Who are you!

Silence.

And, then, as if in reply to his question --

The telephone rings. Shrill and startling.

The man answers it. He listens. Eyes on Danny.

He does not say a word.

He hangs up.

Danny waits.

>   DANNY (CONT'D)
>   (exasperated)
>   Who was that?

>   UNKNOWN MAN
>   That was Alistair's mother.

Danny looks at the now unidentified woman. There's shame
in her face. Danny is amazed that he was right.

>   DANNY
>   His mother?

Silence. Confirmation.

>   DANNY (CONT'D)
>   What does she want?

                        UNKNOWN MAN
           To meet you.

Danny belatedly realizes the implications of the phone
call. Looks around at the room.

Danny sits at the table. The packed lunch is so
desperately ordinary. Danny takes out the pork pie
breaking it in half, crumbling it.

Addressing the room in general:

                        DANNY
           I'll meet her.

EXT. TURNERS' HOUSE. DAY

Danny, with bag, walks towards the car, discretely
checking his phone - no reception.

The unknown couple open the car door for him.

                        DANNY
           How far is it?

                        UNKNOWN MAN
           Not far.

Except there's nothing around but woods.

Danny registers the physical strength of the unknown man.

Danny climbs into the car. The door's shut.

INT/EXT. CAR / COUNTRYSIDE / MANSION GROUNDS. DAY

Danny in the back. The couple in the front.

They pull out of the drive, onto the road and continue
for no more than a few hundred metres.

Up ahead is a grand and dilapidated stone gateway -
wrapped in ivy, crumbling brick.

They turn off the road, underneath the gateway. We pass
through a mangled-branch-forest.

The forest abruptly gives way to the grounds of a
mansion. Shaped hedgerow. Stone fountains. Long lawns.

At the top of a landscaped slope sits a Gothic country
house - two hundred or so years old.

The exterior of the house shows many signs of neglect.
The garden is on the threshold of wilderness.

The car descends the once opulent drive.

From afar, the figure of a woman in her sixties –
dressed elegantly – waits at the front doors.

The car parks. Danny gets out.

EXT. MANSION. DRIVE. DAY

The woman stands at the top of the stone steps looking
down at Danny as he advances towards her.

She's Frances. A magnificently shrewd face with hair,
touched with grey, glorious in its implied wisdom.

Her clothes are vintage designer. Like her house,
splendour mingled with decay. Formidable.

*We realize that Mrs.Turner was wearing this woman's
clothes. And wearing them not very well.*

Seen on their rightful owner they take on a vivid life
of their own. And make sense.

Danny comes face to face with her. Unlike yesterday, when
he was demure, now he's emboldened.

> FRANCES
> We needed to know who we were
> dealing with.

With ironic understanding Danny empties his pockets, for
inspection, tossing the contents on the ground – his
wallet, receipts, a clatter of loose coins.

> DANNY
> Anything else you need to see?

But Danny's retort fades into nothing as Frances is
struck by the dropped coins.

Dirty silver and copper in the gravel. She looks at them
for a moment, her thoughts far away.

And then, a rebuff, almost as an afterthought --

> FRANCES
> Not everyone is comfortable
> inviting strangers into their
> home.

Danny's staggered by the barb. Yet there's a beguiling
quality to her audacity.

> FRANCES (CONT'D)
> We thought, if you saw where we
> lived, you might try to extort us.

                    DANNY
          Why would you think I'm after
          your money?

                    FRANCES
          Because you have none.
                (off Danny's
                 reaction)
          You want an apology? I gave you an
          explanation.

                    DANNY
          You I believe.

Frances reacts powerfully to that statement.

Danny catches sight of a figure at the window --

A hunched man in his seventies. Aged badly. A Tweed
suit. A figure in the shadows, a vision of meanness.

Frances follows Danny's glance.

                    FRANCES
          My husband's name is Charles. My
          name is Frances. And my son's
          name was Alistair. Your name -
          Daniel - we read in the paper.

Danny registers the insult but is beyond hurt. He glances
back at the people who pretended to be Alex's parents.

Dressed in their masters' clothes.

The man drives the vintage car towards the huge garage,
where it belongs.

                    FRANCES (CONT'D)
          My staff, you've met.

The woman sheepishly carries Danny's bag to the house.

                    DANNY
          Where's she taking my stuff?

                    FRANCES
          Surely you're going to stay the
          night?

Frances turns and enters, without waiting for a reply.

After a beat Danny picks up the items he dropped on the
gravel, puts them back in his pocket.

Wary, he follows Frances inside, glancing to the side:
mean Charles still at the window.

INT. MANSION. GRAND HALL . DAY

Danny enters an impressive entrance hall. But we can
see scaffolding up ahead.

Frances moves to the stairs. Danny follows her up.

INT. MANSION. GRAND HALL. DAY

We move through scaffolding and plastic, statues
wrapped in protective coverings take on new forms.

> FRANCES
> We're in the midst of restoring
> this house to its former glory.

Despite her claim there's no sign of any new work being
done. No craftsmen. No builders. The house is silent.

> FRANCES (CONT'D)
> We had hoped Alistair would finish
> the task.

They pass out of the scaffolding area into the main
hall. It's enormous. Alcoves. A fire place.

Danny is dwarfed by the space: his eyes exploring.

INT. MANSION. CORRIDOR. DAY

Danny following Frances through a corridor. She reaches a
door and opens it for him.

INT. MANSION. GUEST BEDROOM. DAY

A second beautifully refurbished room.

High ceilings. Wood panelling. A regal four poster bed.
An antique wardrobe. A grand desk at the window.

Danny inspects the room. Opens the wardrobe. Moth balls
and nothing more. Walks to the huge desk. Touches it.

Looks out the window --

EXT. MANSION GROUNDS. MAZE. DAY

In the grounds there's an ancient and complex maze. The
hedgerow is overgrown. Wild and tangled.

INT. MANSION. GUEST BEDROOM. DAY

Danny turns to Frances. He notices that her fingers toy
with a silver necklace, leading to some pendant
concealed beneath her shirt.

>   DANNY
>   This was his room.

Frances studies Danny with interest.

>   FRANCES
>   How did you know?

>   DANNY
>   Because it's the loneliest room
>   I've ever been in.

She absorbs his observation. A suggestion of sadness in
Frances but she quickly controls it, hiding the emotion.

She lets go of the necklace which disappears.

>   FRANCES
>   Charles was sure that you'd catch
>   the train home today, none the
>   wiser. I was convinced you'd
>   figure it out. It seems you did so
>   not with reason. Or deduction. But
>   with something akin to female
>   intuition.

>   DANNY
>   I won't sleep here.

>   FRANCES
>   I would never have allowed you to.

She leaves. Danny pauses at the door, looking back.

INT. MANSION. SECOND STAIRWAY. DAY

A utilitarian staircase. Narrow, cramped and cold. They
climb up towards the attic. Danny follows Frances.

INT. MANSION. ATTIC BEDROOM. DAY

The top of the house - with low ceilings - a servant's
room. Stark. Functional. Cold. It's deliberately rude.

Danny's bag awaits him.

>   FRANCES
>   Dinner's at eight.

She's about to leave. Danny asks:

                        DANNY
            You're embarrassed by his death?

                        FRANCES
            Yes.

                        DANNY
            Upset, too?

Anger in Frances. A glimpse. Again, she controls it.

                        FRANCES
            Beyond anything you could possibly
            imagine.

She gently shuts the door.

Danny sits on bed - exhausted.

EXT. MANSION GROUNDS. EVENING

Danny exits the house. Surveys his surroundings.

He spots the man who pretended to be Alex's father. In
fact, he's the lone groundsman. With the impossible one-
man task of trying to keep the savage gardens in order.

He's now wearing his regular clothes.

Danny sets off, in the opposite direction.

EXT. MANSION GROUNDS. ENTRANCE TO MAZE. EVENING

Danny stands at the entrance to the maze. Before him is
a tunnel of hedgerow, entwined with brambles.

Only a smudge of light left in the sky. Danny enters.

EXT. MANSION GROUNDS. MAZE. EVENING

Danny reaches the first junction. He turns. He comes to
a brambly dead-end. Danny backtracks --

                                        FLASH TO:

EXT. MANSION GROUNDS. MAZE. DAY (PAST)

Little Alex, running through the maze, his tiny legs
moving at speed, turning right and left with the utmost
confidence. Navigating it expertly.

The dark passage way brightens, opening out into --

                                        BACK TO:

EXT. MANSION GROUNDS. MAZE. EVENING (PRESENT)

Danny at the centre of the maze, standing before a
stone statue - a male statue with arms missing at the
elbows, facial features eroded to smooth-anonymity.

Danny reaches out, touching the stump of the statue's
outstretched arms. He turns to the house.

Frances stands at the window of Alistair's room.
Watching Danny. Upon being seen she pulls back.

INT. MANSION. ATTIC ROOM. NIGHT

Danny changing for dinner. He looks at the clean white
shirt, picks it up and reconsiders.

INT. MANSION. GRAND STAIRWAY. NIGHT

Danny dressed in a T Shirt - bright, tight, appropriate
for a sweaty club. Scruffy jeans. White sneakers.

A wilfully incongruous figure in this mansion.

Passing an antique mirror he regards his reflection. He
has doubts. Mustering courage he continues.

INT. MANSION. GROUND FLOOR HALLWAY. NIGHT

Danny arrives at double height doors. He pushes them
open and enters --

INT. MANSION. DINING ROOM. NIGHT

This room has not been refurbished. Rotten wood
panelling. Cracked floor. Rusted, ancient radiators.

No art on the walls. Just sad shadow marks where
paintings once hung. Implication of artwork sold off.

A formal dining table at the centre.

Frances is at one end. Charles at the other. A place is
set for Danny in the middle. Candles the only light.

Danny walks to his seat. Every step under scrutiny.
Though deliberately dressed as a rebuttal of tradition
he finds his entrance awkward, regretting his decision.

Frances is inscrutable. Danny takes his seat.

>   FRANCES
> Did you realize your provocation
> was infantile before, or after,
> you opened those doors?

Spot on. And crushing.

>   FRANCES (CONT'D)
> Before, I see. And yet you didn't
> decide to change?

Danny accepts his miscalculation.

>   DANNY
> Would you like me to?

>   FRANCES
> No. I think, I prefer you like
> that.

Charles is already eating, fast, slurping, and without pleasure. Something wrong with his demeanour.

The woman who pretended to be Alex's mum serves Danny food. She wears a sad tatty uniform.

Danny finds her reversed position sad and strange. He's polite rather than hostile.

>   DANNY
> Thank you.

She studiously avoids meeting his eye. Around Frances the woman is rigid with formality.

Danny peers down at the chipped china plates. The starter is fussy. But not expensive.

>   FRANCES
> Alistair completed that maze,
> unassisted, three months before
> his fifth birthday.

>   DANNY
> When did you realize he was so
> smart?

Frances considers this.

>   FRANCES
> I always knew. Others consider him
> to be 'disturbed'. But what they
> saw as a disturbance of the mind
> was, in fact, an exceptional gift.
> However, it's not enough, in this
> world, to be born brilliant - you
> need direction and discipline.

>   You need someone who reminds you,
>   day after day, never to waste your
>   talent on triviality.

The word 'triviality' hangs over Danny.

>   FRANCES (CONT'D)
>   How many brilliant minds are out
>   there, right now, rotting in
>   squalor or neglect? It took every
>   ounce of my strength to make
>   Alistair realize his potential. He
>   hated me for it, in the end. You
>   guessed that already?

Danny doesn't reply. Frances accepts it as confirmation.

>   FRANCES (CONT'D)
>   Children are often the worst
>   judges of their own destiny.

>   DANNY
>   Your son was murdered.

Danny lets the statement sit.

Charles stops eating. Frances stops eating.

>   DANNY (CONT'D)
>   The attic was staged.

Suddenly Charles slams a fist against the table, rattling
every item of crockery, demanding silence.

Danny's baffled.

Charles goes back to his food. Head down.

Danny turns to Frances. She's quite calm.

>   FRANCES
>   After dinner perhaps you'll join
>   me for a drink?

Danny nods. Frances delicately continues eating.

Danny turns, catching the 'fake mother' slipping out of
the room. She'd been listening to their conversation.

INT. MANSION. DINING ROOM. NIGHT

At the end of dinner Charles throws down his napkin and
leaves the table without a good-night.

He exits, throwing open the doors, shuffling into the
darkness of his decaying house.

> FRANCES
> It's very sad. He was once an
> important man.

> DANNY
> What did he do?

> FRANCES
> He was head of MI6.

She stands.

> FRANCES (CONT'D)
> Shall we?

INT. MANSION. GRAND HALL. NIGHT

Danny and Frances have retired to the Grand Hall. A
formal and formidable space.

A fire burns.

Danny is seated in a cracked leather chair. Frances
pours him a brandy. She brings it to him.

> FRANCES
> Your number is 82.

Danny doesn't understand.

> FRANCES (CONT'D)
> The sum of the coins you dropped
> on the ground.

Frances pours herself a large scotch.

> FRANCES (CONT'D)
> When he was a child Alistair would
> amuse our guests with a trick --

> FLASH TO:

INT. MANSION. GRAND HALL. DAY (PAST)

Five year old Alex sitting cross-legged in front of the
fire, eyes upwards as a man throws a shower of coins.

In the air - coppers, silvers - of various face values -
rising up, catching the light from the fire.

> FLASH BACK TO:

INT. MANSION. GRAND HALL. NIGHT (PRESENT)

Danny is hungry for these glimpses of Alex's past.

>   FRANCES
>   In a glance he could add up all
>   the coins. He'd rarely bother to
>   remember anyone's name. But he'd
>   never forget their number.

Frances offers Danny a cigarette from a silver box. He
accepts. She also takes one. And sits.

>   FRANCES (CONT'D)
>   You would've been 82.
>   (considers)
>   An easy one.

While she smokes Danny merely holds the cigarette,
waiting to see how this will play out.

>   FRANCES (CONT'D)
>   My son wasn't gay.

Danny tenses: the cigarette disappears into the palm of
his hand.

>   FRANCES (CONT'D)
>   Before you hold some sort of
>   'parade' through the house, hear
>   me out. My son wasn't gay. But I
>   wish he had been.

Danny senses a trap. But is unsure of its nature.

Frances speaks with lethal precision that somehow
sounds casual, fluid and easy.

>   FRANCES (CONT'D)
>   Alistair didn't think like
>   ordinary people. And he didn't
>   feel the way ordinary people
>   feel. In his eyes everyone was a
>   puzzle. He took immense
>   satisfaction from figuring out
>   what a person wanted and then
>   giving it to them. As if we were
>   all computers waiting for the
>   correct code.

The provocation is subtle. Danny holds his tongue.

>   FRANCES (CONT'D)
>   Alistair could be anything a
>   person wanted him to be. In your
>   case, it appears that you craved
>   romance. A good-old-fashioned
>   love story. He gave it to you.
>   Meanwhile, he continued giving
>   other kinds of stimulation to
>   other kinds of people. Men and
>   women.

Danny's finding it harder to control his emotions.

>   FRANCES (CONT'D)
>   If he was involved with someone
>   who hankered after risk he will
>   have provided it. Danger. Pain.
>   Submission. Domination. You see,
>   my son was a mirror to the desires
>   of others - completely free of
>   inhibition. How do I know? It was
>   always this way. Alistair was as
>   precocious sexually as he was
>   intellectually. To him, they were
>   one and the same. Sex was just
>   another form of decryption.

Frances speaks without enjoyment or relish.

>   FRANCES (CONT'D)
>   You think I'm cruel? Perhaps I am.
>   But not in this instance. I wanted
>   to preserve your illusions. We had
>   hoped you'd go home and mourn in
>   the belief that your relationship
>   was perfect. You loved him, I see
>   that. Your love was real, of
>   course it was. As his mother I
>   appreciate your love for my son.
>   However, I cannot allow you to be
>   unaware of the facts in case you
>   blunder further into a situation
>   you simply do not understand.

Frances finishes her cigarette.

>   FRANCES (CONT'D)
>   I'm not surprised he used a
>   different name. He was playing a
>   part - the part of a
>   conventional lover. Ordinary
>   would have been a challenging
>   role for such an extraordinary
>   mind. Soon, he would've become
>   bored. Once he was bored he
>   moved on. And he always became
>   bored in the end.

She is quite brilliant. And with a concluding flourish:

>   FRANCES (CONT'D)
>   I don't know what went on in that
>   attic. And, the truth is, neither
>   do you.

Danny broods, taking it all in - overwhelming.

He opens his closed fist and removes the crushed cigarette. He stands, carefully placing it back in the antique silver box.

He sits back down: opposite Frances. Finally he collects his thoughts enough to speak. With a quiet anger.

> DANNY
> I haven't read many books. I
> haven't been to many places. But I
> have fucked a lot of people. And
> there's one thing you just can't
> fake...
> (beat)
> *Inexperience*. The body's tense
> when it should relax. It hurts
> when it should be fun. And it's
> dirty when it should be clean.

Frances is inscrutable.

> DANNY (CONT'D)
> I don't care how smart you are,
> your muscles don't lie. I'm
> talking about feeling his
> inexperience as clearly as I can
> feel this glass.

Danny raises the tumbler up, on the palm of his hand. His fingers coil around the glass, forming a fist.

> DANNY (CONT'D)
> Do you follow me, Frances?

Frances hasn't moved. Rigid poker face. For the first time since his arrival Danny has her on the back foot.

> DANNY (CONT'D)
> I can see that you do. So, I know,
> for a fact, that you're lying. I
> know, for a fact, that your son –
> the man I loved – was a virgin.
> What I don't know is why you're so
> keen to convince me otherwise.

Danny necks his brandy. Puts the glass down. He stands.

Danny turns his back on her. And Frances is not an easy person to turn your back to.

As he's walking towards the door --

> FRANCES
> Daniel?

Danny stops and turns. Frances is standing, staring directly at him. The full force of her eyes on him.

> FRANCES (CONT'D)
> Amongst all the lies told here
> this weekend recognize one truth --
> 'No fuss' was the best piece of
> advice you will ever be given.

> DANNY
> When he told me you were dead, he
> wasn't lying, was he?

She has no reply.

Danny leaves.

INT. MANSION. CORRIDOR. NIGHT

Alone, Danny leans against the wall, steadying himself.

INT. MANSION. ATTIC ROOM. NIGHT

Danny sitting on the edge of the bed. Not even trying
to sleep. He waits, looking at the clock.

INT. MANSION. STAIRWAY. NIGHT

Danny descends, barefoot, in the darkness.

INT. MANSION. CORRIDOR. NIGHT

Danny approaches a door, quietly. He opens it.

INT. MANSION. ALEX'S BEDROOM. NIGHT

Danny enters - shutting the door behind him.

He stares at the bed. Surprisingly he climbs into it.

In contrast to the 'fake' bed in the hunting lodge, which
meant nothing to him, Danny becomes emotional.

INT. MANSION. ALEX'S BEDROOM. MORNING

Danny wakes. He'd fallen asleep in Alex's bed.

The other side, Alex's side, is untouched and empty.

INT. MANSION. DINING ROOM. MORNING

Danny enters.

The table is set for breakfast. For one. He sits, alone, in this absurdly formal room.

He can't take it any more. He stands, leaves.

INT. MANSION. LOWER STAIRWAY. MORNING

Danny follows the sounds of pots and pans to --

INT. MANSION. KITCHEN. MORNING

An enormous kitchen that once made meals for hundreds of guests. Now only a tiny area is being used.

A vast empty larder. Rat bait. Appliances out of date and broken. A losing fight against disarray and decay.

The woman who pretended to be Alex's mum is preparing Danny's breakfast. She's alone.

In a reversal of roles Danny watches her unobserved. Eventually she turns, shocked to see him.

             DANNY
    I prefer it down here.

Without waiting for permission he sits at the table. She's nervous. He's deviating from plans.

             NANNY
    She won't like it.

             DANNY
    No. I don't think she will.

She reluctantly allows him to remain there, readying his breakfast. Danny ponders and speculates.

             DANNY (CONT'D)
    You cared about him?

She tries not to react but now we realize why she was largely silent in the hunting lodge. She's a lousy actress, a rotten liar, and she hated playing the part.

Danny sees the gap opening. And he takes it.

             DANNY (CONT'D)
    You cared for him?

Danny's intuition is exceptional. And he's so easy to talk to. Good at inspiring confidential conversation.

             DANNY (CONT'D)
    When he had a problem, he came to
    you - didn't he?

          (points upstairs)
   Not her?

The nanny has stopped cooking altogether. Eggs and bacon blacken and burn behind her. She allows them to.

                DANNY (CONT'D)
   You loved him?

Her lips tremble with a desire to speak.

                NANNY
   Alex.

Danny stands.

                DANNY
   Alex?

She nods. A stunned moment. Then happiness and relief.

                NANNY
   He hated the name Alistair.

                DANNY
   What happened here?

                NANNY
   Get as far away from these people
   as you can.

Danny's about to speak when --

The groundsman enters.

The nanny radically adjusts her interaction with Danny from confessional to functional - serving breakfast. Much of it burnt. Her guard is up. Her face impassive.

                NANNY (CONT'D)
   He insisted.

Her movements are clumsy with nerves.

She's afraid.

Danny obliges her performance, mechanically eating the burnt eggs and bacon.

The groundsman watches the two of them.

EXT. MANSION. DRIVE. MORNING

Bag over his shoulder, Danny approaching a small beat up car, not the vintage vehicle.

Neither Frances nor Charles are there to say goodbye.
Or the nanny. Just the groundsman.

Danny looks back at the many gloomy windows. No one is
standing in any of them.

INT/EXT. CAR / MANSION. MORNING

Danny in the cramped back seat. Groundsman in the
front. Danny catches a glance in the rear view mirror.

EXT. RURAL TRAIN STATION PLATFORM. MORNING

The groundsman gives Danny a new set of tickets.

He leaves. Danny watches him go.

INT. MANCHESTER TRAIN STATION. PLATFORM. DAY

Danny walks the length of the busy platform. The
Intercity train is full. A ruckus of passengers.

Reaching his designated carriage a weary Danny boards.

INT. INTERCITY TRAIN. CARRIAGE / STATION. DAY

His carriage is empty.

Every seat is reserved. Paper slips stick out from the
seat tops. As yet no one sitting in any of them.

Checking his ticket, Danny finds his seat. Part of an
arrangement of four. By the window.

INT. INTERCITY TRAIN CARRIAGE / STATION DAY

Danny resting against the window.

The train pulls out.

It dawns on him that he's still the only person in the
carriage. He stands, curious.

The adjacent carriages are completely full.

INT/EXT. INTERCITY TRAIN CARRIAGE / COUNTRY. DAY

A ticket inspector enters the carriage. Apparently also
surprised that the carriage is empty.

He checks some of the reservations slips, finding nothing
amiss. Danny assesses the man carefully.

The Inspector's uniform is suitably drab. Shoes scuffed.

Danny gives him the ticket. He punches it. Hands it back.
And without a word walks towards the next carriage.

INT/EXT. INTERCITY TRAIN / STATION. DAY

The train's stopped. An announcement crackles out.

Passengers board. Some enter the carriage. But all the
seats are reserved and they move on.

Danny is still alone. And increasingly uneasy.

The train pulls out. At this point --

A striking man in his fifties, or sixties, enters.

Dressed in quintessential British attire: Henry Poole of
Saville row suit. Schnieder of Clifford Street shoes. Not
a guy who looks like he'd be in standard class.

The man studies the reservation slips, as many others
have done, paying no attention to Danny. Searching for
his seat number, he eventually finds it --

Directly opposite Danny.

The man squeezes into his allotted seat. The two of them
face to face, knees grazing, in an otherwise empty
carriage. The man seems unaware of any absurdity.

He places his leather satchel on the seat beside him and
smiles at Danny. The smile appears warm and real.

Danny doesn't smile back. The man doesn't notice. Or seem
to mind, instead, he takes from his satchel a small paper
bag. He crinkles it open, offering it to Danny.

Danny peers inside.

It's filled with traditional English boiled sweets.

The man speaks with an American accent - appealing and
melodic - but its precise nature is unimportant.

> THE AMERICAN
> I have a sweet tooth.

Danny's guard is up. He declines the sweets.

> THE AMERICAN (CONT'D)
> It's easier to quit smoking, I
> swear.

The man's engrossed in the sweets and carefully selects
one, putting it in his mouth. Satisfied with his choice.

He sucks.

Danny's eyes never leave the man. Yet the man isn't troubled by the intensity of Danny's stare.

                    THE AMERICAN (CONT'D)
          Not very British, talking to a
          stranger on a train?

Danny doesn't reply. The American continues nonetheless.

                    THE AMERICAN (CONT'D)
          I've worked in this country for
          ten years now --

                    DANNY
               (interrupting)
          What line of work?

In a flash the American produces an elegant business card - 'Insurance Broker'. Various details. Looks real.

                    THE AMERICAN
          Own a house?

                    DANNY
          No.

                    THE AMERICAN
          Car?

                    DANNY
          No.

                    THE AMERICAN
          Valuables?

Danny offers the card back.

                    DANNY
          Nothing.

The American doesn't take the card.

                    THE AMERICAN
          You have your health - that's the
          most precious asset of all.

A faint touch of menace - imagined, or accidental. Sales pitch over, the man contemplates Danny.

                    THE AMERICAN (CONT'D)
          Over the years I've adopted many
          of this country's customs. Except
          for that famous British reserve. I
          enjoy talking too much. Once in a
          while someone...
               (considers carefully)

Unexpected, tells you something...
             (considers carefully)
        Useful.

Danny wonders if this is a cue. He takes the bait.

                        DANNY
        Such as?

The American muses. As if he hadn't expected the
question. A strange dance between these two men. One full
of suspicion. The other excessively innocent.

                     THE AMERICAN
        You've put me on the spot.
             (sucks hard on sweet)
        Okay...

The American leans forward. As though about to impart a
vital secret of some kind. Danny also leans forward.

                  THE AMERICAN (CONT'D)
        Do you mind if I take the sweet
        out of my mouth?

                        DANNY
        Go ahead.

They both sit back.

The American removes the boiled sweet, placing it in the
centre of a white silk handkerchief and neatly depositing
it on the side table.

                     THE AMERICAN
        I was told this story by a
        gentleman I'd never seen before.
        And I'll never see again.

Silence. Danny waits. But the American refuses to speak.

Danny turns around to see --

The Ticket Inspector entering the carriage.

The American has produced his ticket. And waits...

The Inspector clips the ticket. Danny watches the
interaction between the Inspector and the American very
carefully. The Inspector hands the ticket back.

The three hold a moment. And then the Inspector moves on.
Once the Inspector is gone and the carriage is empty --

                  THE AMERICAN (CONT'D)
        There was a farmer living in the
        Greek Peloponnesian Hills.

It had been the hottest-driest
summer for hundreds of years. One
day the farmer saw smoke rising
into the clear blue sky. Out of
the smoke appeared an old man,
riding on the back of a mule. He
said: "*A terrible fire's coming!
The worst I've ever seen. Jump on
the back of my mule!*" The pious
farmer thanked the old man for his
offer but declared: "*I will pray
to God. My faith is strong. He'll
protect me.*" The old man shook his
head at the farmer's folly and
hurried on.
    (beat)
Soon, across the nearby hills,
spread a horizon of flames.
Fleeing the destruction came a
truck carrying many families. They
called out to the farmer: "*A
terrible fire's coming! The worst
we've ever seen. Jump in our truck
or you'll surely be killed.*" But
the farmer said: "*I will pray to
God. My faith is strong. God will
protect me.*" Aghast at this
stupidity, the truck drove off.
    (beat)
Soon the fire arrived at the foot
of the farmer's hill, consuming
every tree and bush and blade of
grass. Miraculously, in the sky,
there appeared a helicopter --
    (breaking flow)
You can guess where this is going?

          DANNY
He said no to the helicopter?

        THE AMERICAN
And sure enough the flames climbed
his hill, scorching his crops,
killing his livestock, burning his
farmhouse. Finally, with the heat
blistering his skin, the pious
farmer cried out to God. But
received no reply.
    (beat)
Soon there was nothing left on the
hill except for smouldering
carcasses, burnt timbers and hot
ash.

The American pauses, as if the story had ended. But just
as Danny is about to react, he continues -

>   THE AMERICAN (CONT'D)
>   In heaven the farmer knelt before
>   God and said: *"I am a pious man.*
>   *My faith is strong. I did no*
>   *wrong. I committed no sin. Why*
>   *didn't you answer my prayers?"*

The American wants Danny to ask the question.

>   DANNY
>   What did God say?

>   THE AMERICAN
>   He said: *"I sent you a mule, a*
>   *truck and a helicopter. Yet still*
>   *you could not be saved."*

The American smiles. The same smile we saw before. But
now doesn't feel quite so warm.

>   THE AMERICAN (CONT'D)
>   *"Yet still you could not be*
>   *saved."*

Like a mirage, the moment of menace passes.

>   THE AMERICAN (CONT'D)
>   Told to me by a gentleman I'd
>   never seen before and will never
>   see again.

The American turns to look out the window. And pays no
more attention to Danny.

INT/EXT. INTERCITY TRAIN. CARRIAGE / LONDON. DAY

Danny seated opposite the American. The man is fascinated
with the view -- the approach into London's outskirts.

>   THE AMERICAN
>   I love this city.

Danny stands, leaving the carriage.

INT. INTERCITY TRAIN. RESTAURANT BAR. DAY

The bar is packed with drunken travellers, returning from
football matches, in contrast to the stillness of the
empty carriage.

Danny buys two miniature bottles of Scotch.

INT. INTERCITY TRAIN. TOILETS. DAY

Danny drinks the first double measure of Scotch in one
gulp. He looks in the mirror.

> DANNY
> Who you are?
> (more assertive)
> *Who are you?*
> *Are you threatening me?*

Danny drinks the second double measure.

INT. INTERCITY TRAIN. CARRIAGE. DAY

Danny returns to his carriage. Only to see that the
American is gone. Danny approaches the seat.

An announcement declares that they're arriving at King's
Cross Station.

Danny looks into the adjacent carriages and sees that the
corridors are full. No one can move. Everyone standing
ready to disembark. Aisles are blocked.

No sign of the American.

Danny's attention returns to his seat.

The American has left behind his white silk handkerchief.
It sits on the side table.

We see the distinct, small curve of an object at its
centre. Around the curve the white material has been
stained an ominous-bloody red.

The train stops. Passengers seep onto the platform.

But not Danny. He sits down. And slowly opens the
handkerchief revealing --

A bright boiled sweet.

At first, relief, then anti-climax. But there's something
unusual about it --

Danny holds it up to the light as though it were a
precious gem.

Encased in the transparent centre is something angular
and blue. We can't see what. Blurred, through the sugar.

The Inspector enters the carriage, taking down all the
reservation slips from the back of the seats.

And looking at Danny.

Danny wraps up the sweet in the handkerchief and puts it in his pocket.

EXT. SCOTTIE'S HOUSE. FRONT DOOR. NIGHT

Danny knocks on the door. Scottie opens up, surprised to see him. He's about to speak when --

Danny shakes his head, indicating a need for silence. He gestures outside.

Scottie obliges, grabbing a coat. He leaves the house, pulling the door shut.

The two stand in his front garden - hidden from the street. Danny's in evident turmoil.

                    SCOTTIE
          You think my home is bugged?

                    DANNY
          It can't be a coincidence... the
          train... the stranger...

                    SCOTTIE
          Danny?

                    DANNY
          They heard us.

                    SCOTTIE
          Who?

                    DANNY
          The people who murdered Alex.

Scottie's thoughtful.

                    SCOTTIE
          Suppose he was murdered. Suppose
          you're right. Then follow it
          through. The implications of what
          you're saying.

Danny nods. Trying to calm down.

                    SCOTTIE (CONT'D)
          You believe you're at the
          beginning of something but really
          you're at the end. It all happened
          whilst you weren't looking. And
          now... It's over. It's done.
          Everything you think of will have
          already been thought of. You know
          nothing about them. And they will
          know everything about you.

If they don't kill you it will be
for one reason - they consider you
less of a nuisance alive than
dead.
          (off Danny's
          reaction)
You're insulted by the idea of
your insignificance? You should
cherish it.

                    DANNY
If the police won't do anything...
Maybe the press will... If the
press won't do anything... Maybe
the parents will... If the parents
won't... who's left?

                    SCOTTIE
No daring journalists will come to
your aid. No rogue police
officers. It will just be you. You
alone. Ask yourself, Danny,
honestly - *who are you*? You're
friends with everyone. You trust
everyone. And you know no-one.

                    DANNY
You know these people --

                    SCOTTIE
I knew them thirty years ago.

                    DANNY
Help me.

Scottie considers. It's hard for him.

                    SCOTTIE
In one way or another I've spent
much of my life being afraid. It
is a privilege spending time with
a man who's never been afraid of
anything. And that's not just
because you were born in a
different time. You're fearless.
I've always wondered how that must
feel. But, Danny, occasionally, it
is right to be afraid.

Danny's unsure.

                    SCOTTIE (CONT'D)
Leave this alone. Promise me?

INT. DANNY'S APARTMENT. BEDROOM. NIGHT

Danny, seated, on the floor of his bedroom. The boiled
sweet is positioned in the middle of plate.

Using a sharp knife, Danny carefully chips away the sugar
shell, chiselling and chiselling, revealing --

A blue pill.

Not an illicit drug. A professionally produced medicine
of some kind. A serial code on the side.

With the pill in one hand, Danny reaches into his pocket,
taking out the American's business card.

He appears to be weighing them in his hands.

INT. DANNY'S APARTMENT. HALLWAY. NIGHT

Danny slips out, in silence.

INT. DANNY'S APARTMENT BUILDING. COMMUNAL STAIRWAY. NIGHT

Danny heads *up* the stairs, towards the fire exit --

EXT. DANNY'S APARTMENT ROOFTOP. NIGHT

The rooftop view of Vauxhall. The park. The pubs. Looming
over the area is the MI6 building.

A light snow falls.

Danny walks to the ledge. Highly visible from every
direction. Directly facing the MI6 building.

He pulls out the insurance business card and slowly -
deliberately - rips it into the tiniest shreds, making
sure his actions can be clearly seen.

He collects the fragments in his hands and raises them up
- offering them to the heavens.

The wind catches them and they blow up, higher and
higher, the paper merging with the snowflakes,
disappearing into the night sky.

END OF EPISODE 2

EPISODE THREE:

"BLUE"

INT. DANNY'S APARTMENT. BEDROOM. DAWN

Danny opens his eyes. He's in bed. It's dark outside. The alarm clock says 5 AM.

His eyes concentrate on the cheap, coarse carpet - tiny flecks of dust rise up, shaken from the fibres.

And now the sound of heavy footsteps, reverberating through the apartment.

Danny sits up as --

The door's kicked open. A shattering noise. And then -

Silence.

A mob of plain clothes police officers enter, shouting instructions we do not hear.

Just angry eyes & angry expressions.

The silence continues as Danny is violently pulled from the bed as if he were a grave and deadly threat.

Danny's head pressed flat on the coarse carpet.

INT. DANNY'S APARTMENT. BEDROOM. DAWN

Silence continues except for one element of sound - Danny's breathing. The effect of disorientation.

Danny under watch as he's handed some clothes. An extreme level of caution, each item is checked by officers.

INT. DANNY'S APARTMENT. BEDROOM. DAWN

Silence except for Danny's breathing, and the addition of a second element of sound --

The metal handcuffs. As Danny's hands secured.

In the background forensic officers have already begun to process his room like a crime scene.

INT. DANNY'S APARTMENT. HALLWAY. DAWN

Silence except for Danny's breathing and Sara's voice, contorted & indistinct - not dialogue, we feel the rhythm of her anger and upset.

Danny being led out. Sara and Pavel being held back by officers, concerned, upset & powerless.

INT. DANNY'S APARTMENT BUILDING. COMMUNAL STAIRWAY. DAWN

Silence except for Danny's breathing and the sound of
doors unlocking --

As Danny's led out, neighbours open their doors, peering.
No sympathy just the presumption of guilt.

INT/EXT. POLICE CAR / LONDON. DAWN

Silence except for Danny's breathing and a siren: warped
and faded and distorted.

Close on Danny against the window, being driven through
near-deserted London, a blur in the background.

INT. POLICE STATION. DETAINEE PROCESSING. DAY

Silence except for Danny's breathing and a particular
sound from each separate part of the sequence.

- Danny photographed.

- Fingerprints taken.

- Information entered into the computer systems.

- a DNA swab from his mouth.

- A health care professional readies a needle, pre-fitted
with a tube, which runs to a 5 millimetre phial - a
modern, sterile, easy-to-use blood-sampling kit.

- The needle enters Danny's vein.

- The plastic tube turns red. The phial's filled. The
needle's removed.

- A barcode wrapped around the blood.

INT. POLICE STATION. INTERROGATION ROOM. DAY

Danny seated. His lawyer, from Episode One, is present.
Detective Taylor and colleague opposite.

The stark white abattoir interrogation room.

Detective Taylor speaks precisely, without bombast. After
beats of silence, her voice hits us like a jolt.

                    DETECTIVE TAYLOR
          The trunk.

She presents a photograph of the trunk. Empty. Just the
trunk. Plain and simple. Lid open.

> DETECTIVE TAYLOR (CONT'D)
> An antique. Wood. Leather. Steel
> frame. Brass locks. Very strong.
> (beat)
> You claim it was used to store
> hiking boots. And other outdoor
> equipment in the back of his car.

FLASH TO:

EXT. ESTUARY. DAY (PAST)

A split second flash from the past - the idyllic country
walk, the trunk filled with maps. Danny & Alex happy.

BACK TO:

INT. POLICE STATION. INTERROGATION ROOM. DAY (PRESENT)

The Detective presents a photo of the trunk as discovered
in the attic. A horrific scene.

> DETECTIVE TAYLOR
> With a man inside oxygen levels
> drop seventeen percent. The
> temperature jumps ten degrees. You
> become breathless. Sweaty. There's
> a moment of euphoria --

FLASH TO:

INT. SEX ATTIC. NIGHT (PAST)

A split second flash of the trunk, discovered by Danny.

BACK TO:

INT. POLICE STATION. INTERROGATION ROOM. DAY (PRESENT)

The word 'euphoria' jars with Danny.

> DANNY
> Euphoria?

> DETECTIVE TAYLOR
> Have you ever experimented with
> erotic asphyxiation?

Danny in disbelief at the line of questioning.

The detective wilfully puts on oversized reading glasses,
making herself bookish & harmless:

                      DETECTIVE TAYLOR (CONT'D)
             (reading from notes)
      "When the brain's deprived of
      oxygen, it induces a semi-
      hallucinogenic state called
      hypoxia. Combined with orgasm --"

       DANNY   DETECTIVE TAYLOR
   (interrupting)   (continuing)
 I know what it is.   "-- the rush is no less
                       powerful than cocaine, and
                       highly addictive."

                      DETECTIVE TAYLOR (CONT'D)
      You know what it is, because
      you've tried it?

The question sounds casual. And lethal.

Danny considers a lie. But decides against it.

                      DANNY
      I used to see a guy.

                      DETECTIVE TAYLOR
      A man called Steve Fields.

Perturbed, Danny can't hide his surprise, looking down at
the sheets of paper, wondering what else she has on him.

                      DETECTIVE TAYLOR (CONT'D)
      Did the two of you use a trunk?

                      DANNY
      We used a belt.
         (embarrassed)
      I didn't particularly enjoy it.
      I've never done it again.

                      DETECTIVE TAYLOR
      We were told you engaged in the
      practice repeatedly.

                      DANNY
      It was three or four times. With
      one man.

                      DETECTIVE TAYLOR
      How close did you come to death?

                      DANNY
      We were careful.

                      DETECTIVE TAYLOR
      Because?

                      DANNY
      He was always watching. Or I was.

                    DETECTIVE TAYLOR
          I see. So if something went wrong,
          he'd step in, or you would?

                    DANNY
               (quick)
          Yes.

                    DETECTIVE TAYLOR
          That means you have personally
          experienced --
               (checks notes)
          "The moment of euphoria before
          conditions become critical",
          haven't you?

                    DANNY
               (less quick)
          Yes.

                    DETECTIVE TAYLOR
          That was the moment you were
          supposed to open the trunk, wasn't
          it?

The trap closes.

                    DETECTIVE TAYLOR (CONT'D)
          Danny, have you ever passed out
          from taking too much 'G'?

Danny stumbles, sensing that she already has the answer.

                    DANNY
          When I first started using it.

                    DETECTIVE TAYLOR
          Repeatedly with one man?
          Repeatedly with different men?

She's brilliant.

                    DETECTIVE TAYLOR (CONT'D)
          More than five times?
          More than five men?

                    DANNY
          It could be.

                    DETECTIVE TAYLOR
          What would you say was a 'typical'
          dose? One and a half millimetres?

She hands him photos of an exquisite glass tumbler by the
mattress. The sequence of photos move progressively
closer until we see fingerprints, lip marks on the rim.

                                        FLASH TO:

INT. SEX ATTIC. NIGHT (PAST)

Danny picking up the glass of 'G' & cola.

                                        BACK TO:

INT. POLICE STATION. INTERROGATION ROOM. DAY (PRESENT)

Detective Taylor ensnaring Danny.

                    DETECTIVE TAYLOR
          5.2 millimetres. Enough for three.

She has him. And she knows it, so she adjusts, becoming
solicitous and understanding.

                    DETECTIVE TAYLOR (CONT'D)
          What happened that night, Danny?
          He asked you to lock him inside
          the trunk. You obliged, sat on the
          bed, waiting for his high. Except
          your high came first, and came
          stronger. You pass out. Nothing
          could wake you. Not his cries for
          help, not the movement of the
          trunk. When you did wake, an hour
          or so later, the attic was quiet.

Danny numb as this alternate reality is laid out before
him. It's so convincing.

                    DETECTIVE TAYLOR (CONT'D)
          You sat up. Saw the trunk. On its
          side. Half way across the attic.
          Now you're panicking. You open the
          locks. You touch his cheeks - he's
          still warm... You consider calling
          an ambulance, of course you do.
          But it's too late. You look around
          at the remnants of your night. The
          drugs. The kink. A jury's going to
          hate you.

Danny shaking his head, but weakly, bewildered by the
completeness of the case against him.

                    DETECTIVE TAYLOR (CONT'D)
          You close the trunk. You leave.
          After all, the guy slept around.
          You didn't even know his name.
          There were others. Maybe we'll
          think it was one of them.

Danny's voice falters. It could be mistaken for guilt.

                    DANNY
          Why would I tell you that there
          were no other people?

                    DETECTIVE TAYLOR
          There are always other people.

INT. POLICE STATION. INTERROGATION ROOM. NIGHT

A rapid, jarring cut forward, slamming into a new part of
the interrogation. The detective is in her element. In
full flow. Danny is looking ragged.

The detective presents Danny with an expensive business
card. Danny studies the enigmatic name.

Classy. Elegant. No phone number.

                    DETECTIVE TAYLOR
          Exclusive. Discreet. A specialist
          escort agency. For the very rich.

                    DANNY
          Alex didn't use escorts.

                    DETECTIVE TAYLOR
          Can we at least use his real name?

                    DANNY
          Alistair didn't --

                    DETECTIVE TAYLOR
          You both enjoyed the company of
          strangers, it would seem.

She presses play on digital device. An audio extract.
It's Danny's voice. It sounds like he's on the phone.

                    DANNY (V.O)
                 (tape recording)
          "I posted an ad online saying
          anyone could come round. I mean -
          any one. I'd be waiting. My only
          condition was that they didn't
          speak. And people showed up."

                                        FLASH TO:

INT. DANNY'S APARTMENT. BATHROOM. NIGHT (PAST)

The scene between Danny and Alex - Alex in the bath.

                    DANNY
          I don't remember much about them.
          There were two older guys.

                                              BACK TO:

INT. POLICE STATION. INTERROGATION ROOM. DAY (PRESENT)

Horrified, Danny stands up, speaking over the recording,
the following dialogue simultaneous and confused.

     DANNY (CONT'D)   DANNY (V.O) (CONT'D)
How do you have this? This   (tape recording)
was a private conversation.   "They arrived together. I
                              didn't turn them away. I
                              didn't ask anything of
                              them. I just reminded them
                              of my rule. Not to speak.
                              And they must have thought
                              their luck was in...
                              Because they didn't make a
                              sound."

The detective pauses the recording. Danny's trembling
with outrage. They're all watching him.

                    DETECTIVE TAYLOR
          You told him that story over the
          phone. The apartment belongs to
          the security services. All calls
          were recorded.

She passes him copies of the call logs. Numbers. Dates.
Times. In black and white. Computerized. One is circled.

Danny stares blankly at the evidence. It looks so real.
Finally, trying to control his emotion.

                    DANNY
          That conversation took place in my
          bedroom. We were face to face.

                    DETECTIVE TAYLOR
          We've just searched your
          apartment. No surveillance
          equipment was found.

Danny looks at the people around the table. Incredulity.

Even his lawyer's stance suggests disbelief.

INT. POLICE STATION. INTERROGATION ROOM. DAY

Later, another jarring cut, slamming relentlessly forward
into a different part of the interrogation

Danny's fingers around a polystyrene cup of coffee. He's unwell, pale, worn down.

Everyone except Danny is wearing different clothes.

Now they're discussing the set of four keys mysteriously given to Danny in Episode 1. They're on the table.

Also the computer handheld device from the warehouse where Danny used to work.

Danny's exasperated, speech fraying at the edges, as if he can hear how implausible reality is starting to sound.

> DANNY
> Alex didn't give me these keys. He
> never gave me a set of keys. They
> were left. In the warehouse. I
> don't know by who. I don't know
> how --
> > (nudging the device)
> You say it can't be done, like
> that's a fact. But it was done!
> They did it! Because they needed
> me to go into the attic so that
> you could believe all -- this --
> > (gestures at the
> > papers & evidence)
> Except it's all a fucking lie.

He's lost control. Danny catches breath.

No one believes him.

INT. POLICE STATION. INTERROGATION ROOM. DAY

Danny has been hollowed out by the process. In fact, he looks gravely unwell. Pale. Shivering.

Detective Taylor remains pristine and precise.

The lawyer checks his watch.

In contrast to Danny's stumbling speech:

> DETECTIVE TAYLOR
> I'm not the one running out of
> time. We both know those attic
> bedsheets - stained with semen and
> shit and blood - are going to come
> back as a match for your DNA. When
> they do, we will charge you.

All eyes on Danny.

Danny overwhelmed. Can't articulate a defence.

INT/EXT. TAXI CAB / LONDON. NIGHT

Danny's sick and shivering.

Scottie registers how ill Danny is.

> DANNY
> A pen?

Scottie has a beautiful pen. He hands it to Danny.

On the back of a tissue, or scrap of paper, Danny starts
to recreate the information from the mysterious business
card that the detective showed him.

Scottie watches.

> DANNY (CONT'D)
> What did the lawyer say?

> SCOTTIE
> He said you should confess.

Danny pauses, looks at Scottie, then continues copying
from memory the information from the escort card.

> SCOTTIE (CONT'D)
> What is that?

> DANNY
> Another lie.

INT. SCOTTIE'S HOUSE. GUEST BEDROOM. NIGHT

Danny's helped into the guest bedroom. He keeps his
clothes on, slipping under the duvet. Scottie finds a
thick throw, placing it over a delirious Danny.

> TO BLACK:

A split second moment of darkness. In which we hear a
loud slam, a noise that jolts us into --

INT. ALEX'S APARTMENT. ATTIC. NIGHT (NIGHTMARE)

A sweat drenched Danny wakes up on his back, on the sex
stained sheets, in the attic, in the gloom.

We hear the slamming sound for the second time.

Danny sits up.

The attic staged as it was before. Orange hubs of
filament light. A tower of babel television sets.

Except the trunk is moving closer and closer to Danny.
Someone's alive inside.

Danny stands, sweating profusely, hurrying forward,
through the harness zone.

Danny reaches the trunk. Sweaty fingers on the brass
locks. We see a human form pressing against the side.

As he opens it --

                                          BACK TO:

INT. SCOTTIE'S HOUSE. GUEST BEDROOM. NIGHT

Danny opens his eyes. The clock says 7.37 PM.

His fever's broken. He gets out of bed. Fragile.

INT. SCOTTIE'S HOUSE. STUDY. NIGHT

Engulfed in an old fashioned dressing gown Danny shuffles
in. The study is dark except for Scottie at his desk, lit
by a pool of intense desk lamp light.

He's working on official looking documents.

Scottie puts the papers aside, turning to see Danny in
the gloom. There's a subtle-but-distinct-distance between
them. Danny's sensitive to it as he takes a seat.

                    DANNY
          Saturday?

                    SCOTTIE
          Sunday.

Silence.

                    SCOTTIE (CONT'D)
          You should eat something.

                    DANNY
          The bedsheets, in the attic -
          they're going come back a match
          for my DNA.

Silence.

                    SCOTTIE
          How is that possible?

                    DANNY
          Alex dry-cleaned everything.
          That's when they were stolen.

Silence.

> DANNY (CONT'D)
> They've been working on this for
> months.

Silence.

> DANNY (CONT'D)
> I'm going to prove --

> SCOTTIE
> (interrupting)
> You can't even prove it wasn't
> you. You're talking about spies
> and conspiracies and --
> (angry)
> Look at you!

Danny looks at himself, a pitiful figure lost in
Scottie's old dressing gown. Scottie's anger melts.

> SCOTTIE (CONT'D)
> (affectionate)
> Look at you.

EXT. EAST LONDON. NARROW STREET. SHOP. DAY

A shadowy side street. A row of old fashioned shops and
craft stores. Cobblers. Locksmiths. Quaint and run down.

Danny stands outside a silversmiths. He checks the street
to make sure he wasn't followed. He enters.

INT. EAST LONDON. SILVERSMITH. SHOP. DAY

Part shop, part workshop - a beautiful bronze bell rings
above the door as Danny enters. He waits at the counter,
standing in front of a wall of keys.

An old man emerges from the back, wearing a cracked,
ancient leather apron, a fine layer of metallic dust on
his clothes and spectacles.

Part wizard, part émigré, a man who has travelled far
and made London his home.

An accent dragged across continents.

The silversmith looks Danny over, unimpressed. Until
Danny places the cylinder on the counter.

The silversmith examines it, bewitched by its complexity
and beauty. After a moment, he reassesses Danny.

                              SILVERSMITH
                    This belongs to you?

Danny nods.

                              SILVERSMITH (CONT'D)
                    Show me your wallet.

Puzzled, Danny hands it over.

The silversmith glances at the cards but seems much more
interested in the wallet itself as a form of ID. Not
leather. Cheap. Synthetic. He picks at stitching.

                              SILVERSMITH (CONT'D)
                    How does a person owning something
                    like this --
                         (the wallet)
                    End up owning something like this?
                         (the cylinder)

                              DANNY
                    It was a gift.

                              SILVERSMITH
                         (incredulous)
                    A gift?

                              DANNY
                    You think I stole it?

The silversmith considers. He doesn't.

                              SILVERSMITH
                    Want to sell it?

                              DANNY
                    Can it be opened?

                              SILVERSMITH
                    If you know the code.

                              DANNY
                    Can't it be picked?

The silversmith lowers his ear to the cylinder, turning
the dials, listening carefully. Delighted.

                              SILVERSMITH
                    Not a sound! Beautiful work.
                    Exceptional.

                              DANNY
                    What about cutting it open?

                    SILVERSMITH
              (with contempt)
          I wouldn't agree to try. Someone
          else might.

About to hand it back but stops.

                    SILVERSMITH (CONT'D)
          But an object such as this was
          made with care. Skill. Love. Most
          of all, it was made with the
          foreknowledge that someone crude
          minded might use brute force. Are
          you sure force won't destroy
          whatever it contains? Or was it
          intended to be opened only by he
          who knows the code? And no one
          else?

He hands it back to Danny.

Danny considers it afresh, daunted by its perfection.

                    SILVERSMITH (CONT'D)
          A gift, perhaps. But perhaps not a
          gift meant for you.

And Danny too has his doubts.

INT. DANNY'S APARTMENT. BEDROOM. NIGHT

Danny seated, copying the emblem for the escort agency
from the fragment of tissue we saw in the taxi.

He's carefully copying it onto a slip of card. Creating a
handmade replica.

Still obviously handmade, coloured in with black biro
ink. But as close to the original as Danny can make it.

Finished, he examines it. Runs his finger over the logo.

What does this mean?

Danny picks up his phone, going through the list of
names.

He stops at Rich. No photo.

Just a number.

Danny seems greatly troubled by the prospect of this man.

EXT. RIVERSIDE APARTMENT BUILDING. NIGHT

A modern block of luxury apartments. Glass. Steel.
Landscaped gardens. Located directly on the riverfront.

An apprehensive Danny stands outside, agonising over a
decision about whether to go in, or not.

In his fingers we see the escort card.

Danny enters.

INT. RIVERSIDE APARTMENT BUILDING. NIGHT

Danny approaches the concierge. He's looked over.

                    DANNY
          I'm here for Rich. He's expecting
          me. I'm a friend.

INT. RIVERSIDE APARTMENT BUILDING. ELEVATOR. NIGHT

A stylish elevator rises up to the Penthouse.

Apprehensive, Danny waits.

The door opens directly into --

INT. RIVERSIDE PENTHOUSE. HALLWAY. NIGHT

The space oozes wealth without style.

Few personal possessions.

Danny knows the way. He threads a path through.

Walking through this space as if it were a bad memory.

He passes a wall of platinum albums.

INT. RIVERSIDE PENTHOUSE. MAIN ROOM. NIGHT

Vast glass windows.

The room itself is sparse. Pre-installed luxury. Shelves are filled with records. A sophisticated music system with decks.

And there, in a chair, at the corner of a dining room table sits Rich. In shadow and light.

Who is this man?

Rich is a record producer. Self made, started his own label, nothing cool, boy bands. Despite the sentimentality of the music he's not sentimental. He's razor sharp shrewd.

He's infamous for discarding bands as they grow tiresome or unpopular. And this fact informs the way he treats people in general - taking what he wants and then moving on.

Rich is as brilliant as he is ruthless. He has charisma and verve and feline savvy.

He knows what people wants. He gives it to them. And in exchange he always gets what he wants.

Formerly a producer who did drugs on the side he sold his label for a vast payoff and he's now a man who does drugs with a bit of producing on the side.

He's a high functioning crystal meth addict: the kind of man who would never accept that he was an addict.

Mid forties, he dresses in Dolce & Gabbana, conspicuously expensively. The clothes look lousy on him. Flash. Glossy. But we shouldn't be laughing at him: he's come up from nothing, why shouldn't he be proud of the money he's made.

He's seated, smoking from an elaborate glass pipe.

It's not chance that he's smoking from this pipe: he knew Danny was coming and this pipe is for Danny.

Let's take a look at the pipe in detail: it's a precise piece of equipment, a narrow cylindrical tube with a round golf ball shaped glass end. It has a fragile beauty.

The crystal rocks are like large salt crystals. They sit in the base of the golf ball curve where they're heated by a flame. The smoke fills the sphere. It's then sucked up through the narrow tube.

Rich exhales: a cloud of smoke. Note the smoke is odourless and not unpleasant.

He puts the pipe down.

The effect this drug has on Rich's character is to make
him sharp, heightened senses, not drowsy, but intense and
crisp. With a voracious sexual appetite.

There is a flood of dopamine to the brain. If Rich were a
first time user he'd be euphoric, 'wasted' but he's been
using for many years and the receptors in his brain have
been desensitized. He smokes now to maintain a level.

This means he's perfectly coherent. But changeable. His
mood can turn on a dime.

Rich is playful only because he's sure that he'll win.
Playful like a snake. Playful like a predator.

He's dangerous. Seductive. And Danny should get as far
away from him as possible. Except Danny can't.

                    RICH
          Dan - ne.

                    DANNY
          Rich.

                    RICH
          It's been a long time.

                                        FLASH TO:

INT. RICH'S APARTMENT BUILDING. ELEVATOR. NIGHT (PAST)

Rich and Danny with just three other guys. None of the
guys are over the age of twenty five. None under twenty.

They feel young in life experience terms, first jobs,
minimum wage, cheap tight jeans and cheap white sneakers.

They should be a "type" - slim, lean muscular,
attractive, and poor, not posh.

Rich is the only one in expensive clothes.

The contrast is sharp and clear.

These young men orbit him like planets around the sun.

All their eyes on Rich.

He has the drugs. He dangles the bag of crystal.

There's laughter. It's shallow. One laughs and another
laughs merely to echo it. There hasn't even been a joke.

Rich is bringing them home, herding them home.

Danny's eyes eager - on the drugs.

                                        BACK TO:

INT. RICH'S APARTMENT. LIVING ROOM. NIGHT (PRESENT)

Danny's eyes wary, nervous.

Rich gestures for Danny to sit beside him.

Which he does.

Very deliberately Rich sets up a white crystal in the
pipe.

The process is as much part of the hit as the drug.

Danny watches.

Rich lights it with care using an expensive sharp blue
flame lighter, a gas blaze. The crystal rock glows.

Precious smoke fills the circular base of the pipe.

Danny's eyes follow the swirls of smoke.

Danny is resisting. Fighting. It's a battle.

Rich spots this reaction, it confuses him.

                    RICH
          You seem tense.

Rich offers his pipe.

                    DANNY
          I'm good, thanks.

Rich's eyes sharpen.

The pleasure flashes into anger. He's confused. He
thought Danny had come here for free drugs in exchange
for sex.

                    RICH
          It's all yours...
               (Danny doesn't move)
          If you don't smoke it it's going
          to be wasted...

Sure enough the smoke begins to seep out of the top.

And Danny's eyes are on the smoke. His brain does
remember this pleasure, some part of him wants to say
yes.

He's fighting it.

                              RICH (CONT'D)
          It's getting away...

                         DANNY
          I'm good.

                              RICH
                    (sharp)
          You're not a man who usually says
          no?

                                        FLASH BACK TO:

INT. RICH'S APARTMENT. LIVING ROOM. NIGHT (PAST)

The three young men and Danny are lined up.

All have their tops off.

All have their mouths open, like sparrows waiting to be
fed.

Rich lights the crystal meth pipe. He inhales deeply.

And then walks down the line of boys, blowing a little
smoke into each of their open sparrow mouths.

Rich reaches Danny. He blows smoke inside his mouth.

And closes his lips around Danny's lips, trapping the
smoke inside. The rush hits Danny.

His pupils explode.

Rich observes.

                                        BACK TO:

INT. RICH'S APARTMENT. LIVING ROOM. NIGHT (PRESENT)

Now Rich sits back, his brilliant mind is reassessing
Danny and wondering what on earth he's doing here.

                         DANNY
          I need information.

                         RICH
          Information? How very grown up
          you've become. What information
          could you possibly want?

Danny puts down the card we just saw him copying out.

The escort card.

Rich stares at Danny a while, still assessing.

                              135

Something's changed about Danny. It's curious.

He has grown up.

Rich finally turns his attention to the card.

He picks it up. Runs his finger over it.

Rich's reaction darkens. He's anxious. Afraid even.

                RICH (CONT'D)
Who sent you?

                DANNY
No one.

                RICH
Who gave you this?

                DANNY
I was shown it. The real thing. I
copied it down.

                RICH
Who showed it to you?

                DANNY
Who are these people?

                RICH
Why are you being so evasive?

                DANNY
Can you help me?

                RICH
You can't be that stupid.

                DANNY
You know them - don't you?

                RICH
          (considers)
No, not stupid. Just blindly
stumbling around...
          (considers)
Yes, I know.

                DANNY
How do I contact them?

                RICH
Impossible.

                DANNY
It's important.

1.1 Danny sad on the bridge. Where it all begins

1.2 Danny and Alex's country walk

2.1 Scottie and Danny in the woods, with secrets to share

2.2 Danny journeys
into the unknown

2.3 Danny meets
Alex's mother

2.4 Alex's mother
is as mysterious as
her son

3.1 Danny arrested

3.2 Danny confronted with the dark side of his past

3.3 The blue room

3.4 Danny's healing

4.1 The professor who taught the genius

5.1 Secrets shared

5.2 Love as decryption

6.1 Author Tom Rob Smith on set

Fan art – Vipada Jakavanphituk

Fan art – Jo Lee

Fan art – Eli Lin

Fan art – Elger Leng

Fan art – Jessica Lucas

Volatile Rich's moods shift again. Danny clearly doesn't know what he's doing. Not a trap. Rich senses opportunity and gestures for Danny to move closer.

> RICH
> Closer.

Danny moves closer.

> RICH (CONT'D)
> Closer!

Danny moves very close.

Rich leans in. He sniffs Danny.

> RICH (CONT'D)
> You have the particular stink of a
> man out of his depth.

The proximity is held for a beat. And we wonder if Rich is going to kiss him. Danny tries hard not to recoil.

> RICH (CONT'D)
> Open your mouth.

> DANNY
> Can you help?

> RICH
> If you open your mouth it might
> become possible.

Rich lights the pipe.

> RICH (CONT'D)
> Open.

Danny weighs it up.

> RICH (CONT'D)
> Open.

Rich inhales, but not for himself, he intends to blow it into Danny's mouth.

Danny can't.

Angry Rich blows it across his face.

> RICH (CONT'D)
> (angry)
> You think I'd give this
> information away for free?

> Do you have any fucking idea how
> upset these people would be if I
> shared their secrets with the
> likes of you? They value privacy.
> They do not take kindly to
> indiscretion.

A cruel smile from Rich.

Despite the abuse Danny is still here. He hasn't left.

Danny's trapped. He wants this badly.

Rich relishes the dilemma.

He changes tack. Becoming charming.

>   RICH (CONT'D)
> Why don't you take a minute?
> Freshen up. And ask yourself: how
> badly do I want this?

INT. RIVERSIDE APARTMENT. BATHROOM. NIGHT

An amazing marble bathroom. A giant bathtub positioned by the window with views over London.

Danny washes his face. Looks in the mirror. Opens the cabinet. Viagra. Valium. Cocaine. Lube. Condoms. Clamps.

           FLASH TO:

INT. RIVERSIDE APARTMENT. LIVING ROOM. NIGHT (PAST)

A vision of hedonism: a post club party, seven-eight-nine guys, various states of undress, music, drugs - happiness of the thinnest kind.

Danny among them. Rich has his hands all over him.

A naked man walks feline like on all fours towards them.

           FLASH BACK TO:

INT. RIVERSIDE APARTMENT. BATHROOM. NIGHT (PRESENT)

Danny's thoughts are interrupted by an awful laugh. Rich is at the door. Watching him.

He enters, squeezing past, hands on Danny's hips. He climbs into the tub, despite it being empty.

> RICH
> I'm going to die in this tub.
> Heart attack. Or a stroke. They'll
> find me here, tongue hanging out,
> my little dick bobbing about in
> the bubble bath. Four strong men
> will heave me out. My flesh will
> slosh and slop on the marble
> floor. And they'll write about me:
> "he was a man who always got what
> he wanted".

He laughs. And smokes. Regarding Danny's dilemma.

> DANNY
> I can't.

Rich turns mean. He was sure Danny would say yes.

> RICH
> Then fuck off.

INT. DANNY'S APARTMENT. BATHROOM. NIGHT

Danny in the shower, under a dribble of tepid water,
scrubbing the night's sleaze from his skin.

> FLASH TO:

EXT. ESTUARY. DAY (PAST)

Danny and Alex walking by the sea - happy.

> BACK TO:

INT. DANNY'S APARTMENT. BEDROOM. NIGHT (PRESENT)

Danny enters his bedroom. In jogging pants, ready to
sleep. However, he finds Sara sitting on his bed.

She's been waiting for him. She seems anxious.

Even though he's exhausted, Danny joins his troubled
friend putting an arm around her - ready to help.

> DANNY
> What's wrong?

She's upset. And nervous.

> SARA
> Why didn't you tell me?

Danny's surprised - this is about him.

                    DANNY
          Tell you what?

Sara's sad eyes stare into his. Trying to make sense of
his response.

                    SARA
          Nothing would change between us,
          you know that, don't you?

Danny's perplexed.

                    DANNY
          Sara, I don't know what you're
          talking about.

Sara searches his expression: blank incomprehension. She
becomes embarrassed. And apologetic.

                    SARA
          You're not ready. I'm sorry. I
          shouldn't have...
                    (hugs him)
          I love you.

There are tears in her eyes. She stands, intending to
leave. But Danny gently takes her hand. Stopping her.

                    DANNY
          Hey?

She's confused by the signals.

                    DANNY (CONT'D)
          Tell me.

                    SARA
          Danny, I found it.

                    DANNY
          Found what?

                    SARA
          Your medication.

Sara's beginning to doubt herself.

In contrast, Danny becomes assertive.

                    DANNY
          Sara, what did you find?

She walks to Danny's desk. Opens the drawer, reaches in.
Pinched between her fingers is the pill from episode 2.

Danny's confusion transitions to fear.

INT. SOHO. SEXUAL HEALTH CLINIC. RECEPTION. DAY

Danny at the reception. Filling in a form.

*"Do you have any particular reason for wanting an HIV
test today?"*

Danny stares at the Yes or No answer.

INT. SOHO. SEXUAL HEALTH CLINIC. WAITING AREA. DAY

The room's bright and clean. Effort has been spent on
making the space welcoming. However, a waiting room it
remains. With an anxious energy.

Danny's seated. He steals glances at the other people.

The room is full. A mix of older and younger, a few
couples. Predominantly men.

Very little conversation. Some are there for support.
Even so, only a few whispered words.

On a digital screen is a notice: 'Had sex without a
condom? Fill in a survey to win an Ipad'.

A sexual health clinician appears. A middle aged woman.
She's reading from the form he filled in.

> CLINICIAN
> Danny?

Danny hears his name. No surname. A fractional pause
before he stands. Eyes land on him, briefly, curious.

The woman smiles, professionally. Unusually for him,
Danny doesn't smile back.

INT. SOHO SEXUAL HEALTH CLINIC. TESTING ROOM. DAY

A desk. An ancient computer. An examination bed. Blue
plastic shelves full of testing equipment. A sink.

A narrow window with a view over Soho.

The room is narrow and rectangular. Standing in the
middle with arms outstretched you could touch both walls.

Danny seated.

The clinician at the desk, glancing over his form.

> CLINICIAN
> Last test was eight months ago.
> Since then, one sexual partner.
> And you're always safe?

> DANNY
> Always.

The clinician reacts to his unusually forceful emphasis.

> CLINICIAN
> Do you use a condom during oral
> sex?

> DANNY
> No.

> CLINICIAN
> It's low risk but not 'no risk'.

She stands. Readying the test. There's a ritual. The commentary is always spoken, no matter how many tests you have. Like airline safety procedures.

> CLINICIAN (CONT'D)
> We're going to use a finger prick
> test. This isn't a test for HIV
> but for the antibodies produced in
> response to the infection. It will
> detect infections six weeks after
> exposure --

> DANNY
> I haven't had sexual contact - of
> any kind - for over six weeks.

Again, she's sensitive to his emphasis.

> CLINICIAN
> Then this result will be up to
> date. I need to ask, before the
> test, if the result comes back
> positive is there someone you can
> phone?

The question hits Danny hard. Danny manages a nod.

The clinician puts her plastic gloves on.

> CLINICIAN (CONT'D)
> We have a support network. No one
> is ever alone. Just so you know.

She takes Danny's hand, pushing down all his fingers except for the middle.

> CLINICIAN (CONT'D)
> Going to feel a slight scratch.

A finger prick stamp on the tip. A bubble of blood. She gives it a squeeze and fills a very thin glass tube.

She places a bud of cotton on the top of his finger.

She's finished. Blood taken. Easy. Quick. Sample ready.

                    CLINICIAN (CONT'D)
          This will just take a few minutes.

She leaves.

Danny alone.

There's no clock on the wall.

We should not jump cut out of this wait. Play it in real time, feel every beat with Danny. Discount how quickly it reads on the page - this should be roughly two minutes.

- Danny looks out of the window. Coffee shops and passers-by. He watches the random street interaction. The fragments of conversation.

- He turns back and stares at door.

- He looks at the blue plastic shelving units full of different testing equipment.

- Notices a box of free condoms and lube on the desk.

- Glances at the battered ancient computer. His information on screen.

- Spots a water mark on the ceiling. Searches for other signs of funding constraints. Scuffs on walls, etc.

- Removes the cotton bud from his finger tip. Looks at the blood-stained fibres. Throws it in the orange bin.

- Stares at the pin prick on the tip of his finger.

The door opens.

The clinician returns.

She's carrying the test. A small petri dish. Her body language is impossible to read.

                    CLINICIAN (CONT'D)
          The result is reactive.

The word 'reactive' sounds oddly blank.

                    CLINICIAN (CONT'D)
          We use the word 'reactive' because
          7 out of a 1000 results come back
          with 'false reactive' result so
          what we're going to do now --

Understanding, Danny stands up, sharply, the chair pushed back. The noise is unsettling. His movement abrupt.

Silence.

The clinician is delicate with him.

> CLINICIAN (CONT'D)
> Danny, why don't you take a seat
> for me?

Danny's in shock.

He looks directly at her. She remains careful with him.

> CLINICIAN (CONT'D)
> Danny?

He slowly sits down.

She also sits, putting the test down on the desk.

A small petri-dish with clear fluid. And through the
liquid are two small dots.

> CLINICIAN (CONT'D)
> Two dots indicate the presence of
> antibodies to the HIV virus.

Danny stares into the two blue dots. They're like two
little eyes looking back at him - he stares and stares as
if they were the eyes of his enemy.

> CLINICIAN (CONT'D)
> I need to take a second sample.
> And run a second test to rule out
> the chance of a false result.

He's still staring at the two blue dots. Danny looks at
her. His mouth is dry. He shakes his head.

So many people lie about their sex lives that the
clinician is accustomed to a disconnect between a
reactive test and claims about their sexual activity.

> DANNY
> It's not possible.

She presumes he's in denial.

> CLINICIAN
> Let's run the second test.

The second test.

She readies the equipment.

This time no talking. And the atmosphere is very
different. From both of them. Fraught.

Plastic gloves on. She takes Danny's other hand, his left one. This time his hand is trembling.

She waits.

Danny steadies himself.

She pushes down all his fingers except for the middle.

A finger prick stamp on the tip. A bubble of blood. She gives it a squeeze and fills a thin glass tube.

She gives him a bud of cotton to put on the top of his finger. She's finished. Blood taken.

Second sample ready.

> CLINICIAN (CONT'D)
> Would you like someone to wait
> with you?

Danny shakes his head.

She leaves.

We do not cut out of this second wait. We must feel it in real time. Beat for beat. Again, discount how quickly it reads - this is another two minutes.

But the energy of these two minutes is completely different. Tension no longer subsumed. On the surface.

As soon as the door is shut Danny stands and paces.

- He stops at the desk. Stares intently at the two implacable blue eyes in the petri dish.

- Walks to door. Places hands on it. Pushing against it.

- Walks back to the desk. Stares again at the two blue eyes in the petri dish. Unable to believe them.

- Removes the cotton bud from his finger tip. Sees the bloody fibres. Throws it away. In the orange hazard bin. And this time his eyes linger on the hazard symbol.

- Suddenly he seems to lose all of his frantic energy, short of breath, he sits at the desk.

- Close on the ancient computer screen: his health records. A large amount of text. He reads, blankly at first, then with more concentration.

- A long list of entries.

Danny scrolls up:

"Syphilis. Chlamydia. Hepatitis B. Hepatitis C."

It all looks so absolute and real on screen. Dates.
Antibiotics. On and on and on...

Danny scrolls up faster and faster, over a sexual health
history packed with incident, until Danny reaches his
name at the top of the screen.

He stands, stepping back from the computer, as if it were
a threat to him. And, in many ways, it is.

And now he sees, in the blue plastic shelves --

A blood testing kit.

Danny takes it out. Removes the packaging. A needle
combined with a tube that leads into a 5 millimetre
plastic phial. An all in one unit.

It's the exact same piece of kit used by the medic at the
police station. From the opening sequence.

Danny holds the needle up to eye level. The moment of
full comprehension.

Slowly his fingers tighten around the needle. Until it
disappears within his clenched hand.

The door opens.

The clinician is surprised to see Danny so close to the
door, holding that piece of kit, his expression full of
fear and fury. She's startled.

An uneasy stand-off.

> DANNY
> I know how they did it!

> CLINICIAN
> Danny --

> DANNY
> I know!

Danny's emphasis changes with each exclamation,
modulating from anger to despair.

> DANNY (CONT'D)
> I know!

> CLINICIAN
> Danny --

                        DANNY
         I know.

                        CLINICIAN
         Danny --

                        DANNY
         I know...

He isn't listening. He raises his fist, containing the
needle and phial to his head. Frozen in this position.

The clinician peers out into the corridor. She gestures
for help.

A friendly male member of staff joins her. They stand at
the door. Some form of silent communication. He
understands. Both trained in distress.

                        CLINICIAN
         Danny?

She does not touch him. They hold back.

Slowly Danny lowers the needle and phial from his face.

                        CLINICIAN (CONT'D)
         Danny, why don't you take a seat?

Now numb and compliant Danny steps back, perching on the
edge of the bed, still holding the needle.

The clinician cautiously steps closer.

The second member of staff remains at the door.

                        CLINICIAN (CONT'D)
         Danny, why don't you give me the
         needle?

It takes a moment for Danny to process the request. An
all consuming weariness has come over him.

He opens his hand. The needle has sunk into his skin.
There's blood. The glass phial has broken.

She places the second test result down on the table. Next
to the first.

She puts on a fresh pair of gloves, taking a tissue in
order to remove the bloody needle.

She moves gingerly. Warily.

She throws the needle into the hazardous orange bin. She
returns, to tend to his minor injury.

Meeting her glance Danny understands that she'll never believe him. Nor will the man at the door.

Danny slowly turns to the second test result on the desk - a second set of blue eyes watching him, beside the first set - two pairs of enemy eyes now on him.

Confirmation.

>   CLINICIAN (CONT'D)
>   Is there someone we can call?

INT. SCOTTIE'S HOUSE. LIVING ROOM. EVENING

Scottie stands by the window, looking out. His hands are clasped behind his back. It's dusk. He's in shadow. His stance appears formal and objective.

Danny is seated on the sofa. He's been crying. And remains on the brink of tears.

His dialogue is muddled - he knows what is true but can't explain how it is so. The monologue veers wildly between compelling and implausible.

>   DANNY
>   When he took my blood at the
>   station they must have injected me
>   at the same time --
>   (sudden thought)
>   The virus can't survive outside
>   the body --
>   (sudden thought)
>   They must have kept it heated --
>   (sudden thought)
>   And I know it hasn't been six
>   weeks and it takes that long to
>   show up in the test --
>   (beat)
>   Maybe they found a way --

But Danny doesn't have the answers.

>   DANNY (CONT'D)
>   (abandoning the
>   explanation)
>   I don't know how. I don't know how
>   they did it. But they did it.
>   (pitiful)
>   They did it.

Scottie makes no attempt to console or comfort Danny. He isn't even looking at him.

Sensing that the situation is slipping away Danny rallies, trying to compose himself.

>   DANNY (CONT'D)
>   Please Scottie. You have to
>   believe me.
>   (beat)
>   Please...
>   (beat)
>   Please...

But Scottie doesn't turn around. In sharp contrast, Scottie's response is precise & composed.

>   SCOTTIE
>   I remember taking you to hospital
>   all those years ago. When there
>   was a chance you were infected. We
>   barely knew each other. You were
>   so young. More child than adult. I
>   made you promise to never take a
>   risk like that again. And you
>   promised. You promised me, Danny.

Danny breaks down at the thought of Scottie not believing him. The tears that follow are from the very depth of his soul, wrenched up in the most awful way.

Scottie does not move to comfort him.

Danny repeats his petition but, this time, through the tears and snot, he's barely comprehensible:

>   DANNY
>   Scottie-I-swear-to-you-I-never-
>   broke-that-promise-I-swear-Scottie-
>   please-believe-me-because-I-don't-
>   have-anyone-else-if-you-don't
>   believe-me-I-don't-have-anyone
>   else...

A desperate plea. One Danny thinks will never be believed. He lapses back into tears.

He has no hope.

Scottie doesn't budge from his position. Doesn't rush to offer any soothing reassurance. Doesn't even turn around.

Finally, quietly, still looking out the window --

>   SCOTTIE
>   I believe you.

Danny doesn't quite hear, or understand. He wipes his eyes, trying to catch up. He waits. Unsure.

>   SCOTTIE (CONT'D)
>   I knew that you were a young man
>   who'd make a lot of mistakes. But
>   never the same one twice.

> (beat)
> I believe you, Danny. I believe
> that they deliberately infected
> you.

Danny is blank. Numb. No longer crying. He can't fathom that Scottie is on his side. Or what this means.

Scottie still hasn't altered his position, still isn't looking at Danny.

> SCOTTIE (CONT'D)
> Not to kill you, obviously. With
> medication you'll live a long and
> normal life. They did it to
> discredit you. They'll say you
> took risks with your own health.
> You were reckless and
> irresponsible. Perhaps they'll
> even say you infected Alex.

> DANNY
> No, he was --

> SCOTTIE
> Negative?

Danny silent. Reconsiders.

> SCOTTIE (CONT'D)
> The story of you two has been
> written. It was written many
> months ago. A sordid tale, the
> details of which will leak into
> the public sphere. People will
> recoil. Many will think that you
> got what you deserved. No one will
> campaign for answers. No one will
> demand justice.

Scottie's voice remains calm and analytical. Dissecting the situation carefully. Without emotion, like a professor presented with a problem.

Danny sits back in his chair, eyes on the ceiling. He's suddenly so incredibly exhausted.

> DANNY
> These people...

> SCOTTIE
> Yes.

> DANNY
> ...They'll do anything.

> SCOTTIE
> Yes.

>   DANNY
> I can't...

>   SCOTTIE
> No.

For the first time we witness Danny utterly defeated.

>   DANNY
> I can't.

He closes his eyes.

It's over.

And then --

>   SCOTTIE
> A long, long time ago I had a
> lover.

Danny opens his eyes.

Yet to his surprise Scottie still hasn't moved to comfort
or console him. He remains at the window, in the shadows.

Danny wondering what Scottie's talking about.

>   SCOTTIE (CONT'D)
> He was an aspiring artist. Quite
> promising. Extraordinarily
> beautiful. He had countless
> admirers, of course. And rightly
> so. I didn't begrudge him that. I
> was the man he phoned when he
> wanted a good meal. Tickets to a
> West End show. I was stability.
> Domesticity, which he liked to dip
> his toe into every now and again.
> I was more than happy with the
> arrangement.

Exhausted, Danny listens to the seemingly irrelevant
story without a trace of impatience.

>   SCOTTIE (CONT'D)
> His name was Raphael. Not his real
> name, one he'd chosen for himself,
> as he reshaped his suburban
> background into something more
> fitting for an avant-garde
> metropolitan artist.
>   (beat)

1983, and he was among the first
in London to fall ill. Back then
it didn't even have a name. There
was no information. No leaflets.
No warnings. No answers. You'd
watch the news and hear no mention
of it. A secret plague.

Danny's now listening in earnest.

                    SCOTTIE (CONT'D)
          I visited him as often as I could,
          with as much fresh fruit and
          vegetables as I could carry.

                                        FLASH TO:

INT. HOUSING ESTATE. CORRIDOR. DAY (PAST)

Moving down a wretched, gloomy communal corridor. Grey.
Dark. Without colour. We're almost floating, dreamlike.

The door to an apartment opens to reveal --

INT. HOUSING ESTATE. BEDSIT. DAY (PAST)

A tiny studio apartment. Little bigger than the bed at
its centre. No bathroom. No kitchen unit. A sink.

Poverty, squalor and yet this room is remarkable --

The bed is blue, not painted, blue sheets, blue pillows.
Lying on top of it is a beautiful gaunt young man.

The young man is painted one shade of blue, in thick oil
paints, encrusting him, cocooning him in blue.

His hair is painted blue, not dyed. His pubic hair too.
The paint is days old, cracked and dry.

Aside from being wisp-thin, the man has no other outward
signs of sickness.

Painted on the back wall, emerging at the exact point
behind his head, is a pyramid of blue - spreading out,
narrow at first, expanding across the back wall, and up
onto the ceiling, which is almost completely covered.

Within this pyramid is every shade of blue known to man,
swirls, lines, Pollack splatters, always abstract.

The effect is both magical and disturbing, as if all this
blue burst out of the man's mind, as if he'd blown his
brains out and the result was not blood, but blue,
covering the back wall and ceiling.

Outside of the brain splatter of blue, which is painted with mania and genius, the remaining three walls are one shade of blue and low key.

The blue continues across the floor - carpet painted one shade of blue, covered with a hard blue crust. Again, low key shades, so the ceiling and back wall dominate.

Clothes on a painted blue rack are all blue, either originally blue or dyed blue.

In shock, at the door, we see a brown paper bag being dropped, hitting the floor, different coloured fruit rolling across the blue carpet.

                                                    BACK TO:

INT. SCOTTIE'S HOUSE. LIVING ROOM. EVENING (PRESENT)

Scottie remains at the window. He still has not turned around, arms behind his back, looking outside as though he stood at the doorway to the blue room.

                    SCOTTIE
          He'd been given a book on colour
          therapy. In it blue was described
          as having healing properties. Blue
          - blue alone - was able to fight
          infections. Blue - blue alone -
          could save him. Blue and blue
          alone. The idea no doubt appealed
          to his artistic sensibilities. In
          those days mysticism and magic
          stood in for medicine. He wouldn't
          accept the fruit and vegetables
          because they weren't blue. But -
          since water was blue - he
          eventually agreed to a bath.

                                                    FLASH TO:

INT. HOUSING ESTATE. COMMUNAL BATHROOM. DAY (PAST)

A grubby communal bathroom. Cracked tiles. Dirty. Without a window. No natural light. No colour.

Scottie is bathing the beautiful man. Tenderly, as if afraid the man will break. We don't need to see Scottie, just the man and a younger Scottie's caring hands.

The oil paint breaks off in uneven fragments.

As the blue paint dissolves Scottie reveals, across the man's back, skin lesions: Kaposi's Sarcoma.

A purple color. But subtle and real, unlike the vivid blue, this can't be washed away.

The permanence of this purple.

Scottie's fingers pass over them.

The beautiful man's expression is serene. At peace.

BACK TO:

INT. SCOTTIE'S HOUSE. LIVING ROOM. EVENING (PRESENT)

Scottie in the same position, at the window.

> SCOTTIE
> I told him that he'd given up. I told him to fight.
> (reenacting)
> *"Let's find some better answers than the colour blue."* But he refused. He said that I'd never faced the inevitability of defeat. He was going to die. He was going to suffer. And suffer terribly. There was nothing he could do. There was nothing anyone could do. He was right. On both counts. He did suffer terribly. And I have never faced the inevitability of defeat.

For the first time, in this exchange, Scottie turns around to face Danny. Close on Scottie's eyes.

FLASH TO:

INT. HOUSING ESTATE. BLUE ROOM. DAY (PAST)

The blue room.

The bedsheets have been stripped so the bed is now white. The carpet has been unevenly scratched clean of most of the blue paint. The room emptied.

All that remains is the blue brain burst - the pyramid of mania-blue across the back wall and ceiling.

Cracked. Fracturing. A single autumnal blue flake falls.

BACK TO:

INT. SCOTTIE'S HOUSE. LIVING ROOM. EVENING (PRESENT)

Scottie stands before Danny & gestures for him to rise.

Danny stands.

Face to face with Scottie.

Scottie kisses Danny's lips. Not sexual. Platonic love.
An acceptance of Danny's body. A healing act.

> SCOTTIE
> It is impossible. We will lose.
> But we will fight.

INT. LONDON BATHS. SWIMMING POOL. DAY

Underwater. All is blue.

At the bottom of a beautiful public tiled swimming pool.
The noise of the world is muted.

Danny and Scottie are swimming at the deepest point -
side by side. The two friends. Together.

The world has slowed.

Scottie turns upwards and surfaces.

But Danny remains a moment longer. He can't face
returning to the surface. He can't face returning to the
world.

Not yet.

He grips onto the bottom of the pool, the draining grill,
or whatever, looking down.

Still sad.

He doesn't want to go up.

And then he turns to see --

A young girl swimming along the bottom of the pool. She's
only seven or eight years old.

She's wearing a comically huge snorkel as if she were
deep sea fishing. It makes her eyes bulbous.

She's wearing a bright glittering swimming costume,
sparkling, decorated with wonderful silvery sea
creatures.

She shimmers in the water. Her long beautiful hair flows
around her head like silk.

She sees Danny.

And waves at him.

Danny waves back.

And the little girl returns to the surface.

Danny looks up for the first time in this sequence.

We see the surface packed with people.

And now, finally, Danny kicks up.

And we follow him up. And up. And up...

And he breaks the surface.

INT. LONDON BATHS. SWIMMING POOL. SURFACE. DAY

Danny on the surface.

He looks around. At all these people.

There's the muscular fitness fanatic.

There's an overweight individual.

There's a family.

There's an elderly man.

There's an elderly woman.

There's an eccentric woman.

There's a man with a missing limb.

There's a young straight couple kissing.

There are children playing.

Danny searches for the little girl with the snorkel but she's nowhere to be seen.

Danny turns to see Scottie.

Scottie is sitting on a bench by the side of the pool, wrapped in towels. Patiently waiting for him.

Danny swims towards him.

INT. LONDON BATHS. SWIMMING POOL. BENCH / LEDGE. DAY

Danny gets out and sits beside Scottie, both wrapped in towels, looking out over this pool.

It's busy with every kind of person from every walk of life, from places all over the world.

Behind Danny and Scottie is a sign that reads:

LONDON BATHS

And the whole of London is represented here. With Danny too.

> DANNY
> I'm ready.

Scottie nods, observing his friend.

> SCOTTIE
> Are you going to tell me?

Danny glances at Scottie.

> SCOTTIE (CONT'D)
> The secret you've been keeping.

Danny smiles.

> DANNY
> How...

He thinks better of the question.

Of course Scottie sensed something.

Danny nods.

Scottie raises a finger to his lips.

> SCOTTIE
> Not here. Downstairs.

Scottie stands.

Danny follows. They leave the pool

INT. PUBLIC BATHS. STEAM ROOM. DAY

Dense plumes of steam. Thick stone walls drip with condensation. Moody gloominess.

Danny and Scottie are at the back, in the darkest corner. Except for the hiss of vapour - there's silence.

Danny and Scottie wait for the only other shadowy figure to leave. The man stands, stretches, and walks out.

The door closes. They're alone.

> SCOTTIE
> Tell me.

                    DANNY
          I lied.

                    SCOTTIE
          About?

                    DANNY
          I stole something. From the attic.

Scottie's impressed.

                    SCOTTIE
          You lied well.

                    DANNY
          A locked cylinder.

Danny marks a small line in the condensation.

                    SCOTTIE
          You lied wisely.

                    DANNY
          It needs a code.

                    SCOTTIE
          Which you don't know?

                    DANNY
          No.

                    SCOTTIE
          Did Alex intend it for you?

                    DANNY
          He told me where to look.

                    SCOTTIE
          Then he must have believed you
          capable of opening it.

Danny's exasperated.

                    DANNY
          I've gone over every word. Every
          conversation.

                    SCOTTIE
          Go over them again. Remember he
          will have been aware you were
          under surveillance.
                 (beat)
          Danny, you must figure it out.
          You're the only one who can.

Danny pulls himself together. He nods, about to speak
when a man enters the steam room.

Scottie and Danny abruptly fall silent.

The man misinterprets the awkward silence and presumes Danny and Scottie were fooling about.

The man huffs, in disgust, and leaves, shaking his head.

Scottie and Danny are briefly amused.

The door closes. The conversation continues.

> SCOTTIE (CONT'D)
> Where is it now? You can't have
> kept it in the flat?

Danny shakes his head, about to answer --

> SCOTTIE (CONT'D)
> You were right to be cautious.

Scottie sounds genuinely afraid.

> SCOTTIE (CONT'D)
> If they knew that you had this...
> (trails off)
> They would have behaved quite
> differently.

Scottie ponders deeply.

> SCOTTIE (CONT'D)
> Secrets have changed. They used to
> be typed documents, stashed inside
> manila files. Pages stamped
> 'Confidential'. Rolls of
> microfilm. Now they're numbers.
> Algorithms. The contents of that
> cylinder will almost certainly be
> incomprehensible. At least to us.
> We need an ally. A great mind.

Scottie stands, taking the precaution of wiping away the cylinder marked on the condensation.

INT. PUBLIC BATHS. MALE CHANGING ROOM. DAY

Danny and Scottie wrapped in towels. At the lockers. Scottie hands Danny a suit bag.

Danny's surprised. He opens it.

A new set of clothes. Smarter. Formal. Expensive. Understated tailoring. Trousers. Shirt. A jacket.

                  SCOTTIE
Some of the people we need to
speak to care very much about
appearances. They'll look at the
cut of your suit before they
listen to what you say. It's not
about wealth. It's about a set of
signals. They require a lifetime
of study, which is precisely the
point. Wealth can be acquired in
an instant.

Danny stares at the outfit, processing the request.

                SCOTTIE (CONT'D)
Tonight we must play by their
rules.

INT. PUBLIC BATHS. MALE CHANGING ROOM. DAY

Danny in new attire. A radically different proposition.
Fantastically handsome.

Scottie's impressed. Danny remains circumspect.

                DANNY
They fit.

                SCOTTIE
What kind of spy would I be if I
couldn't guess a man's shirt size?

But Scottie's joke can't conceal the problematic My-Fair-
Lady dressing up of Danny.

EXT. UNIVERSITY OF LONDON. MAIN QUAD. NIGHT

Stone pillars. Columns. The grand dome. History.
Prestige. Hugely Impressive.

The quad at night. Spot lit. Dramatic. No one around.

Danny and Scottie walk up the stairs towards the grand
main building.

                DANNY
Who is she?

                SCOTTIE
She's the President and Provost
Professor of the University of
London.

                DANNY
Can we trust her?

                         SCOTTIE
There's no art in trusting nobody.
The craft of a spy has always been
choosing the right people to
trust.

                        DANNY
You two are friends?

                        SCOTTIE
Friends... Yes.

Scottie drifts off. Danny waits.

For once Scottie is reluctant to tell his story.

And in the end, says nothing, surprising Danny.

Danny glances back.

People on the street. People in the quad.

INT. UNIVERSITY OF LONDON. MAIN QUAD BUILDING. RECEPTION.
NIGHT

While Scottie is talking to the receptionist, Danny hangs
back, his attention caught by the poster board, crammed
with University society notices --

Travel. Screenings. Debates. Theatre. Politics. Sport.

Curious, he explores the flyers. A new world to him.

                        SCOTTIE
Danny?

Scottie registers Danny's interest in this board.

Danny rejoins Scottie.

They pass a Security Guard. The Guard's eyes follow them
further inside.

A cleaner uses a machine to polish the stone floor.

INT. UNIVERSITY OF LONDON. ELEVATOR. NIGHT

Danny and Scottie in the creaky old elevator.

The elevator arrives. Doors open --

INT. UNIVERSITY OF LONDON. MAIN BUILDING. CORRIDORS.
NIGHT

Scottie and Danny step out into a deserted corridor. A
long line of identical doors.

Their shoes clip on the hard stone floor, echoing around
the maze-like space.

As they turn a corner, reaching another long line of
doors, Scottie comes to an abrupt stop.

We hear the distinct clip-clip-clip of an unseen person
walking somewhere in this maze of corridors.

The footsteps are getting closer.

Suddenly the sound stops.

The clip-clip-clip sound starts again. But the sound is
getting softer. Going in the opposite direction.

Troubled, Scottie continues.

INT. UNIVERSITY OF LONDON. MAIN BUILDING. CORRIDOR. NIGHT

Danny stops outside the President's office. A sign on the
grand door.

                    SCOTTIE
          They'll be aware of my connection
          to her. They will have anticipated
          this meeting. Her office will be
          almost certainly be bugged.

Scottie gestures away from the office.

INT. UNIVERSITY OF LONDON. RARE BOOKS LIBRARY. SECURITY.
NIGHT

Scottie and Danny at the entrance to the rare books
library. A guard. A librarian. A metal detector. More
like entering a vault than a library.

They must leave their phones and wallets behind. Emptying
their pockets. Airport style screening.

They pass through the detector.

Scottie and Danny put plastic dust covers over their
shoes. They're both given a pair of gloves.

The solemn librarian, gravely unhappy at their admission,
escorts them through.

INT. UNIVERSITY OF LONDON. RARE BOOKS LIBRARY. SECURITY.
NIGHT

The hum of rarified air, humidity controlled.

A secure archive. Not academic romantic.

Stark steel shelves are filled with books many hundreds
of years old. Priceless. Irreplaceable.

Harsh fluorescent lights on the ceiling.

Sterile and austere, impossible to see all the corners
and aisles, filled with hidden spaces.

The President of the University of London - Claire -
waits for them. In many ways Claire is a reflection of
Scottie. Same age. A mix of brilliance and eccentricity.

Scottie and Claire hug - an embrace full of warmth and
love. Danny observes. It has the feel of former lovers.

A mystery.

Claire offers a hand to Danny. He shakes it.

She turns her attention to the librarian, lingering at
the back of the room.

> CLAIRE
> Thank you.

The librarian leaves, reluctantly.

We hear a door shut. And seal.

> CLAIRE (CONT'D)
> You haven't lost your taste for
> theatricality.

> SCOTTIE
> For once it's justified.

The fond reunion atmosphere changes.

> CLAIRE
> What is this about? Why couldn't
> you tell me on the phone?

> SCOTTIE
> A former student of your
> university. A prodigy.

> DANNY
> You might have known him as
> Alistair Turner. But he preferred
> the name Alex.

Claire regards Danny with exacting scrutiny. Catching up with the gravity of the situation.

>   CLAIRE
>   Let's walk.

INT. UNIVERSITY OF LONDON. RARE BOOKS LIBRARY. MAIN CHAMBER. NIGHT

The three conspirators on the move, through the steel maze of bookshelves, weaving an unpredictable path.

Their voices are low.

>   CLAIRE
>   I didn't know Alex personally.
>   Only by reputation. There aren't
>   many students who start their
>   degree at the age of fifteen.

>   DANNY
>   He was murdered.

Claire turns to Scottie for confirmation.

>   SCOTTIE
>   He was murdered, Claire.

Scottie gives no evidence. Nothing to back up the claim. Yet Claire nods, accepting. His words are enough.

Danny follows the mechanics of credibility.

>   CLAIRE
>   I take it you want to speak to
>   Alex's professor?

>   DANNY
>   Marcus Shaw.

>   SCOTTIE
>   What do you know about him?

>   CLAIRE
>   Brilliant. Difficult.

>   SCOTTIE
>   And his relationship with Alex?

>   CLAIRE
>   They were close.

>   SCOTTIE
>   Sexual?

Danny's about to object. Scottie stops him.

                    CLAIRE
          I'm confident their intimacy was
          purely intellectual.

                    DANNY
          Will he talk to us?

                    CLAIRE
          Marcus is precise. He won't
          'chat'. Unless you're talking
          about mathematics the discussion
          will be a waste of time.

                    SCOTTIE
          Is it possible Alex confided in
          him?

                    CLAIRE
          That's a very serious allegation.

                    SCOTTIE
          I'm just thinking aloud.

                    CLAIRE
          Marcus admired Alex. On some
          level, he might have envied him.
          But I can't believe he would've
          harmed him --

Suddenly the entire archive is plunged into darkness.
Then, slowly, the fluorescent lights reboot.

Aisle by aisle until the table is in light again.

They're spooked. They've stopped walking.

                    SCOTTIE
          Can you arrange a meeting?

                    CLAIRE
          Then you do have something
          specific to speak about?

Scottie glances at Danny.

Danny must decide. Does he trust her?

                    DANNY
          We will.

Claire processes this revelation. Inscrutable.

INT. UNIVERSITY OF LONDON. RARE BOOKS LIBRARY. MAIN
CHAMBER. NIGHT

Danny, Scottie and Claire about to leave.

> SCOTTIE
> Don't send emails. Don't make
> calls. They'll have access to your
> computers. Your office. Your
> phone.
>   (grave)
> Claire, I should warn you --

> CLAIRE
>   (interrupting)
> He was my student, Scottie.

Scottie nods.

The door opens.

The librarian is standing outside.

EXT. UNIVERSITY OF LONDON. NIGHT

Scottie hails a black cab.

> DANNY
> Where now?

> SCOTTIE
> A club, I thought.

EXT. MAYFAIR. EXCLUSIVE MEMBERS ONLY CLUB. NIGHT

Embassies and tax avoidance offices. Boutique shops. Fine
dining establishments.

The streets are silent. And immaculate.

A beautiful period building. All front curtains closed.
No glimpse inside. No sign.

Danny and Scottie at the gate.

> SCOTTIE
> Don't admire your surroundings.
> Affect an air of mild boredom. But
> don't take it too far. It needs to
> feel effortless. Making an effort
> is the surest give away.

> DANNY
> This isn't going to work.

> SCOTTIE
> All we need is enough uncertainty
> for them to allow you inside. The
> advantage is on our side: more
> than anything they despise making
> a scene.

They open the gate.

INT. MAYFAIR MEMBERS ONLY CLUB. RECEPTION. NIGHT

Dickensian. Dark timbers. Candle light. Antiques. Art on
the walls: paintings of naval battles. Polished bronze
busts of historical figures in glass cabinets. All men.

We could be a hundred years in the past.

At the front desk stands one young man and one older
gentleman: both dressed in long-coat black tie.

Their solemn faces greet Scottie as he signs the leather
bound ledger using a fountain pen.

> FRONT OF HOUSE
> Good evening, sir.

> SCOTTIE
> Good evening. One guest.

In synchronicity the two men turn to examine Danny.

He tries hard not to recoil under the stare. And does
well. Yet they're not convinced.

Scottie moves towards the next room.

As Danny passes the desk the younger man hands him a
cream card with the rules neatly printed on it:

*"No phones. No photographs. No electronic devices of any
kind. Ties must be worn at all times."*

INT. MAYFAIR MEMBERS ONLY CLUB. LOUNGE. NIGHT

Danny and Scottie seated in deep leather chairs. A real
fire burns. No artificial light.

Bookshelves hold leather volumes but we sense they
haven't been read.

The lounge is full. Danny's the only person under the age
of fifty. Everyone wears a suit. Saville Row. Nothing
flashy. No gold watches. No bright colours.

Danny's socks - exposed as he's seated - are Christmas
novelty. A ring of reindeer. He spots them and sits
forward so that his trousers sink back over the reindeer.

Trying to ignore that he's under scrutiny, Danny studies
the menu. No prices. They talk in hushed tones.

          DANNY
How do you know what anything
costs?

          SCOTTIE
Everything goes on account. It's
presumed each member can always
pay his way. Money's never
mentioned. Seen. Or discussed.

Danny can't help but glance about the room.

          DANNY
There are more women in a gay
club.

          SCOTTIE
Women are not allowed.

          DANNY
Is that legal?

          SCOTTIE
How many women do you think apply?

An elegant man in his fifties enters, bespoke tailoring,
nodding hellos to most in the lounge.

He spots Scottie and joins them. He's James. Regal.
Angular. Good looking. Groomed. Sensational waves of
glossy grey hair. And full of apparent good cheer.

He shakes Scottie's hand.

          JAMES
Good to see you.

          SCOTTIE
You look fantastic as always,
James.

James smiles, placing a gracious hand on Scottie's arm.
Instantly the social order is established.

James turns to Danny. Offering his hand and silently
assessing this young man. Unfavourably.

His good cheer takes a small but noticeable knock.

          DANNY
Danny.

He regrets not using 'Daniel' but too late. James doesn't
even give his name.

They sit. But there's already tension. James can sense
something's wrong, some rule broken, or about to be.

Scottie tries to maintain a breezy air, turning to Danny.

>   SCOTTIE
>   James and I have worked together
>   for over thirty years.

>   JAMES
>   Not really together, Scottie.

Said lightly, but sour underneath.

>   SCOTTIE
>   No, I suppose not.

We sense James is much higher up, a great success,
whereas Scottie has remained stuck in the middle.

>   SCOTTIE (CONT'D)
>   James, I'm afraid I need to ask a
>   favour.

>   JAMES
>   A favour?

>   SCOTTIE
>   Afraid so.

Another rule broken. James's mood darkens again.

>   JAMES
>   Scottie, this is unlike you.

>   SCOTTIE
>   The situation is exceptional.

James weighs up the situation carefully.

>   JAMES
>   Very well.

>   SCOTTIE
>   What can you tell me about the
>   murder of Alistair Turner?

As outrageous a comment as could be imagined. Even Danny
is taken by surprise.

James is appalled. And furious. Although his expression
has barely changed. He leans forward. In a low voice:

>   JAMES
>   Have you lost your mind?

Silence.

James stands, about to leave.

                    SCOTTIE
        I'm asking you to be indiscreet.
        The quid pro quo is that I will
        not be.

James stops, looking down at Scottie. Weighing up all the
secrets that he contains. He's not sure.

James sits. Eyes on Danny. Then Scottie.

                    JAMES
        You've been hanging around too
        many street corners, old friend.
        Your acquaintances are beginning
        to rub off on you.

                    SCOTTIE
        Oh no. I learnt these tricks from
        the top.

                    JAMES
        You're sure you want to continue
        down this road?

                    SCOTTIE
        Quite sure.

                    JAMES
        That's an awful shame.

James carefully calculates.

                    JAMES (CONT'D)
        I'll tell you a joke. How about
        that?

                    SCOTTIE
        It would depends on how funny I
        find it.

                    JAMES
        It's hysterical.

Said without a trace of humour.

Scottie nods. Deal agreed.

Danny can't follow the logic of this peculiar exchange.

                    JAMES (CONT'D)
        An Englishman, a Chinaman, a
        Frenchman, an American, a Russian,
        an Israeli and a Saudi walk into a
        bar.
                (beat)
        And they all agree.

That was the punch-line.

Danny's baffled. But Scottie acts as if he's heard the most disturbing piece of information. Disconcerted, he nods, solemnly. Transaction concluded.

James glances at Danny.

> JAMES (CONT'D)
> You'd better explain it to your
> boy at a later stage.

Danny should be offended but isn't. He's watched this whole exchange as though he were a visitor to a zoo.

James stands.

> JAMES (CONT'D)
> Like I said, old friend, an awful
> shame.

James leaves.

And now everyone in the lounge is staring at them. As if they can sense that the club rules have been shattered.

> SCOTTIE
> Time to go.

INT. MAYFAIR MEMBERS ONLY CLUB. RECEPTION. NIGHT

As Scottie and Danny leave, the older staff member gently intercepts Scottie, remaining polite.

> FRONT OF HOUSE
> If I could ask you to settle up,
> Sir?

Scottie takes a beat.

> SCOTTIE
> Of course.

He heads to the desk.

EXT. MAYFAIR MEMBERS ONLY CLUB. NIGHT

Danny and Scottie stand outside.

> DANNY
> What did it mean?

> SCOTTIE
> That my membership has been
> cancelled with immediate effect. A
> pity: they did a marvellous eggs
> Benedict.

> DANNY
> The joke, Scottie, the joke.

> SCOTTIE
> I thought it was perfectly clear.

> DANNY
> No.

> SCOTTIE
> Substitute the nationality for the
> security agency. British MI6. The
> Chinese Ministry for State
> Security. Israeli Mossad. American
> CIA. Russian FSB. And Saudi GIP.

> DANNY
> Okay?

> SCOTTIE
> The punch line was that they all
> agree.
>   (beat)
> Danny, they've never agreed on
> anything. Ever. Until now, it
> seems. Whatever Alex discovered -
> whatever it was, whatever it is -
> no one wants in the open. We're
> not up against one intelligence
> agency. We're up against them all.
> What does it mean? It means we're
> quite alone.

And the two of them are alone - the only people standing
on this sleepy exclusive street.

EXT. VAUXHALL. NIGHT

Danny walking in his expensive suit. Casual party crowd
pass him by. Self conscious, he takes his tie off.

Gradually he becomes aware that an expensive car is
trailing him. Or is he imagining it? Not sure.

He turns a corner.

EXT. VAUXHALL. DANNY'S APARTMENT BUILDING. NIGHT

Danny can see his home, not far.

The expensive car following also turns the corner.

Danny checks, and stops, alarmed.

The car accelerates, straight towards him.

Danny pulls back as if expecting the car to mount the pavement and crash into him.

But the car parks beside him. The back door opens.

Danny steps forward. He sees Rich in the back seat. There's a no-nonsense driver in the front.

                         RICH
          Get in.

Danny is unsure.

                         RICH (CONT'D)
          Get in the fucking car.

Danny obeys.

INT/EXT. RICH'S CAR / VAUXHALL. NIGHT

As soon as Danny shuts the door Rich's driver pulls out, accelerating at great speed. Running a red light.

A radical contrast to his previous manner, Rich seems rattled and on edge.

He eyes Danny's natty suit.

                         RICH
          Found yourself a rich Daddy, my
          fun-loving-friend?

Studying Danny's expression.

                         RICH (CONT'D)
          Or is it fun no more, Danny? Have
          you fallen out of love? With fun?
                    (assessing)
          You have.
                    (as if betrayed)
          Some call that growing up. I call
          it growing old. Once you let fun
          go you never get it back. And over
          and above everything - or anybody -
          I choose fun.

A declaration about fun spoken with darkness.

Rich gestures to the back seat pocket.

                         RICH (CONT'D)
          For you.

Danny reaches in. He pulls out --

A large padded envelope. Sealed. He takes it. And is about to open it.

> RICH (CONT'D)
> Not here.

> DANNY
> What is it?

> RICH
> It's 'the impossible'.

> DANNY
> Why did you change your mind?

> RICH
> I didn't.

At great speed the driver pulls into a service station.

> DANNY
> I don't understand.

> RICH
> I'm sure you don't.

The driver parks.

> RICH (CONT'D)
> Get out.

Danny is confused. He lingers.

> RICH (CONT'D)
> Get out the fucking car.

Just as Danny is about to get out.

> RICH (CONT'D)
> Oh, Danny?

Danny looks back.

> RICH (CONT'D)
> Have fun.

Rich's face is knowing and mean.

Danny gets out.

EXT. VAUXHALL. SERVICE STATION. NIGHT

Danny under the alien service station lights.

Rich's car accelerates away.

Danny looks at the padded envelope in his hand.

He spots the service station toilets.

INT. VAUXHALL. SERVICE STATION STORE. RESTROOM. NIGHT

Danny locks the door.

The toilet should be horrendous, concrete, grim.

He stands in front of the mirror. Envelope resting on the sink. He uses his key to rip the tape.

He reaches inside --

A cheap mobile phone.

The keypad has been doctored so none of the buttons can be used apart from the 'accept call' button.

It's on. Fully charged.

Then - shrill and startling - the telephone rings. No caller ID. Danny stares at it.

The phone continues to ring.

Danny presses accept.

END OF EPISODE

EPISODE FOUR:

"I KNOW"

EXT. OMINOUS HOTEL. LONDON. NIGHT

Danny stands outside a rundown and ominous hotel.

He holds the doctored phone from the previous episode to
his ear, hearing instructions from a scrambled voice:

> SCRAMBLED VOICE (V.O.)
> Room 116.

INT. OMINOUS HOTEL. CORRIDOR. NIGHT

Room 116 - numbers hang loose on the door.

Danny has the key in hand, phone to ear. He checks the
bleak-empty-corridor. He unlocks the door --

INT. OMINOUS HOTEL. ROOM 116. NIGHT

Danny tentatively enters the dark hallway. Lights reveal
a squalid room. Fraying carpet. Stained walls.

> SCRAMBLED VOICE (V.O.)
> The bathroom.

Danny turns, opening the door to --

INT. OMINOUS HOTEL. ROOM 116. BATHROOM. NIGHT

Fluorescent lights flicker. A plastic floor.

The bathtub is filled to the brim - water steaming,
recently filled, implying near-by presence.

> SCRAMBLED VOICE (V.O.)
> Get in.

Danny hesitates, unsure of the instructions.

> SCRAMBLED VOICE (V.O.)
> Clothes on.

Danny realizes he's being watched. His eyes glance
around, unable to find the concealed camera.

INT. OMINOUS HOTEL. ROOM 116. BATHROOM. NIGHT

Danny steps into the bathtub, fully clothed, including
shoes, submerging up to his neck.

The phone remains by his ear, above the water.

INT. OMINOUS HOTEL. ROOM 116. BEDROOM. NIGHT

Dripping wet, fully clothed, Danny stands by the bed.
Laid out before him are a new set of expensive clothes.

An unusual & immaculate suit. Mauve, perhaps.

INT. OMINOUS HOTEL. ROOM 116. BEDROOM. NIGHT

Danny dressed in new clothes. Shirt. Tie. Suit. Shoes.
They fit perfectly. He looks terrific. And troubled.

He picks up the phone --

                  SCRAMBLED VOICE (V.O.)
        Outside.

EXT. OMINOUS HOTEL. STREET. NIGHT

Downstairs a black cab pulls up in front of Danny.

The cab seems ordinary.

INT/EXT. BLACK CAB. LONDON. NIGHT

Danny in the back, phone to his ear, apprehensive,
waiting to see where in London he's being taken.

His eyes glance about the cab's interior.

Oddities start to make the cab feel less ordinary. No
door handles. No way out. The windows are plexiglass. The
screen between driver and passenger is reinforced.

This is no ordinary cab.

The driver glances at Danny in the rear view mirror. Mean
eyes: all we see of his face.

INT/EXT. BLACK CAB. CHELSEA. NIGHT

The cab parks in a sleepy and exclusive residential area.

Danny waits. One last glance from mean-eyes-driver. The
door unlocks. Danny gets out.

EXT. CHELSEA. NIGHT

The cab drives off.

Danny knows this area well --

The street where Alex lived. The house where he died.

A police cordon remains in place. A police officer stands guard outside.

The street itself is eerie-quiet. No one around. Old fashioned street lamps fuzz a faint orange glow.

> SCRAMBLED VOICE (V.O.)
> Walk.

Right past the house.

Uneasy, Danny considers refusing.

> SCRAMBLED VOICE (V.O.)
> Walk.

Logically, Danny must be under surveillance. He tries to find them. Eyes search. He can't see anyone.

Reluctantly, Danny starts to walk towards Alex's house. The first time he's been back.

Danny reaches the house, of such significance and pain. The officer regards him with suspicion.

No instructions from the phone. Not told to stop. He continues walking.

He reaches the end of the street.

EXT. FASHIONABLE RESTAURANT. NIGHT

To the right, around the corner from Alex's house, is the restaurant where Danny and Alex first ate breakfast.

It's now in dinner mode, with dimmed lighting. Not part of a high street, singular, like Hopper's 'Nighthawks'.

> SCRAMBLED VOICE (V.O.)
> A reservation. For two.

The phone dies. Danny regards it, lifeless in his hand.

Danny stares at the restaurant --

> FLASH TO:

EXT. FASHIONABLE RESTAURANT. MORNING (PAST)

A bright sunny morning, Danny and Alex on their first date, walking towards the restaurant.

Their innocent early interaction.

Alex holds the door open for Danny as he enters --

                                    FLASH BACK TO:

INT. FASHIONABLE RESTAURANT. NIGHT (PRESENT)

Danny enters alone - his state of mind radically changed
from that first date. Guarded & unsure.

He surveys the scene. Tables are full: a young & wealthy
crowd. A few glance at him, at his attire, they approve.

Danny wonders if this is real or staged, a trap. A
hostess appears and smiles. But Danny's sure of nothing.

                                        FLASH TO:

INT. FASHIONABLE RESTAURANT. MORNING (PAST)

The restaurant is busy. A few glance at Danny, at his
clothes. And they do not approve. Danny's self-conscious.

Danny and Alex are guided to a table in the far corner --

                                    FLASH BACK TO:

INT. FASHIONABLE RESTAURANT. NIGHT (PRESENT)

Danny has been shown to the same table in the far corner.
He looks at the hostess, struck by this choice.

She appears oblivious of any significance.

Danny sits down, looking at the empty space opposite --

                                        FLASH TO:

INT. FASHIONABLE RESTAURANT. MORNING (PAST)

Alex seated opposite Danny, at the exact same table, on
their first date. Danny eyes the expensive prices listed
on the menu. Establish how expensive it is.

Alex has observed his concerns, about to speak --

                                    FLASH BACK TO:

INT. FASHIONABLE RESTAURANT. NIGHT (PRESENT)

Danny seated, as he was in the past, thoughts in past.

His doctored phone rests on the table.

                            182

An identical phone, doctored in an identical fashion, is placed beside it.

Danny looks up to see his 'guest'.

We don't yet see who they are.

Amazed, Danny stands, coming face to face with --

A man similar in appearance to Danny.

Same build, same age, same hair colour - dressed in an identical, expensive, mauve suit.

Same shirt, same tie, same tie clip, same shoes.

With the two directly opposite each other, tailored identically, we marvel at their parallels.

Although not strictly a doppelganger, we'll use the name.

> DOPPELGANGER
> Well, this is weird.

The doppelganger tries hard to sound sophisticated, in fact, he's street, poorly concealed by a patchwork of gentlemanly traits. But the man has edge & darkness.

That said, he is very, very handsome. And exudes a powerful sexual presence.

The doppelganger takes a seat.

Danny sits opposite, wary, but accustomed to these games.

> DOPPELGANGER (CONT'D)
> I've never done anything like this
> before --

> DANNY
> Like this? What is this?

> DOPPELGANGER
> A job. And my job - this evening -
> is to tell you a story.

> DANNY
> About?

> DOPPELGANGER
> Boy meets boy.

> DANNY
> Who?

> DOPPELGANGER
> Me.

                    DANNY
          And?

                    DOPPELGANGER
          Alex.

Danny isn't surprised by the use of Alex's name and
remains cool, playing along, with wry distance.

                    DANNY
          Where?

                    DOPPELGANGER
          Right here.

                    DANNY
          This table?

                    DOPPELGANGER
          His regular.

                    DANNY
          You're right. It was.

                    DOPPELGANGER
          Where he'd order his usual --

                    DANNY
          You're going to tell me what that
          is.

                    DOPPELGANGER
          Poached eggs. Rye toast. Steamed
          spinach. And one pot of strong
          coffee. With cream, on the side.

The details are correct. But Danny doesn't yet give any
clue that's he concerned. Or hurt. Or upset.

                    DOPPELGANGER (CONT'D)
          Your boyfriend ate breakfast here
          almost every morning, for a while.

                    DANNY
          You were watching him?

                    DOPPELGANGER
          Serving him.

                    DANNY
          You're a waiter?

                    DOPPELGANGER
          At that time, pretending to be.

                    DANNY
          Who pretends to be a waiter?

The Doppelganger places on the table the elegant business
card that Detective Taylor showed Danny in Episode Three.

Danny is struck.

>   DOPPELGANGER
>   My agency specializes in a very
>   particular and expensive service:
>   one where the recipient, of my
>   talents, is entirely unaware that
>   they're dealing with an escort.

>   DANNY
>   How is that possible?

>   DOPPELGANGER
>   We pretend to meet them by chance.
>   We pretend to be won over by their
>   charms. We pretend to fuck them
>   for pleasure. We pretend.

Danny holds back, refusing to be pulled in. He observes
how that pretence has hollowed this man out.

>   DANNY
>   How are you paid?

>   DOPPELGANGER
>   Correct. Our clients aren't the
>   people we sleep with. And their
>   motives, for employing us, are not
>   normally very nice. They want
>   secrets. How they use those
>   secrets is entirely up to them.
>   Blackmail. Divorce. Entrapment.
>   (shrugs)
>   Not my business.

>   DANNY
>   You just do the fucking.

>   DOPPELGANGER
>   Exactly.

Though the doppelganger speaks without emotion, he's not
malicious or cruel. Matter of fact.

>   DOPPELGANGER (CONT'D)
>   Alex was a job.

>   FLASH BACK TO:

INT. FASHIONABLE RESTAURANT. MORNING

Without dialogue.

Alex on his own, eating breakfast, reading an
incomprehensible academic paper.

Doppelganger serving him. He wears a cute waiter outfit,
tight white shirt. Very attractive.

He appears frazzled and spills a drink it. He apologizes
profusely, tidying, fluttering about - disarming.

Alex is clearly reassuring him that it's alright and not
to worry. Doppelganger is ever-so grateful.

INT. FASHIONABLE RESTAURANT. NIGHT

Danny listens and is finding it increasingly difficult to
hold his emotions in check.

                DOPPELGANGER
      To speed the process along, I was
      given a persona.

                DANNY
      Who?

                DOPPELGANGER
      You.

                DANNY
      And who am I? When played by you?

                DOPPELGANGER
      Plucky. Friendly. Street-smart. A
      romantic. With a shambolic love
      life. Downtrodden. Yet never self-
      pitying.

A fake persona modelled on Danny. A character
distillation as written by his enemies.

                DOPPELGANGER (CONT'D)
      Acting like that, Alex wasn't a
      particularly difficult job.

Doppelganger is casual with that observation.

                DOPPELGANGER (CONT'D)
      The key to him was that he needed
      to believe he was being good even
      when he was really being bad.

                        FLASH TO:

EXT. FASHIONABLE RESTAURANT. MORNING (PAST)

Alex leaving the restaurant, alone.

Doppelganger is in the back alley, smoking a cigarette, forlorn, clearly troubled.

Alex sees him. They begin to talk. Alex listening patiently to Doppelganger's 'problems'.

FLASH BACK TO:

INT. FASHIONABLE RESTAURANT. NIGHT (PRESENT)

Danny listening, part measured, part agitated.

> DANNY
> I don't believe you.

> DOPPELGANGER
> They warned me you wouldn't. That
> I'd have to work hard.

> DANNY
> I won't listen to any more--

Danny fully intends to leave but not because he doesn't believe - *he's afraid of being convinced.*

> DOPPELGANGER
> When I asked Alex to write down my
> phone number, he told me he didn't
> need to. He said: 'Numbers, I have
> no problem with'. It sounded like
> he'd said it before...

With the details Danny's defences are being broken down. He looks to the door.

> DOPPELGANGER (CONT'D)
> We both know you want to hear how
> this story ends.

Danny desperately wants to leave but desperately wants to know. He remains seated.

> DOPPELGANGER (CONT'D)
> I rang Alex a few days later. I
> made up some personal-life crisis.
> He offered to come round, under
> the pretext of wanting to help.

FLASH TO:

INT. RUNDOWN APARTMENT. DOPPELGANGER'S ROOM. DAY (PAST)

An apartment staged to look much like Danny's apartment, tiny rooms, cramped and chaotic.

Alex is standing in Doppelganger's bedroom. His possessions are ramshackle, eclectic and endearing.

Doppelganger in revealing jogging pants and a T Shirt. Casual, not overt, yet calculating.

Alex sits on the bed, earnestly listening as the doppelganger paces the room, telling some made-up tale of woe, with the energy of a person under pressure.

Alex listening, trying to appear helpful, but eyes give him away, stealing glances up and down.

Tempted & unsure.

With perfect & professional timing, the doppelganger stops pacing, standing close to Alex.

                                        FLASH BACK TO:

INT. FASHIONABLE RESTAURANT. NIGHT (PRESENT)

Danny listens, grim faced. The doppelganger speaks as though describing a mere chore. Which it was.

                    DOPPELGANGER
          They told me his sexual preference
          was for confidence. Experience.
          Dominance. A fancy way of saying
          he liked to be...

Danny's about to ask a question but catches himself.

                    DOPPELGANGER (CONT'D)
          You want details? Proof? A
          birthmark? Some sensitivity? The
          smell of his skin? Anything, you
          need, Danny, like I said, my job,
          tonight, is to convince you.
               (beat)
          He was passive. But very
          responsive. Had a thirst, like a
          man late to the game, catching up
          on all those missed years...

                                        FLASH TO:

INT. RUNDOWN APARTMENT. DOPPELGANGER'S ROOM. DAY (PAST)

Alex having sex with the doppelganger, who is expert, and in great shape.

Alex is enjoying it.

                                        FLASH BACK TO:

INT. FASHIONABLE RESTAURANT. NIGHT (PAST)

Danny fighting back belief.

And these two men, dressed the same, so physically
similar, couldn't be further apart in terms of character.

>   DOPPELGANGER
>   For what it's worth, it was only
>   that one time. Well, a few times
>   that one time, it has to be said,
>   but never repeated. I rang him,
>   afterwards. He didn't answer. The
>   client wanted more. But Alex
>   wasn't interested --

Danny leaps on this.

>   DANNY
>   Why wouldn't you tell me that he
>   loved it so much he kept coming
>   back? Unless it was all a lie?

>   DOPPELGANGER
>   (impressed)
>   Very smart, Danny. But I can see
>   you're good at sussing a lie. So
>   I've told you the truth.

>   DANNY
>   You tell them, I know --
>   (voice cracks)
>   I know it's not true.

But Danny now believes.

>   DOPPELGANGER
>   I'll finish this quick.
>   (beat)
>   To avoid me, Alex stopped eating
>   here, at this table. What did he
>   tell you? That he wanted breakfast
>   at home? That he didn't feel the
>   need to eat out so much?

The pain in Danny is sharp and precise. We realize that
this must have happened. Those words were said.

>   DANNY
>   Why did they hire you?

>   DOPPELGANGER
>   I don't know - I don't care.

>   DANNY
>   Who hired you?

<pre>
                    DOPPELGANGER
          I don't know - I don't care.

                    DANNY
          Why are you telling me --

                    DOPPELGANGER
          I don't know -

                    DANNY
          And you don't care?

The doppelganger tries to be reasonable.

                    DOPPELGANGER
          It's a job. Not much of a job, you
          might say. Maybe I agree. But I've
          done worse. For worse money.

And we believe he has.

                    DOPPELGANGER (CONT'D)
          You might find this hard to
          comprehend, because, I can see you
          care lots about things, but -
          honestly - deep down - all there
          is to me is this:
                    (beat)
          I don't know and I don't care.

                    DANNY
          He's dead.

The doppelganger reacts. He didn't know. A flash of fear.

                    DANNY (CONT'D)
          Your 'job' - Alex.
                    (beat)
          He was murdered.

The doppelganger is troubled.

                    DANNY (CONT'D)
          Do you think you're not involved?

The doppelganger stands, sharply. He throws down a
hundred pounds, with no joy, completing his task.

                    DOPPELGANGER
          I was instructed to pay for
          dinner.

He leaves, walking away.

Danny grabs the doctored phone he left behind. He stands.

                    DANNY
          Hey?
</pre>

The doppelganger turns.

Danny throws him the phone, not aggressively, across the restaurant. The doppelganger catches it.

> DANNY (CONT'D)
> How else you going to tell them
> what a great job you've done?

Other customers are staring at these two handsome, similar looking guys in identical clothes.

The doppelganger nods: he quite likes Danny.

The doppelganger leaves.

Danny remains, standing, upset, all eyes on him.

EXT. HAMPSTEAD HEATH. DAY

On the heath. A secluded area.

Scottie and Danny walk.

> SCOTTIE
> You were Alex's first experience
> of love. If he enjoyed a second
> would you seem less important?
> Could the thrill of the new
> replace the comfort of the old?
> Would he realize there were others
> like you? That what felt unique,
> and special, could easily be
> replaced?
> > (beat)
> In the end your relationship
> became a threat to their
> relationship with him. He changed
> you. You changed him. Priorities
> altered. Loyalties altered. I
> noticed it in our friendship...
> > (Danny can't deny it)
> The two of you were... besotted.
> The rest of the world ceased to
> exist. But Alex was one of their
> most important minds. Did you
> imagine they'd allow him to drift
> away?

> DANNY
> I didn't think about it.

> SCOTTIE
> That's all they would've thought
> about. What binds this brilliant
> young man to us? The Queen? Our
> history? His parents?

Yet Danny remains troubled and distant. Scottie observes.

>   DANNY
>   I accept that I didn't know about
>   Alex's work. His job. But the
>   truth is that I didn't really know
>   him as a person. Either. I didn't
>   know him.
>   (beat)
>   *I don't know him.*

Scottie's tone changes. He's unimpressed.

>   SCOTTIE
>   Of all the attacks they've used,
>   including your health, the one
>   which has proved most effective is
>   smut. For you, of all people.

>   DANNY
>   He made a mistake, that's not it.
>   But why didn't he tell me? Some of
>   it? Any of it?

>   SCOTTIE
>   Because you wanted him to be
>   perfect. He saw that more clearly
>   than you.

>   DANNY
>   It was his funeral last week. Do
>   you know how I found out? I heard
>   about it on the news. He was
>   buried at a private ceremony. For
>   close friends and family.

>   SCOTTIE
>   I can't count how many men I've
>   comforted when their partners died
>   and the families refused to allow
>   them into the hospital, or the
>   church where they're buried. I'm
>   tired of it. Tired of hearing
>   about it. He wasn't close to his
>   parents. He was close to you. Hold
>   your own funeral. Say your own
>   goodbye.

>   DANNY
>   (exasperated)
>   That's what I should be doing!
>   Saying goodbye. What am I doing
>   all this other stuff for? Because
>   Alex discovered some government
>   secret? So what? So they lied
>   about a war? So they spy on us?
>   What's it got to do with me?
>   (beat)

> And, you know - *I don't know* any
> code. I don't. So, maybe, whatever
> those secrets are, maybe they
> weren't meant for me.

Scottie notes his resignation. It's unlike Danny.

>   SCOTTIE
> Then, that's that.

INT. DANNY'S APARTMENT. BEDROOM. NIGHT

Danny seated on the floor, cross-legged.

In front of him is a shoebox. He opens it.

Inside are items that belonged to Alex. The everyday
possessions of someone who regularly stayed over.

A T shirt for sleeping in. Expensive aftershave.

A collection of receipts. Meals they've eaten. Shows
they've seen. Movies ticket stubs.

A razor. A tub of shaving cream.

Danny picks up the cream, unscrews the lid. There's a
distinct finger indent where a scoop was last taken.

Danny puts it down, next to a paperback novel - Isaac
Asimov. The first part of his Foundation trilogy.

Dog-eared at the page Alex reached. We see the number.

Danny studies the spine: the demarcation line between the
read and unread part of the novel.

The last item is an Ordnance Survey map of the estuary
walk. Danny's eyes glance across the contours.

He places his finger on one of the latitude lines, moving
up the map --

                                           MATCH TO:

EXT. COUNTRYSIDE. ESTUARY. DAY (PAST)

Danny's finger moving up one of the latitude lines on the
same map. Into frame comes Alex's finger, moving along
one of the longitude lines.

They almost touch. But not quite. Pull back to reveal
their first date. At the end of the picnic scene.

Danny smiles at Alex's hesitation to touch.

EXT. COUNTRYSIDE. ESTUARY. DAY

Danny stands with that same Ordnance Survey map in hand.
A return to their first walk.

An emptiness. Whereas it had magic with the two of them,
on his own this landscape is melancholy.

EXT. COUNTRYSIDE. ESTUARY. DAY

Danny at the same spot where he was once with Alex. From
Episode 1. An empty grey sky merging with the grey sea.

                                            FLASH TO:

EXT. COUNTRYSIDE. NIGHT (PAST)

A camp fire burns. Not the estuary but we can't see the
landscape beyond the flames.

Alex and Danny are seated beside the fire.

                     DANNY
            Do you believe in soulmates?

                     ALEX
            No. Not only do I not believe in
            them - it's not even a nice idea.

                     DANNY
            Not a nice idea?

                     ALEX
            That there's just one other person
            out there for you? The 'perfect
            partner'? What are the odds this
            person would be in the same
            country? Or the same city? That
            your paths would cross? It would
            mean almost everyone in the world
            is with the wrong person. If it's
            a way of saying 'we're good
            together' why not just say 'we're
            good together'? But if you mean it
            literally --

                     DANNY
                (interrupting)
            You think there are better people
            out there for you?

                     ALEX
            There might be. For both of us.
            But since we don't know them, it's
            just a theoretical.

Alex has overstated the case. His intellectual rigour is sharp. And in this instance a little cruel.

> DANNY
> It's a sentimental idea... The
> maths doesn't add up. But... we're
> sitting by the fire... under a
> night sky... couldn't you have
> just said yes?

Alex asks with curiosity rather than petulance:

> ALEX
> Is that what your soulmate
> would've done?

Alex immediately regrets his statement. Danny doesn't take the bait - he doesn't say 'yes'.

> FLASH BACK TO:

EXT. COUNTRYSIDE. ESTUARY. NIGHT

Danny by a fire of his own creation. On his own.

Danny opens the bag. Slowly, thoughtfully, he starts burning Alex's few remaining possessions.

A farewell, an improvised funeral. No anger. The actions are heavy with defeat. First is the T shirt.

Then the various stubs and tickets and receipts. Each a moment. An event. A point in time. With him.

Then the tub of cream, the fingerprint, the plastic burning blue and green, contorting in the flames.

The aftershave bottle goes in, the glass cracking, the alcohol burning bright. Danny inhales the smell.

Danny can't bring himself to throw the book in. He puts it to one side.

He does, however, throw the laminated estuary map into the fire, watching the flames take it.

We see the various numbers melt.

And the spot where their fingers almost met.

EXT. COUNTRYSIDE. ESTUARY. DAWN

Danny has been awake all night. The fire's dead. Just ash and blackened shards of glass.

He stands, stiff. The ash is cold. Danny takes a handful.

A partial fragment of a burnt number among the ash.

Danny walks away from the fire, into the estuary mud flats and holds his hand high above his head.

He releases the ashes as though they were the ashes of Alex's body.

They catch in the wind: a bold grey upward streak in the sky. And then they're gone.

Danny looks down at his hand.

A single flake stubbornly remains.

                                        FLASH TO:

EXT. SOHO YARD BAR. NIGHT (PAST)

Yard bar, Soho. An outdoor courtyard. The bar on several levels. We're upstairs. It's busy.

Danny is artfully trying to carry two drinks through the crowd, spilling a little here and there.

He reaches the balcony and looks down, among the crowd. Many faces. Old and young.

Danny's eye searches --

Until he sees Alex by a tree filled with lights.

A handsome man is hitting on Alex. A flicker of powerful sexual chemistry between them.

Danny observes, not jealous, or angry, but thoughtful.

EXT. SOHO YARD BAR. PASSAGEWAY & STREET. NIGHT (PAST)

Lively. Many couples.

Danny and Alex leaving. Danny is unusually serious. And detached. Alex is concerned.

                    DANNY
                (struggling)
          I've tried a lot of things with a
          lot of people. That's part of the
          reason I'm so sure we're something
          special. But for you...

These are some of the hardest words he's spoken. He's trying to sound unemotional.

                    DANNY (CONT'D)
        I don't want you to stay with me
        just because I'm the first.

They've reached the street. Alex stops walking. Giving no
reaction. Danny pushes the point.

                    DANNY (CONT'D)
        You should see other people.
            (beat)
        You should.
            (beat)
        And, I hope, afterwards, you'll
        decide to come back to me...

The emotion starts to come through from Danny.

But not from Alex. He holds the same expression.

                    DANNY (CONT'D)
        I'll wait. For as long as it
        takes.
            (beat)
        And maybe...
            (emotional)
        Someone else...
            (emotional)
        I don't know...
            (beat)
        But you need to know...
            (beat)
        I need you to know.

Alex remains unemotional. Inexpressive. And then --

To Danny's amazement an apparently unemotional Alex looks
directly up, staring at the night sky.

Baffled, Danny is on the verge of being angry when --

Alex looks down. He's crying.

The first and only time we've seen him cry. And, it's as
if they're new to Alex too.

                    DANNY (CONT'D)
        Hey?

Danny wraps his arms around Alex.

                    DANNY (CONT'D)
        What is it?

With tears, but calm, as if he's done the maths and --

                    ALEX
        I don't want to.

                         DANNY
          I only meant --

                         ALEX
          I don't want to.

                         DANNY
          Okay.

                         ALEX
          I don't need to.

                         DANNY
          Okay.

Referring to their relationship --

                         ALEX
          I know.
               (subtle variation)
          I know.

                         DANNY
          I know too.

The swirl of people around them on the street.

                                        FLASH BACK TO:

INT. CENTRAL LONDON TRAIN STATION. DAY (PRESENT)

The swirl of people around Danny on the concourse. The
station is crowded with evening commuters.

He's returned from the walk.

He appears to have stopped in the middle of the concourse
among the flow of people. In the way. Nudged impatiently.

So many different lives. Passing each other unconnected.

Danny turns his head in a specific direction, staring at
the flow of people. Waiting --

Until they break and we catch a glimpse of a bench.

                                           FLASH TO:

INT. CENTRAL LONDON TRAIN STATION. DAY (PAST)

Same station.

Danny sitting on that bench, dressed for a hike, bag
packed and ready by his side.

He's waiting, watching the crowd of commuters and then, among them, he sees Alex. Out of the many.

A moment of relative insignificance at the time.

FLASH BACK TO:

INT. CENTRAL LONDON TRAIN STATION. DAY (PRESENT)

Danny looking at the bench. The crowd reforms and the bench disappears behind the mass of people.

Danny starts walking again, slowly at first, then faster, and faster. Pushing his way through. Until he's running --

EXT. EAST LONDON. HIGH STREET. NIGHT

Danny running --

An impoverished area. Pawnbrokers. Betting shops.

Danny makes sure he isn't being followed, and moves with great speed and determination.

He hurries into a fast food restaurant --

EXT. EAST LONDON. SIDE ALLEY. NIGHT

Danny clambers out of the back window, into an alley with no CCTV. He retreats, away from the main road.

EXT. EAST LONDON SCRUBLAND. NIGHT

Danny climbs over a fence and into scrubland. Abandoned washing machines. Burnt mattresses. He arrives at --

The skeleton of a former factory where he hid the cylinder in episode 2.

INT. DERELICT INDUSTRIAL WAREHOUSE. MACHINE ROOM. NIGHT

Danny nimbly clambers up the shell of a long-dead furnace towards the ceiling. Rusted pipes crisscross.

He finds a section of the pipe and removes the bolts. Inside is a diary wrapped in plastic. He removes the plastic. Inside the spine is the cylinder.

He holds it for a moment, studying the elegant seven digit dial code lock. A random spread of numbers.

He adjusts the first dial to zero, then the second, the third, fourth, fifth and the sixth - all to zero.

000000

Finally, with the last dial, he turns it to number --

0000001

A click. The cylinder unlocks.

A final message from Alex.

Danny's excitement modulates into sadness.

And now, finally, Danny opens the cylinder, revealing --

INT. SCOTTIE'S HOUSE. FRONT DOOR. NIGHT

Danny rings the doorbell, excited, the cylinder in the palm of his hand. No reply. He rings again.

He peers through the letter box.

EXT. SCOTTIE'S HOUSE. BACK GARDEN. NIGHT

Climbing the side gate, like a burglar, Danny tries the back door. It's locked.

He finds the spare key, hidden in one of the pots.

INT. SCOTTIE'S HOUSE. KITCHEN. NIGHT

Danny enters. The lights are off. But a saucepan is on the stove. The gas blazes underneath it.

Danny peers into the saucepan only to find it's empty. Red hot. Forgotten about. He turns the gas off.

He's afraid.

INT. SCOTTIE'S HOUSE. UPSTAIRS HALLWAY. NIGHT

Danny reaches the landing. He sees a shard of cracked mirror on the floor outside the bathroom.

Danny hurries forward to see --

INT. SCOTTIE'S HOUSE. BATHROOM. NIGHT

The mirror smashed. Pulled from the wall. Blood on it.

                DANNY
Scottie!

INT. SCOTTIE'S HOUSE. UPSTAIRS HALLWAY. NIGHT

Danny searching the house at speed.

He hears a thud from the bedroom. He runs --

INT. SCOTTIE'S HOUSE. SCOTTIE'S BEDROOM. NIGHT

Danny opens the door to find Scottie sprawled on the
floor, one hand bleeding profusely. In the other hand is
a near empty bottle of Scotch.

He's horribly drunk - the drinking of a sick man.

*Nothing comedic about this moment. Scottie, normally so
impressive, in a dreadful self-medicating state.*

Danny rushes to help. But Scottie's difficult to move.

Scottie takes a while to register Danny, but when he
does, he smiles warmly.

                    SCOTTIE
          I was...

Not listening, Danny examines the cut to Scottie's hand.
A lot of blood, though not too serious.

                    SCOTTIE (CONT'D)
          Remembering...

Danny tries to take the bottle.

                    SCOTTIE (CONT'D)
          A place...

                    DANNY
          We need to go to a hospital.

                    SCOTTIE
          Listen to me. For once, Danny.

Danny relents, observing that his friend is not well.
Having presented Scottie with so many of his own problems
this is a pivotal reversal for Danny.

Danny tries to recall what Scottie was trying to say.

                    DANNY
          You were remembering a place.

Scottie's eyes light up. As the memory returns --

Scottie trying to tell the story but forgetting to speak.
Instead, performing various disconnected actions. The
saddest, most broken down version of his storytelling.

With a bloody hand, he lamely, incompetently rolls up one trouser leg. It makes no sense.

And then --

Scottie points to the wall, as though pointing to something completely other. With great wonder.

And then --

His wonder turns to sadness.

An incomprehensible pantomime. Danny remains focused on his friend. With no idea what is being communicated.

Scottie, as if he's concluded his story:

>   SCOTTIE
>   A place where no one cares.

Scottie turns to Danny. And lurches towards him, kissing him. Danny doesn't recoil. He gently, slowly, takes hold of Scottie and separates them.

Scottie shakes his head at himself. Ashamed. Pitiful.

>   SCOTTIE (CONT'D)
>   Pathetic.

He goes to take another swig from the bottle but Danny catches it, again gently.

>   SCOTTIE (CONT'D)
>   Pathetic.

Scottie allows Danny to have the bottle.

>   SCOTTIE (CONT'D)
>   Path --

Before he can say it a third time Danny puts a finger on his lips, stopping him.

Danny stands, offering his arm. Scottie pulls himself together and stands, resting on Danny for support.

INT. HOSPITAL. A&E. NIGHT

Scottie and Danny are waiting: a busy night. Chaotic scenes around them.

Scottie sobering up. But a melancholy sickness remains.

>   SCOTTIE
>   My parents used to chide me -
>   (wistful)

"You used to be such a happy child".

> DANNY
> How long?

> SCOTTIE
> Like this?

Danny nods.

> SCOTTIE (CONT'D)
> The past three weeks... worse and worse... each day... as bad as it's ever been.

Danny silent.

> SCOTTIE (CONT'D)
> It can't be a coincidence? Can it? Thirty years, and I've been okay. And now, like this?

Danny and Scottie ponder.

INT. HOSPITAL. TREATMENT ROOM. NIGHT

Scottie's hand examined by a doctor. Danny standing in the corner, with other things on his mind.

> DANNY
> (to the doctor)
> Why might someone who's managed depression for thirty years, suddenly suffer a relapse? For no reason?

The doctor turns to Danny, then looks at Scottie.

INT. SCOTTIE'S HOUSE. KITCHEN. NIGHT

Danny and Scottie at the table.

Scottie is sober. His hand has been bandaged.

On the table in front of them is a pack of prescription pills. A blister pack with only two left.

The pills are branded. Unremarkable. Yet Danny and Scottie are staring at them as though they were a puzzle.

The box has a standard printed prescription label with Scottie's name and address.

Anti-depressants.

Danny picks up the pack, pushes out a pill. He twists the capsule apart - a powder spills out.

They peer at the contents. Scottie dabs some. Unsure.

Danny becomes practical. Sensible. Efficient.

>   DANNY
>   This is what we're going to do:
>   we'll get new pills. Real pills.
>   From a different doctor. You can
>   keep them on you at all times...
>   (re-thinking)
>   Unless they're switched before
>   they're given to you...
>   (re-thinking)
>   We can buy them illegally. I know
>   someone. He can get anything.

Scottie seems removed, deep in thought. With an exploratory knuckle he taps the table, testing it.

>   SCOTTIE
>   ...On your shell. Until they find
>   a crack. A frailty. A
>   vulnerability. No matter how
>   small. And then they pick away.

Scottie still not well.

EXT. RUN DOWN SHOPPING CENTRE. DAY

A grim concrete building. A grotty carpark.

Danny waits, beside his bicycle. A car pulls up.

INT/EXT. DRUG DEALER'S CAR / SHOPPING CENTRE. DAY

Danny studying a box of prescription anti-depressants. He opens them, looking at the blister pack. Intact.

They're the same kind that Scottie uses.

The drug dealer sits beside Danny, tetchy.

>   DANNY
>   Where did you get them?

The dealer's speech is a near incomprehensible gabble.

>   DEALER
>   People-tell-the-doctor-whatever-
>   story-collect-the prescription-
>   sell-them-to-me-they're good-all-
>   good-always-good-with-me-want
>   something else?

Danny realizes that this man is a relic from his past.

                    DANNY
          No, nothing else.

INT. SCOTTIE'S HOUSE. BATHROOM. DAY

Scottie swallows one of the new anti-depressants. Danny
watching. Scottie turns to him.

Unsure whether he should, because of Scottie's state of
mind, Danny opens the palm of his hand, showing Scottie
the unlocked cylinder.

We see the contents for the first time: a data stick.

Scottie stares at it.

INT. HAMPSTEAD CHURCH. DAY

Scottie and Danny at the front pew of an otherwise empty
church. They face the altar - deep in thought.

Scottie holds the data stick, turning it over in his
fingers as though it were a religious trinket.

                    SCOTTIE
          You've examined the contents?

Danny nods.

                    DANNY
          We're going to need help.

                    SCOTTIE
          With help comes risk. With each
          new person we involve...

Scottie remains scared by his depressive relapse. A haze
of fear surrounds him. He struggles with it.

                    SCOTTIE (CONT'D)
          Look at what they've done to us.
          Before they even knew we had this.

Danny considers his friend, not yet well.

                    DANNY
          I can do this alone.

Hearing that, Scottie embarks on an act of self-
regeneration. He uses the following narrative - an
archetypal Scottie story - as a form of self healing.

He begins unsteadily, growing in fluency and assurance.

                    SCOTTIE
               (unsteady)
     There are rumours... About how the
     Kremlin guarantees the loyalty of
     its most important citizens. Under
     the pretext of celebrating an
     election to the State Duma, the
     individual is treated to the
     finest meal Moscow has to offer...
               (improving)
     At some point during that night,
     this prized individual blacks out,
     waking up in a hotel suite. On a
     bed. Beside a terrified naked
     child. Before they can say a word
     the FSB storm the room and arrest
     them, taking them to an
     interrogation cell in Moscow's
     Butyrka prison where the
     individual swears that he's not a
     pedophile --
               (vivid)
     "My drink must have been spiked!"
     "I've been framed by my enemies!"
     He doesn't know. He can't explain.
     "But it is a mistake!"
               (near perfect)
     To their surprise the FSB officer
     agrees: *it is a mistake.* But a
     mistake they will hold on record
     forever, a mistake no one will
     ever see, unless, of course, they
     make a mistake of a political
     kind. And with that, the
     individual's choice is clear -
     privilege or disgrace. Destruction
     or survival. The officer believes
     he's won. And the individual
     believes he's lost. But those
     systems of oppression - ruthless
     as they appear, unbeatable as they
     seem - never hold, never last,
     never survive.
               (at full force)
     For we will not live in fear.

Danny amazed by this act of self-creation, and it's not
the anti-depressants - it's Scottie pulling himself out
of a dark hole. And it's breathtaking.

                    SCOTTIE (CONT'D)
     I'd very much like to finish this
     particular adventure with you,
     Daniel Edward Holt, if you'll have
     me.

Scottie offers Danny his hand. Danny accepts.

EXT. SCOTTIE'S HOUSE. FRONT GARDEN. DAY

Danny exits the house, readying a rickety old bicycle. A
moment later Scottie exits.

Scottie gets into his car, an off beat vintage car.

The two part without a word, in opposite directions.

EXT. WOOLWICH FERRY DOCKING AREA. DAY

Danny waits at the docking area for the Woolwich Ferry.

Scottie's car pulls up beside him.

Danny puts his bike in the back.

EXT. WOOLWICH FERRY. DAY

Danny and Scottie at the back of the ferry as it crosses
the Thames. They stare into the churning murky water.

Danny's uncertain whether to bring the subject up,
expecting it to be a painful subject.

                    DANNY
          The place where no one cares?

To his surprise Scottie's amused.

                    SCOTTIE
          I've always taken comfort from the
          idea of people not caring, that
          they have better things to do,
          that there are more important
          matters to worry about. I like it
          when people walk past me and
          couldn't care less what I was
          wearing, or whose hand I was
          holding. *The place where no one
          cares.* When I was young I spent a
          lot of time searching for it,
          promising myself that if I ever
          found it - if it ever existed -
          I'd make it my home.

London in the background. The murky Thames. Not a
romantic image of the city. An ugly one.

Yet, perhaps, our most celebratory.

EXT. EAST LONDON. DERELICT INDUSTRIAL WAREHOUSE. EVENING

The abandoned factory where Danny stored the cylinder. A
bleak outline against the darkening sky.

Danny and Scottie stand outside.

INT. DERELICT INDUSTRIAL WAREHOUSE. EVENING

Holding flashlights, moving through rubble and rats,
Scottie and Danny pass the graffiti wall. Danny makes no
mention of it. But Scottie spots Danny's name.

              SCOTTIE
You?

              DANNY
Me.

Scottie's curious, comparing the two, name & man.

INT. DERELICT INDUSTRIAL WAREHOUSE. MACHINE ROOM. EVENING

Danny and Scottie sit on the carcass of an old machine.
Scottie's reading Danny's teenage diary. We should see,
in detail, the content of the crinkled pages.

Breezy, as though he didn't care:

              DANNY
What do you think?

              SCOTTIE
Ambition. But no conviction. You
skip from short stories to lyrics,
from poems to sketches, hoping the
world will tell you who you are.
But you must tell the world.

Danny not remotely offended. We should feel an echo of
Alex's directness in this reply.

Reaching the end, Scottie puts Danny's old note book down
and picks up the faded porn magazine.

              SCOTTIE (CONT'D)
This - on the other hand - knows
exactly what it is.

They hear footsteps on rubble.

Both Danny and Scottie stand.

Claire, the Provost of UCL, appears. She assesses the
space. The two of them. The porn magazine.

Scottie discards the magazine.

He and Claire hug.

Danny watches their interaction, assessing the nature of their friendship. Extremely close.

> SCOTTIE (CONT'D)
> Were you followed?

Claire adjusts to these spy requirements.

> CLAIRE
> I don't believe so...
> (beat)
> I don't know...
> (beat)
> How does one know?

> SCOTTIE
> Will he help us?

> CLAIRE
> He didn't say.

INT. RUINED INDUSTRIAL WAREHOUSE. MACHINE ROOM. NIGHT

Scottie and Claire working on a cryptic crossword. Filling in alternate answers. At speed. Danny watches.

> DANNY
> Where did you two meet?

Scottie and Claire pause.

> SCOTTIE
> At Cambridge.

Scottie is unusually cagey and abrupt. However, Claire warms to the subject.

> CLAIRE
> I was the first person he shared
> the secret of his sexuality with.

> SCOTTIE
> At that time 'it' was illegal. And
> there were rumours.

> CLAIRE
> I agreed to play the part of his
> lover. We walked arm in arm, took
> picnics in the scholar's garden.
> It was supposed to be for no more
> than a few months. Enough to keep
> the whispering at bay.

> SCOTTIE
> It lasted two years.

> DANNY
> (to Claire)
> Are you gay?

> CLAIRE
> No.

> DANNY
> Did you see other people?

> CLAIRE
> No.

Silence.

Scottie remains unusually tongue tied. As if this is the only story he can't bring himself to tell.

> SCOTTIE
> I tried to become the man I was pretending to be...
> (to Claire)
> You know, I even prayed? For the right kind of desire?
> (she never knew)
> A sham romance, you might say.

> CLAIRE
> No.

> SCOTTIE
> No.

They kiss. The kiss of celibate lovers.

Finally Scottie turns to Danny and smiles.

> SCOTTIE (CONT'D)
> But we're friends. We've remained friends for many years. How can you be sad about that? No, I refuse to be sad about that.

Danny and Scottie hold a look.

And in that instant Claire catches Scottie's affections for Danny clearly too.

Claire smiles at Scottie. He smiles back at her, a daisy chain of unrequited physical attraction.

Broken by --

> MARCUS
> It's all very touching.

Alex's professor - Marcus Shaw - has been standing in the gloom, watching for we don't know how long.

Late fifties. Stern & brutally so. No hint of whimsy or
nerdy intellect. Physically in excellent shape.

He assesses the three conspirators, in particular -
Danny. He's unimpressed.

Claire introduces them.

> CLAIRE
> Marcus, this is Danny, Alex's
> partner. And this --

Interrupting, Marcus cuts to the chase:

> MARCUS
> Where is it?

INT. RUINED INDUSTRIAL WAREHOUSE. MACHINE ROOM. NIGHT

Danny takes out a laptop, improvising a desk from the
ruins. He inserts the data stick and loads the file.

On screen - in the darkness of this disordered space - we
see beauty and order. A stream of mathematical formula.

Danny's eyes fill with the glow of Alex's numbers. He's
beguiled by them, even if he can't understand them.

Marcus takes his turn at the laptop, effectively brushing
Danny out the way.

And Marcus's stern expression softens for the first time.

Danny remains close by, his presence irritating Marcus.

> MARCUS
> This will take time.

Danny backs off, reluctantly.

INT. RUINED INDUSTRIAL WAREHOUSE. MACHINE ROOM. NIGHT

Marcus at the laptop.

He stops working, offering no explanation.

He heads off. Scottie and Danny share a glance.

Danny follows the Professor.

EXT. RUINED INDUSTRIAL WAREHOUSE. NIGHT

Danny sees Marcus smoking outside.

He approaches, covering his ulterior motive by indicating
that he'd like a smoke too.

Marcus isn't surprised, or annoyed, when Danny appears, a
subtle implication that he even intended to lure him out.

He offers a cigarette and lights it for him.

The two men stand opposite - as opposites - considering
each other.

> MARCUS
> You didn't know, did you? How
> smart he was?

> DANNY
> I knew.

> MARCUS
> But, not really?

> DANNY
> Not in the way you did, no.

> MARCUS
> (toying with word)
> His 'partner'
> (beat)
> Without any appreciation of his
> intellect? Beyond some generalized
> sense that he was good with
> numbers. Love without knowledge.
> Popular culture might depict that
> as a romantic notion, I suppose.

> DANNY
> He never spoke about his work.

Marcus finds that fact incredible.

> MARCUS
> What did you talk about?

Danny tries not to sound defensive.

> DANNY
> Everything else.

> MARCUS
> I see.
> (beat)
> No. I don't. I don't see at all.

> DANNY
> What did you two talk about -
> outside of work?

> MARCUS
> We didn't.

Danny finds that fact incredible.

> MARCUS (CONT'D)
> Try to understand I was sure -
> absolutely certain - he was going
> to change the world in some way.
> Not *my* world - *the* world. Can you
> comprehend the enormity of that
> feeling? Being in the company of
> someone like that?

> DANNY
> We knew different people.

> MARCUS
> The man I knew was exceptional.
> The man you knew was not.

Danny about to reply. Marcus cuts in.

> MARCUS (CONT'D)
> Or are you going to tell me how
> many sugars he took in his tea? Or
> how he liked to be fucked?

Danny has teased from Marcus unresolved, closeted
feelings. And Marcus senses he's revealed too much.

> MARCUS (CONT'D)
> Do you think these are the details
> that define us?

> DANNY
> I think being admired is lonely.

> MARCUS
> You're right, I'm sure. But that
> was the price he had to pay. The
> ordinary world was not for him.
> And his flirtation with it was
> always going to end badly.

Marcus stubs out his cigarette, leaving Danny behind.

> DANNY
> Professor?

Marcus looks back, expecting an insult.

But Danny surprises him.

> DANNY (CONT'D)
> I miss him too.

Marcus registers Danny's loss. And underneath all his
great intellect, a pulse of emotion.

INT. RUINED INDUSTRIAL WAREHOUSE. MACHINE ROOM. DAWN

Marcus still working at the laptop. Fragments of daylight
creep through the broken walls.

Danny waiting, watching, never far away. Claire and
Scottie are huddled beneath a coat.

Abruptly Marcus stands from the laptop. He seems to have
forgotten about Danny, Claire and Scottie.

He finally turns to them.

                MARCUS
     He did it.

INT. RUINED INDUSTRIAL WAREHOUSE. MACHINE ROOM. DAWN

Marcus searches for a surface to write on, animated in a
way we haven't seen. The barbed aloofness is gone.

We glimpse the Marcus that Alex loved. A radically
different proposition.

Excitable. As he scrambles about, followed by Danny,
Scottie and Claire.

                MARCUS
     The 9/11 attackers sent emails
     using pre-arranged code words.
     "Faculty of Urban Planning" was
     the World Trade Center. The
     Pentagon was "The Faculty of Fine
     Arts".

Marcus takes out a felt pen, trying to write on the
rusted surface of a machine. It doesn't work.

                MARCUS (CONT'D)
     Mohammed Atta's final message to
     the other terrorists referred to
     their semester beginning in three
     weeks. In faculty of urban
     planning. And fine arts.

Suddenly he sees, in the adjacent room, a huge broken
mirror, or glass partition window.

He hurries towards it.

INT. RUINED INDUSTRIAL WAREHOUSE. MIRROR ROOM. DAWN

Marcus writing on the mirror or window. His audience
expect him to write an algorithm.

Instead Marcus writes:

"Meet you at the Zoo".

Marcus then writes the identical sentence underneath:

"Meet you at the Zoo".

> MARCUS
> In this email -
> (points to first)
> Zoo means Zoo. In this email -
> (points to second)
> It means airport.
> (beat)
> How can you tell them apart?

His audience have no idea.

Marcus rubs out all the words except for 'zoo'.

He adds the words 'museum', 'child' and 'charity'
allocating numbers above each of the words.

> MARCUS (CONT'D)
> People who go to the zoo also
> visit museums. Watch animated
> movies. Buy children's clothes.
> Donate to animal charities.

Zoo 113 Museum 72 Child 44 Charity 9

> MARCUS (CONT'D)
> Now convert our entire online
> history into numbers.

Marcus rubs out the text, leaving only the numbers,
hastily adding rows of other numbers, several repeating.

Marcus draws a pentagon around the number 113 linking it
to other repeating numbers.

> MARCUS (CONT'D)
> A real visit to the zoo looks like
> this.

A 'molecular structure' of different numbers.

Now Marcus wipes the steel clean, writing the number 113,
repeating it at random spots across the steel.

> MARCUS (CONT'D)
> A coded message looks like this.

He draws a pentagon around the number 113. Except there are no other numbers to attach. No 'molecular structure'.

> MARCUS (CONT'D)
> The 9/11 terrorists used
> 'innocent' words. But they didn't
> use them like everyone else.

Marcus fills an entire window pane with a chain of numbers, very quickly, speaking at the same time.

> MARCUS (CONT'D)
> We like to think of ourselves as
> individuals. But we're a pattern.
> Married. Professional. Rich. Poor.
> Gay. Straight. Our online DNA.
> Revealing our true nature, even
> when we lie.

The first detail Danny has heard about Alex's work. A side to him never explored. A kind of magic.

> MARCUS (CONT'D)
> I told him he'd change the world.
> I just never told him how
> dangerous that would be.

He turns, abruptly, leaving the room, hurrying up the stairs, towards the roof.

Danny hurries after him, followed by Claire and Scottie.

EXT. DERELICT INDUSTRIAL WAREHOUSE. ROOF TOP. DAWN

Danny emerges onto the roof to see --

Marcus standing on the edge, staring at the sunrise.

Danny joins the Professor. They look out together. Marcus turns to Danny, without hostility.

> MARCUS
> You're a 'thoroughly nice guy',
> aren't you, Danny?

It doesn't seem like an insult. Danny waits.

> MARCUS (CONT'D)
> So was Alex. For all his
> intellect, an innocent, really.
> When he told me that he was going
> to work for GCHQ, I knew it was a
> mistake. That he didn't belong in
> that world. And I could feel him
> wanting me to tell him so.

                    DANNY
        Why didn't you say something?

                    MARCUS
        We didn't have that kind of
        relationship.

Claire and Scottie arrive, joining them. A little out of
breathe having climbed the flight of stairs.

                    SCOTTIE
        Why did they kill him?

EXT. DERELICT INDUSTRIAL WAREHOUSE. ROOF TOP. DAWN

The team are seated, huddled. Marcus smokes.

                    MARCUS
        He decided to apply his concept to
        speech.

Scottie, Danny and Claire can't see the connection.

                    MARCUS (CONT'D)
        Words don't occur in isolation.
        They're part of a series of
        actions. Your intake of breath.
        Facial gestures. Pupil dilation.
        Hand movements. Alex theorized
        they form patterns. And these
        patterns would be different if you
        were telling the truth or telling
        a lie.

                    CLAIRE
        A lie detector?

                    SCOTTIE
        Important lies are told by
        important people. They'd never
        consent to a test of any kind.

                    MARCUS
        Alex didn't need their consent.
        That was the genius of it. They've
        already provided all the
        information. The world's most
        important people are also the most
        documented.

We follow Danny's eyes to the precise movements of
Marcus's lips: the physicality of his speech.

                    MARCUS (CONT'D)
        Study every word they've ever
        spoken - mundane, profound - it
        doesn't matter.

Analyze as many variables as
possible. Translate the
information into numbers. And
identify the patterns. A
fingerprint. For our truths. And
our lies.

                    CLAIRE
We'd be able to analyze every
statement?

                    MARCUS
Every political claim. Every case
for war. Every court case verdict.

                    SCOTTIE
The end of lies.

                    MARCUS
If the four of us survive a week,
I'll be surprised.

And now excitement adjusts to apprehension.

EXT. RUINED INDUSTRIAL WAREHOUSE. DAY

The conspirators are getting ready to leave.

                    MARCUS
I take it you have some sort of
'plan'?

                    SCOTTIE
We must prove it works.

Marcus's sceptical. But Scottie is such an authoritative
presence he's swayed. With reluctance, Marcus nods.

THIS SCENE IS CUT

INT/EXT. SCOTTIE'S CAR / LONDON. DAWN

Scottie driving. Danny in the passenger seat.

                    DANNY
You don't have a plan, do you?

                    SCOTTIE
No. But he needed to believe I
did. And we need him.
          (beat)
You see? Proof that the orderly
functioning of society depends on
our ability to lie.

These aren't secrets we can peddle
to our nation's enemies. Given the
choice of 'no lies', or 'lies',
every organization, every person
of power - without exception -
will choose lies.

                DANNY
Maybe Alex imagined a better way
of doing things.

Scottie considers Danny for a moment. He's an instinctive
idealist. A romantic.

                SCOTTIE
I wonder when he began work on
this project.

The subtext of the observation slips Danny by.

                DANNY
Why does that matter?

                SCOTTIE
        (musing aloud)
Maybe Alex was ashamed of the lies
he'd told you. Ashamed that your
relationship was built on lies.
Maybe he even thought, on some
level, he was making amends.

                DANNY
To who?

                SCOTTIE
To you.

Thoughtful silence.

Danny processing the notion. Scottie suddenly realizes
how enormous a revelation it is. Too late.

Tense silence.

              SCOTTIE (CONT'D)
Danny --

Danny abruptly, in a kind of haze, opens the car door,
about to get out, even though the car is still moving.

Scottie slams on the brakes just as --

EXT. SCOTTIE'S CAR / LONDON. DAWN

Danny gets out, unsteady on his feet. We're on the
fringes of the decaying former industrial area.

Danny in great turmoil.

Scottie steps out, apologetic.

> DANNY
> I'm to blame?

> SCOTTIE
> Danny, I'm sorry --

> DANNY
> I'm to blame?

Danny refuses to let him back away from the idea.

> SCOTTIE
> I never said to blame.

Danny rephrases.

> DANNY
> He did it for me?

Scottie can't deny it.

> SCOTTIE
> It's possible.

> DANNY
> I didn't ask for it.

Danny looks at the cylinder, now attached to a piece of string, around his neck. The intricate number dials, code - 0000001. Proof of Love.

> SCOTTIE
> He knew you were going to find out
> that he'd lied about much of his
> life. He must have worried that
> you'd end up hating him. He must
> have worried about that moment
> every day. Will he still love me,
> if he knew? Could he still love
> me, if he knew? Or would you re-
> examine your love story - Alex's
> only love story - and decide it
> was, in the end, nothing but a
> lie.

This notion causes great sadness in Danny.

> DANNY
> He was never sure?

> SCOTTIE
> How could he be?

              DANNY
I wish, I could've told him...
That the lies, the mistakes - that
none of it mattered. That I loved
him, just the same. That I love
him. Still. Now. Knowing it all. I
wish he could've heard me say it.

              SCOTTIE
Yes.

              DANNY
He'll never know.

              SCOTTIE
No.

                                    FLASH TO:

INT. DANNY'S APARTMENT. BEDROOM. NIGHT (PAST)

In bed, Danny on his side regarding Alex, who is on his
back, staring at the ceiling.

It's clear that Alex has a great deal on his mind.

              DANNY
      What are you thinking?

Alex breaks from his thoughts, facing Danny.

They are as close as they can be without actually
touching. The thinnest of gaps between them.

For a second it looks like Alex might actually answer the
question seriously, unravelling his innermost thoughts.

And close the gap.

              ALEX
      Say it again.

Danny smiles, puzzled. Alex watches him carefully --

              DANNY
      What are you thinking?

Alex understands the question as a cue for attention.
He's disappointed. But covers. Close and yet apart.

Alex kisses Danny.

*The moment shouldn't feel heartwarming or sentimental. It
should play like a missed opportunity.*

              ALEX
      Nothing.

But Danny, unaware, is happy & glibly content. He has what he wants - attention.

FLASH BACK TO:

INT. SCOTTIE'S HOUSE. GUEST BEDROOM. NIGHT

Danny perched on the edge of the bed, unable to sleep.

Troubled, he gets up.

INT. SCOTTIE'S HOUSE. HALLWAY & BEDROOM. NIGHT

Danny approaches Scottie's bedroom. Scottie sitting on the edge of the bed.

Danny about to enter --

When he spies that Scottie's eyes are closed. His hands clasped. He's praying.

Something Danny has never seen Scottie do before. He decides not to disturb him and backtracks.

However, Danny rethinks, and returns to the doorway, standing there, quietly, until Scottie notices him.

> DANNY
> This is going to sound...
> (struggles)
> But it occurred to me that I've
> never said it aloud, before...
> (beat)
> I love you very much.

Scottie remains silent.

A profound sense of calm seems to come over both of them.

TO BLACK:

The harsh, rhythmic sound of steel capped footsteps on a stone floor.

Clip-Clip-Clip.

FADE IN ON:

INT. POLICE STATION. CORRIDOR. DAY

Danny walking down a bleak-bright-white corridor.

Unseen, behind him, the sound of steel capped shoes clipping on the stone floor.

Up ahead, a door opens, harsh white light --

INT. POLICE STATION. INTERROGATION ROOM. DAY

The strange abattoir room.

Danny seated at a table, braced for the worst. Police officers stand, in the corner, sentries.

Cameras on him.

Detective Taylor sits opposite.

> DETECTIVE TAYLOR
> You're not going to be charged.

Danny can't believe it.

Silence.

Danny remains in disbelief.

> DANNY
> That's it?

> DETECTIVE TAYLOR
> You're free to go.

Danny doesn't move. Looking from face to face. He doesn't trust this news. Expects a trap. A trick.

> DANNY
> You brought me in, like *this*, to say *that*?

Detective Taylor reacts. It's very unusual. And she's been told to do it, but doesn't understand why.

> DANNY (CONT'D)
> Will anyone be charged?

Silence. Which Danny understands as a "no".

> DETECTIVE TAYLOR
> Danny, for you, this is over.

Danny still hasn't moved.

> DANNY
> (softly)
> This isn't over.
> (to the room)
> This isn't over.

INT. THE BALLROOM. GAY CLUB. STAGE. NIGHT

Dazzlingly bright spotlight on stage.

A typical female magician assistant type; archetypal
femininity, skimpy glittery dress, long blonde hair, etc.

Except there is no male magician on stage, no one she's
assisting. She's performing alone.

The actual magic should exhibit genuine wonder and verve.

As she performs she removes her wig, revealing cropped
black hair. Transforming herself in conjunction with her
magic show: *she is part of the magic.*

The accompanying music is a relentless tribal drumming
performed by three women at the back of the stage.

INT. THE BALLROOM GAY CLUB. BOOTH. NIGHT

In one of the shadowy booths is Danny, alone, watching.

He checks his watch and heads out.

EXT. BALLROOM GAY CLUB. FIRE ESCAPE. NIGHT

Danny on the fire escape in the secretive darkness.
Lashing rain. He's indifferent to it.

*The relentless drumming from the stage show plays over
the sequence.*

Danny has a view over the seedy entrance to the club.

Claire arrives, hurries in through the main entrance,
unaware of Danny's presence.

Danny observes. Doesn't move.

INT. THE BALLROOM GAY CLUB. STAGE. NIGHT

The magician is now in a state of androgyny. Out of the
glittery dress. She's wearing white boxers and a white
vest. Her padded bra has been removed.

As a woman, she's thin and flat chested and incredibly
striking. And the drumming continues.

EXT. BALLROOM GAY CLUB. FIRE ESCAPE. NIGHT

Danny on the fire escape, in the darkness, watching. This
time it's Marcus who arrives.

Drumming continues.

Wrapped up against the cold, he hurries into the club.

Danny is pleased. He returns inside, through the fire
exit door, which had been propped open with a brick.

INT. BALLROOM GAY CLUB. STAGE. NIGHT

The female magician is transforming herself into black
tie attire. A typical male magician's outfit.

From assistant to magician.

She's in the middle of performing an elaborate show
stopping trick. Her finale is building.

The drumming continues.

INT. BALLROOM GAY CLUB. BOOTH. NIGHT

Danny joins Marcus and Claire at the booth.

Marcus, drinking whiskey, watches the magician with a
surprising degree of interest rather than disdain.

Danny looks at Marcus.

Marcus gives Danny a small nod.

Claire smiles. A buzz of anticipation.

They wait for the fourth member of their team.

Danny looks at the empty space where Scottie should be.

INT. THE BALLROOM GAY CLUB. NEAR STAGE. NIGHT

Magician in the background, Danny on the phone, walking
away from the booth, towards a quieter corner.

> DANNY (ON PHONE)
> Scottie?

INT/EXT. BLACK CAB / BACK STREETS OF LONDON. NIGHT

Scottie in the back of a black cab, on the phone to
Danny. But his eyes are very much focused on the driver.

Scottie is afraid.

> SCOTTIE (ON PHONE)
> Danny --

His eyes assess the cab --

No door handles. No way out. The windows are plexiglass. The screen between driver and passenger is reinforced.

This is no ordinary cab.

It's the cab that took Danny to the restaurant in the opening of this episode.

The driver glances at Scottie in the rear view mirror. Mean eyes. All we ever see of this man's face.

Scottie's eyes meet his in the mirror.

They both know the truth about each other.

                    DANNY (V.O.)
          Scottie?

The cab is picking up speed: faster and faster.

In contrast, Scottie becomes quite calm.

He sits back, looking out at the blurring night view of London, no longer concentrating on the driver.

                    SCOTTIE (ON PHONE)
          Danny...

Scottie accepts it's over.

                    SCOTTIE (ON PHONE) (CONT'D)
          There will be a note.

INT. BALLROOM GAY CLUB. STAGE. NIGHT

The magician's imaginative act is concluding.

She's now fully transformed into a 'male' magician. With black top hat and black tie.

Unrecognizable from the 'assistant' who opened the show.

Drumming getting faster and faster.

INT. SCOTTIE'S HOUSE. LIVING ROOM. NIGHT

The drumming continues over

Midnight. Darkness in the house.

Danny runs into the room. He sees the pills on the table.

INT. SCOTTIE'S HOUSE. HALLWAY. NIGHT

Sound of drumming continues.

Danny cries out for Scottie but we only hear drumming.

EXT. SCOTTIE'S HOUSE. FRONT GARDEN. NIGHT

Drumming continues.

Danny running towards the heath.

EXT. HAMPSTEAD. NIGHT

Drumming continues.

Danny running.

EXT. HAMPSTEAD HEATH. NIGHT

Danny running along an established path, he turns off, onto the grass, heading towards the trees.

EXT. HAMPSTEAD HEATH. CRUISING AREA. NIGHT

Danny passes through bushes and trees.

Lingering in the darkness a lonely male figure emerges, soliciting. Danny shakes his head, abrupt, dismissive.

Stung by the manner of the rejection, the figure retreats into the shadows.

Danny pauses, emotional, before continuing his search.

INT. BALLROOM GAY CLUB. FIRE ESCAPE. NIGHT

Drumming coming to a climax.

The magician steps into a box.

The doors close.

EXT. HAMPSTEAD HEATH. CRUISING AREA. NIGHT

Up ahead, Danny spots a coat folded neatly on the ground. Danny comes to a stop.

Scottie's jacket. Beside his exquisite shoes.

Danny's fingers are tight around the jacket, understanding exactly what the discovery means.

With effort, Danny turns his eyes upwards to see --

In the darkness, a shadow, a form - a man, hanging from one of the low branches of a tree.

An abrupt burst of energy, Danny hurries forward, grabbing Scottie's legs, trying to take the strain off his neck, as if it were possible to save him.

It's too late, but Danny refuses to accept that fact.

He climbs the tree, reaching the noose, scrambling at the knot. He unties it, lowering Scottie's body.

Danny climbs down.

He feels Scottie's pulse. The action is futile. But Danny behaves as if a rescue were possible.

He tries to breathe life into Scottie - with paramedic zeal - until the third attempt and reality sinks in.

The exact same action becomes distraught. A kiss of extraordinary grief.

His friend is dead.

Danny is strangely calm, suffering from a surfeit of sadness, an emotional shutdown, resting his head on Scottie's chest, as though listening to his heart.

The sound of drumming stops.

INT. BALLROOM GAY CLUB. FIRE ESCAPE. NIGHT

On stage the magic act comes to an end.

The box opens --

The stage is empty.

END OF EPISODE

EPISODE FIVE:

"IF THIS IS
A LIE"

INT. CHURCH. DAY

Scottie's church. Scottie's funeral.

Danny walking towards the lectern --

EXT. HAMPSTEAD HEATH. NIGHT (PAST)

Danny running as fast as he can towards desolate trees.

INT. CHURCH. DAY (PRESENT)

Danny stands at the lectern.

Before him many empty pews. In the front row are Claire,
Sara & Pavel. From the ballroom club an older barman.

Two elderly women: regular church attendees. Behind them:

Three men in their sixties. Civil service aura. Dressed
like Scottie. Exquisite English tailoring --

INT. HAMPSTEAD HEATH. WILDERNESS. NIGHT (PAST)

Scottie's exquisite wool jacket neatly folded on the
ground. Beside his leather shoes.

Red faced, out of breath, Danny drops to his knees,
grabbing the jacket, hands tight on the material --

INT. CHURCH. DAY (PRESENT)

Danny's fingers tight on index cards densely packed with
clumsy handwriting.

A great deal of labour and toil.

EXT. HAMPSTEAD HEATH. WILDERNESS. NIGHT (PAST)

Sparse, delicate, effortless fountain pen handwriting, on
elegant cream letter paper - addressed to Danny.

A suicide note.

As if scolded Danny lets it fall.

INT. CHURCH. DAY (PRESENT)

Under Danny's fingers the ink on the index cards is
starting to smudge. He's unable to read his first line.
Instead, he looks up, at one of the empty pews --

INT. CHURCH. DAY (PAST)

Same church, same pew.

The moment from episode 4. Scottie and Danny seated.
Scottie offers Danny his hand. Danny accepts.

INT. CHURCH. DAY (PRESENT)

Danny's eyes on the empty pew --

EXT. HAMPSTEAD HEATH. WILDERNESS. NIGHT (PAST)

Danny's eyes on the 'sadness' tree.

The shadowy form of a man hanging from a low branch.

INT. CHURCH. DAY (PRESENT)

Danny at the lectern.

And still he can't speak.

We see Sara worrying in the front row, looking to Pavel,
unsure whether she should intervene.

Danny's thoughts revert to the past --

EXT. HAMPSTEAD HEATH. WILDERNESS. NIGHT (PAST)

Danny's face pressed against the gnarled bark as though
listening for a heartbeat.

INT. CHURCH. DAY (PRESENT)

Danny pulls his thoughts back to the present. He ignores
his smudged index cards. Pushing them aside.

Words that follow are more like interior dialogue, nudged
out from his head, rather than regular speech.

> DANNY
> I have a question.
> (beat)
> How do we live without the people
> we love?
> (eyes on empty pew)
> I can hear his reply --
> (Danny listens)
> "We must figure this question out
> for ourselves." He's right. He was
> always right. Except, my friend, I
> don't want to know.

EXT. LONDON. THAMES RIVERBANK. DAWN (PAST)

River shoreline. Centre of London. Beside the Oxo Tower.

Danny, dressed as he was on the heath, sits on the sand in front of a gentle ebb of water. He hasn't slept.

He takes off his shoes. He's walked all night. He puts aside the trainers, an emblem of youth.

A bleak dawn.

He stands, edging into the freezing Thames. The murky water washes over Danny's feet.

We hear music from the church, not a hymn, something Scottie would have loved --

INT. CHURCH. DAY (PRESENT)

Danny seated with Sara, Pavel & Claire.

Continuing from the previous scene we see the musician at the front of the church, playing the piece of music.

Which continues into --

EXT. HAMPSTEAD HEATH. WILDERNESS. DAWN (PAST)

Background: a blur of police activity in the trees.

Foreground: on the grass, the delicate suicide note, ripped into ragged, angry fragments. Discarded by Danny.

The music from the church plays over this.

The shards flutter in the wind, into the cold grey sky, dispersing across the heath.

And the music stops.

PAST/PRESENT
SEQUENCE ENDS

INT. CHURCH. RECEPTION. DAY (PRESENT)

A buffet spread. Far too much food for the number of guests. Most of it untouched.

Claire talks to Pavel and Sara.

The civil servants huddle as a group.

The barman talks to the elderly ladies. Danny is with them but removed, his thoughts elsewhere.

INT. CHURCH. RECEPTION. DAY

Reception over. Danny alone with Claire. He surveys the
leftover food. Untouched remnants. Dips discolouring.

Professor Marcus Shaw enters. Dressed formally. In black.

Claire and Danny are both surprised to see him. He
approaches. Claire guesses his intentions.

> CLAIRE
> Marcus, this isn't the time --

> MARCUS
> Yes it is, Claire. It's exactly
> the right time.

Marcus turns to Danny, addressing him, but addressing the
room in general, careful with diction and volume.

> MARCUS (CONT'D)
> I've destroyed my copy of Alex's
> research.
> (beat)
> You should destroy yours.

Marcus speaks as though he believes the room is bugged.
And that whoever was behind Scottie's death is listening.

> MARCUS (CONT'D)
> You asked for my advice. There it
> is. You can take it. Or not.

And then, again, for emphasis and clarity.

> MARCUS (CONT'D)
> But I won't help you --

> CLAIRE
> (interrupting)
> That's enough.

Silence.

Danny and Marcus stand opposite each other - as
opposites. One a realist. One an idealist.

Marcus turns and walks away.

Danny has to say something, to try and change the
Professor's mind. *He cannot let him walk out the room.*

But Danny says nothing.

Marcus at the door, hesitates. He looks back.

> MARCUS
> It was... a nice idea.

With that, he leaves. The door shuts.

When Danny looks back he sees that Claire is inscrutable.

INT. DANNY'S APARTMENT. BEDROOM. DAY

Alone, Danny sitting on the floor, in the corner of the
bedroom. The room stripped bare.

He runs his hand along the coarse carpet. Fine flecks
of dust rise up: all that remains.

Danny pulls back the corner of the carpet, exposing the
floorboards. Underneath a loose board is an album.

Instead of photos it contains press cuttings concerning
Alex's death. Meticulously clipped and saved.

Each of the articles is annotated with red ink. Sentences
underlined. With the repeating line of commentary:

"This is a lie"

Page after page. The same commentary.

INT. DANNY'S APARTMENT. HALLWAY. DAY

Album under his arm, Danny walks through, contemplating
an era over. He examines damage from a raucous party.

INT. DANNY'S APARTMENT. BATHROOM. DAY

Danny at the window, looking out --

EXT. DANNY'S APARTMENT BUILDING. COURTYARD. DAY

The surveillance apartment, also empty. Shutters open.

EXT. DANNY'S APARTMENT BUILDING. COURTYARD. DAY

Danny in the courtyard, standing at the window to the
empty surveillance apartment, peering in.

There's a gap under the window. Emboldened, Danny pries
his fingers under the frame and lifts it up.

INT. SURVEILLANCE APARTMENT. LIVING ROOM. DAY

Danny nimbly climbs inside, discovering --

Imprint lines on the carpet where heavy equipment had
once been placed. Not ordinary furniture. Strange shapes.

INT. SURVEILLANCE APARTMENT. BEDROOM. DAY

Paint scarred by tape. A collage once covered this wall.
Danny peels off a remaining strip of masking tape. It
coils lifelessly in his hand. A trace of text underneath.

A knock on the window. Danny's startled. Sara is outside,
in the courtyard, beckoning him to get out.

EXT. DANNY'S APARTMENT BUILDING. DAY

Danny, Pavel, Sara on the street. Scottie's car parked
nearby, loaded with a few of Danny's belongings.

Pavel and Danny hug. Sara doesn't wait her turn, joining
them. Tender & sad. The only one crying should be Pavel.

                    PAVEL
          Sorry... Goodbyes...

                    DANNY
          I'll see you all the time!

                    SARA
          You better believe it.

But they don't believe it, sensing their time as intense
friends is over. As they separate, Sara whispers:

                    SARA (CONT'D)
          Be careful.

INT/EXT. SCOTTIE'S CAR / SCOTTIE'S HOUSE. DAY

Danny parks Scottie's car, now his car, in the drive.

And sits there.

EXT. SCOTTIE'S HOUSE. DAY

Danny, holding a box of belongings, before the house.

And stands there.

INT. SCOTTIE'S HOUSE. HALLWAY. DAY

Danny regarding the boxes, the album, the bin bag of
clothes - out of place in Scottie's immaculate home.

INT. SCOTTIE'S HOUSE. LIVING ROOM. DAY

Danny exploring the bookshelves. He picks out books that
catch his eye, flicking through.

Danny is about to put the last book back when he notices in the space behind where this book was kept --

A glass jam jar. Danny reaches in, takes it out.

Holding it to the light, we see, inside the jar, a large flake of mania-blue-paint-work from Raphael's blue room.

Blue and blue alone. Preserved in this wax sealed jam jar. Danny on the verge of crying.

EXT. SCOTTIE'S GARDEN. EVENING

Wrapped up, Danny sits in the corner of Scottie's barren winter garden regarding this house.

He toys with the cylinder, tied around his neck on a piece of string like a gap year student travel trinket.

INT. SCOTTIE'S HOUSE. STUDY. NIGHT

Danny at the computer. He loads Alex's research. A stream of baffling numbers.

Danny presses 'Print'.

INT. SCOTTIE'S HOUSE. STUDY. NIGHT

The printer spewing out the research. Danny collates the pages, binding the research.

INT. SCOTTIE'S HOUSE. STUDY. DAWN

Danny has produced fifty or so manuscripts. They're stacked. Addressed. Neat & careful work.

EXT. POST BOX. HAMPSTEAD. DAY

Danny sending several manuscripts abroad to international newspapers. NY Times, La Monde, etc.

EXT. SECOND POST BOX. LONDON. DAY

Danny in the centre of town, posting manuscripts.

EXT. THIRD POST BOX. LONDON. DAY

Contrasting location. Danny takes the last manuscripts from the boot of Scottie's car. He posts them.

All gone.

EXT. THAMES RIVERSIDE. DAY

Danny sits at the bench where he once waited for Alex.

Detective Taylor arrives, alone, holding her copy of the
manuscript that Danny produced.

She assesses the location - the MI6 building, the river
pathway - before sitting down.

> DETECTIVE TAYLOR
> This is where you two met.

Not a question. She seems in no particular rush. A
melancholy energy about the scene.

She glances through the manuscript. Danny is hopeful. But
she hands the document to Danny. He's confused.

> DETECTIVE TAYLOR (CONT'D)
> Look closely.

As Danny studies the pages, Detective Taylor observes him
with the nearest to tenderness we've seen.

Close on the pages: a series of random equations cut and
pasted together. Every six pages the mass of numbers
repeat. A worthless document.

> DANNY
> This isn't what I gave you.

> DETECTIVE TAYLOR
> But this is what I have.

Danny about to suggest some plan but she speaks first.

> DETECTIVE TAYLOR (CONT'D)
> I visited the nurse who took your
> blood sample.

For the first time she allows Danny a glimmer of her
character, wry, thoughtful and practical.

> DETECTIVE TAYLOR (CONT'D)
> I was curious. Because it's not
> procedure. So I asked a
> straightforward question. "Why did
> you do it?" And it's not what he
> said. *This man was afraid.*
> (beat)
> Afterwards, I'd barely walked out
> the door and my phone rang. It's
> my superiors demanding to know why
> I'm interrogating him. And you
> know what I said? *"No reason"*. It
> wasn't much. But it's as far as
> I'm prepared to go.

Danny understands. She believes. She just won't help.

> DETECTIVE TAYLOR (CONT'D)
> Fifteen years a detective. All the
> cases I've solved... When accounts
> are written about the death of
> this spy, I'm going to end up as
> the simple minded copper.

We should love her, in this moment, as she understands
her entire career will be defined by this case.

INT. UCL. CLAIRE'S OFFICE. DAY

In an impressive office Danny sits in front of Claire. On
her table is a manuscript. She flicks through. Closes it.

Says nothing.

Danny reaches over, takes it, examining it - the pages
doctored as Detective Taylor's manuscript had been.

The numbers repeat every six pages.

> DANNY
> I'll get you another one.

> CLAIRE
> With Scottie we had a chance.
> Without him we don't.

Danny stops examining the pages. He looks at Claire.

> DANNY
> (gentle)
> I don't accept that. We knew him
> better than anyone. What would he
> have done?

And now a glimpse of why she's head of UCL.

> CLAIRE
> You're confused, Danny. Between
> trying to prove how much you love
> him. And trying to prove a
> conspiracy. *You're confused*. And I
> wonder if you haven't always been.

> DANNY
> What's that mean?

> CLAIRE
> Scottie was sentimental about you.

And she's not.

>   CLAIRE (CONT'D)
>   You're doing this for him. He was
>   doing this for you.

A moment of softness.

>   CLAIRE (CONT'D)
>   Maybe I was doing it for him.

Tough again.

>   CLAIRE (CONT'D)
>   But it's not real, Danny. It won't
>   work. Whatever you do. Whatever
>   you try.
>   (emphatic)
>   *It wont work.*

Nudging the manuscript aside, she opens her drawer,
retrieving an envelope of her own.

It's been sent to her, stamped, addressed, etc. She
places it in front of Danny.

>   CLAIRE (CONT'D)
>   He sent it to me.

*Inside is Danny's notebook from the factory. His teenage
jottings. Sketches. Poems. Lyrics. Etc.*

Danny had no idea Scottie had even taken it from the
abandoned factory. He holds it, emotional.

Claire stands.

>   CLAIRE (CONT'D)
>   Walk with me.

INT. UCL. LIBRARY. DAY

Through the entrance, bustling with students, the energy
of hopes and ambitions, towards --

The central chamber with many levels, a cathedral to
education and knowledge. Danny and Claire stand together.

Not a fusty library: modern with glass and sunlight.

The sound of pages turning. Books being moved. The
scratch of pens. Surreptitious student whispers.

She allows the location to do all the work.

Danny remains guarded. Claire sad at his mistrust.

>   CLAIRE
>   I'll be here, when you're ready.

She turns and leaves.

Danny lingers, listening to the enticing library noises --

INT. SCOTTIE'S HOUSE. GUEST BEDROOM. NIGHT

A disturbing noise --

Danny sits up in bed. The middle of the night.

INT. SCOTTIE'S HOUSE. STARIWAY. NIGHT

Danny descends the stairs, investigating, from room to
room, unable to find anything amiss.

The noise again. Coming from outside.

INT. SCOTTIE'S HOUSE. HALLWAY. NIGHT

Danny unlocks the front door. He opens it --

EXT. SCOTTIE'S HOUSE. NIGHT

Danny steps out, peering at the deserted street, before
noticing that the garage door is slightly raised.

Uneasy, he moves towards the garage, lifting up the door.
The hinge isn't oiled and screeches - the noise we heard.

INT. SCOTTIE'S GARAGE. NIGHT

Danny turns on the lights, they hum and flicker,
revealing no one.

The garage is full of Scottie's curious odds and ends.

*And a box marked fragile: newly deposited, taped up,
sitting in the middle of the space.*

Danny crouches, nervous, breaking the seal, opening it.
He stares into it, troubled.

We still haven't seen what the box contains.

INT. SCOTTIE'S HOUSE. STUDY. NIGHT

The box carried inside, by the desk. Danny tips the
contents onto the floor. Out of it spill --

The envelopes he delivered. His handwriting. The stamps.
Post marks. All collected. And returned. All fifty.

He rips one open. A neatly bound manuscript. Except all the pages are blank. The research is gone.

He opens another, and another, and --

INT. SCOTTIE'S HOUSE. STUDY. NIGHT

The fifty blank manuscripts on the floor around Danny.

Refusing to give up, he's at the computer. The cylinder is in the drive. On screen is Alex's research.

Danny attaches it to an e-mail.

INT. SCOTTIE'S HOUSE. STUDY. DAY

Bleary eyed, Danny at the computer. His 'sent box' shows the hundreds of documents he's mailed overnight.

His inbox shows no replies.

Danny hears the sound of a car in the drive.

He stands, walking to the window --

EXT. SCOTTIE'S HOUSE. DAY

A bashed up car parked in the drive.

A woman, in her fifties, is helping a man in his seventies, towards the front door.

They move slowly. The man appears infirm.

INT/EXT. SCOTTIE'S HOUSE. FRONT DOOR. DAY

The doorbell rings.

Danny lingers, near the stairs, refusing to answer.

The doorbell rings again.

Danny again, doesn't move. But he's tormented.

The doorbell rings a third time.

Unable to stop himself, Danny opens the door.

A couple stand before him.

The man, in his seventies, has part of his throat missing. He breathes through a plastic tube affixed to where his larynx once was. A sad, soft wheezing sound.

The woman, in her fifties, has beauty but no warmth. Both rough edged. Both smartly attired in inexpensive clothes.

Danny displays hostile unease.

INT. SCOTTIE'S HOUSE. KITCHEN. DAY

The three sit at the table. The awkward silence is punctuated with the slow-sad rhythm of the man's wheeze.

Danny refuses to make polite chit chat. No tea, no coffee, no hospitality of any kind.

The atmosphere is excruciating.

The woman is about to make an observation, regarding the lovely kitchen, or whatever, when Danny cuts her off.

>   DANNY
>   How did you find me?

Danny studies their reaction carefully.

>   WOMAN
>   You gave us this address.

The woman takes out her address book, offering it to Danny. He views it, as he views them, with suspicion.

Danny glances inside the book: he finds his name and Scottie's address. Crinkled and faded.

Wary of its apparent plausibility, he returns it.

>   DANNY
>   Eleven years.

>   WOMAN
>   (weakly)
>   A long time.

>   DANNY
>   And now?

>   MUM
>   Dan, your Dad's dying.

These are his parents.

Danny's instinct is sympathy. He guards against it, looking at his dad's sick-yellow-tinged eyes. A body wracked by anger, booze and cigarettes.

>   MUM (CONT'D)
>   We weren't much as parents.

Danny realizes he's being sucked into an exchange he doesn't even believe to be real. He pulls back.

> DANNY
> You read about me in the paper?

> MUM
> We read about you.

> DANNY
> But that's not why you're here?

She doesn't seem to understand. And is about to answer --

When his dad's breathing interrupts. Danny's mother needs to clean the pipe. Phlegm. And mucus. It's graphic.

Danny can't decide - could this be real?

> DANNY (CONT'D)
> You need money?

> MUM
> No.

> DANNY
> No?

> MUM
> No.

Danny muses. Incredulous.

> MUM (CONT'D)
> This was a mistake.

She stands, helping her husband up - they're leaving.

Danny allows them to.

INT. SCOTTIE'S HOUSE. HALLWAY. DAY

Danny watching his parents leave. He stands at the back of the hall. The front door opens.

Some deeper childhood connection pulls at Danny. He can't allow it to end like this. Despite his better judgement.

> DANNY
> Tell me why.

His mum turns to Danny.

> DANNY (CONT'D)
> Why now?

Maintaining a hard line.

> DANNY (CONT'D)
> Why today?

> MUM
> Weeks, that's all he's got left.

That revelation causes Danny to rethink.

> DANNY
> (without conviction)
> We've said goodbye.

> MUM
> Want to do a better job of it?

Danny desperately does.

> MUM (CONT'D)
> There's something we'd like to
> show you.

INT/EXT. DANNY'S PARENTS CAR / LONDON. DAY

A beat-up car. Danny's mum driving. His dad in the
passenger seat. Danny in the back.

A family.

Danny snoops through the items in the backseat pocket. A
take away menu. A pack of gum. A tatty street map.

Yet at this ordinariness Danny seems to falter, becoming
paranoid and unsure.

> DANNY
> If this a lie please stop the car
> and let me out. Because I've been
> through too much for this to be
> another lie.
> (beat)
> I won't be angry. It's not your
> fault. Just stop the car. And let
> me out.
> (beat)
> But if you drive me home, when I
> gave you this chance...
> (beat)
> Mum, is this is a lie?

He looks at his mum in the rear view mirror. She looks at
him in the rear view mirror. And does not stop the car.

EXT. EAST LONDON. TERRACE STREET. DAY

Danny stands outside his childhood home. A row of terrace
houses, once near-worthless now property-boom-gentrified.

Danny follows his parents inside, past the tidy front
garden, with some flower pots. A welcome mat.

INT. DANNY'S CHILDHOOD HOUSE. LIVING ROOM. DAY

Danny stands in a neat, clean, ordinary room. A
television. Some DVDs on the bookshelves. Cookbooks.

Three separate geraniums planted in a single decorative
rectangular pot.

His mum helps his dad to a comfy chair, adapted to his
physical needs with hospital equipment.

His mum takes up an ordinary digital camera. Busy with
the timer. Checking with Danny.

> DANNY'S MUM
>> Alright if I?

Danny can't form a response, positive or negative.

INT. DANNY'S CHILDHOOD HOUSE. LIVING ROOM. DAY

An awkward & bizarre family photo. Danny next to his dad
in the chair. His mum on the other side.

The camera on the shelf. The flash --

INT. DANNY'S CHILDHOOD HOUSE. LIVING ROOM. DAY

Danny seated near his dad. Larynx or not, these men have
nothing to say to each other.

His mum enters with a tray of tea and classy biscuits.
She places it on the coffee table.

Danny picks up the porcelain milk urn shaped like a cow.
He pours, fascinated, as the milk flows through the cow's
mouth into a dainty cup.

Danny continues to pour until it spills over. Even as it
overflows, he doesn't stop. Milk puddle growing larger.

His parents stare.

> DANNY
>> (gentle)
>> I wish this could be true.

Danny puts the urn down. He stares at his dad wheezing,
with yellow tinged eyes. At his mum.

Danny's attention concentrates on the geraniums behind
her. He stands and walks to them. Touching their leaves.

Then, taking hold of the base of one of the plants, Danny gently lifts the geranium clean out of the decorative pot. It emerges from the loose soil easily.

He places it on the table.

The root system is smooth & precise. It was re-potted recently. And its roots haven't spread.

Danny repeats this for the other plants so they're side by side. All three recently moved from plastic pots.

Danny turns to his parents. His mum is about to speak. Danny raises a finger to his lips. No more lies.

Danny studies the room.

                    DANNY (CONT'D)
          People can change this much. For
          real, I mean.

He looks at his dad.

                    DANNY (CONT'D)
          You're not dying, are you?

His wheezing, although exactly the same sound, now feels less sad, and a little more menacing.

                    DANNY (CONT'D)
          Not right now. Not next week.

Her respectability slipping. Roughness creeping back in.

                    MUM
          They're scary people, Dan. They
          know everything about us. Every
          thing we ever done wrong. What-did-
          you-do? This isn't like pinching
          stuff from the shops.

                    DANNY
          Why am I here?

And in a flash of anger. Shrill and sharp.

                    MUM
          Why are we here? Being made to do
          this? Being threatened? What have
          you dragged us into?

His mum continues speaking, vicious tongued, but Danny stops listening, instead, observing the movement of her lips, her frown, a particular flush to her neck.

He's seen it countless times before. But this time it has no impact. As she finishes we fade back in.

                    MUM (CONT'D)
And you have the cheek to ask:
          (imitating)
Why am I here?

And in this speech we have a potted history of Danny's
childhood. An angry mum interested only in herself.

Understanding that there's no way on earth this woman
would want a family photo Danny turns to the camera.

He picks it up. Heavier than it looks. He checks the
photo on the display.

On screen we see the awkward and bizarre family photo.

With curiosity, not aggression, Danny breaks the camera
apart snapping the shell, revealing a high tech interior.

We can't be sure & Danny can see that neither of his
parents know what it really is. He puts it down.

About to leave. But a thought strikes him.

                    DANNY
          I always wanted to know...
          Wouldn't it have been easier to
          love me?

His mum is less aggressive now.

                    MUM
          I can't say why we never did.

Danny puts a gentle hand on his mum's cheek. She's
surprised.

                    DANNY
          (emotional)
          I'm not angry anymore.

But he is sad. At the confirmed absence of real parents.

He walks towards his dad. The man is frail, and afraid,
expecting to be punched, to reap what he sowed.

Instead, Danny kisses his cheek. And sheds a tear.

EXT. DANNY'S CHILDHOOD HOUSE. FRONT GARDEN & STREET. DAY

Danny walking away from the house. When he glances back
his mum has already shut the front door.

They'll never see each other again.

Understanding that fact, Danny takes a beat to say goodbye to this street - this place - before continuing on his way. He takes out his phone.

It's stopped working. The screen is blank. He tries to turn it on. Nothing. Takes out the battery, tries again.

The phone's dead. Danny's troubled.

He touches the cylinder around his neck --

INT. SCOTTIE'S HOUSE. STUDY. DAY

At the computer Danny slots in the data stick. Only to discover it's been wiped clean.

Danny accesses his e-mail. His account has been purged. None of the sent messages. Nothing in his inbox.

Nothing remains.

And then an email appears. The only one in his inbox. Sender: unknown. No text. Just an attachment.

Danny presses on the attachment.

On screen we see the bizarre family photo taken only a few hours ago. Danny. Mum. Dad.

A provocation. An explanation.

Suddenly the printer comes to life. And prints a colour copy of the family portrait.

Danny sits back, tight with anger. And notices that --

Every book on the shelves has been turned upside down.

Amazed, Danny stands, walking down the length of the bookshelves, only to find, incongruous among Scottie's first editions -- the photo album of press cuttings.

INT. SCOTTIE'S HOUSE. STUDY. DAY

Danny ripping out pages from the album of press cuttings. He feeds them into the shredder.

The black and white text spews out in thin lines. "This is a lie" reduced to thin red streaks.

Danny feeds in his family photo.

INT. SCOTTIE'S HOUSE. STUDY. DAY

Danny sitting on the floor. Opposite him is a mountainous heap of shredded press clippings.

And now - truly - nothing remains.

Danny's exhausted. A spent force. It's over.

INT. COMMUNITY CENTRE. ROOM. EVENING

Danny at his regular HIV support group meeting. On the whiteboard we see info about employment laws and HIV.

A new attendee. A young man, only 17 years old, shy and embarrassed. The friendly chair addresses this young man.

> CHAIR
> I'd like us to welcome Ryan.

There's applause.

> CHAIR (CONT'D)
> A lot of people don't speak until
> they've been a few times. So you
> shouldn't feel any pressure. But I
> wanted to give you the chance.

Most eyes on Ryan - friendly - a few don't look, deliberately, not wanting him to feel under pressure.

Ryan struggling with what to say. Such a familiar reaction no one is surprised. Everyone empathetic.

> CHAIR (CONT'D)
> And remember there's no point
> talking unless you feel able to
> tell the truth.
> (beat)
> Maybe you're not ready?

Ryan shakes his head. Not ready.

Danny sits forward.

> DANNY
> I'll go.

Everyone in the group is pleasantly surprised, as though these were among the first words Danny has spoken.

> GROUP CHAIR
> Danny.

Danny considers where to begin.

                                        FLASH TO:

EXT. VAUXHALL BRIDGE. DAWN (PAST)

Danny on the bridge, that morning. He turns to see Alex.

The first time. That first look.

                                    FLASH BACK TO:

INT. COMMUNITY CENTRE. ROOM. EVENING (PRESENT)

The group in stunned silence. They all believe him.

Danny has finished his summary. He's holding the
cylinder. He puts it back, around his neck.

Finally, the oldest member of the group, a black man in
his seventies, speaks out, with gravitas.

                    OLDEST GUY
          What are you going to do now?

The first time he's articulated his defeat aloud:

                    DANNY
          I'm going to do nothing.

INT. COMMUNITY CENTRE. CORRIDOR. EVENING

Danny leaving the session.

In the corridor, waiting for their seventeen year old
son, are Ryan's parents.

Mother and father side by side, as if waiting to pick
their child up from after-school music practice.

We wonder if they're angry, disapproving, ashamed.

The parents walk with their son, silently. And as they
walk out, the mother rests a hand on her son's shoulder.

A family.

INT. SCOTTIE'S HOUSE. STUDY. NIGHT

Danny crouching over the heap of shredded pages. He picks
out the shredded colour lines of his family photo.

INT. SCOTTIE'S HOUSE. STUDY. NIGHT

On a flat sheet of card Danny's positioning the strips.

INT. SCOTTIE'S HOUSE. STUDY. NIGHT

Danny has assembled and glued down all the vertical
strips of his 'family photo'.

Except he's wilfully misaligned the strips. Mum is
mingled with Dad is mingled with Danny.

A family messed up.

EXT. SCOTTIE'S HOUSE. NIGHT

Danny getting into Scottie's car. He has the copy of fake
research manuscript. And the mixed up family photo --

EXT. MOTORWAY. NIGHT

Danny driving along the motorway at night.

EXT. MANSION. NIGHT

Danny driving towards the mansion.

EXT. MANSION. GARDENS. DRIVEWAY. NIGHT

Danny getting out of car, holding a copy of the research
manuscript and the messed up family portrait.

The mansion is in darkness.

Danny turns towards the intimidating front doors.

EXT. MANSION. FRONT DOORWAY. NIGHT

Frances opens the doors, inscrutable as ever, except,
perhaps for the faintest trace of admiration.

> FRANCES
> I rather thought it might be you.

She looks him over, registering his seriousness of
purpose. And the man himself - older, wiser, sadder.

> DANNY
> Is it too late to talk?

> FRANCES
> (with sadness)
> Too late? Perhaps it is.

She steps back, leaving the doors open for him.

Danny enters the mansion.

INT. MANSION. GRAND HALLWAY. NIGHT

Frances less formally dressed compared to episode two.
Not hiding behind any imposing outfit.

At the top of the stairs, looking down, stands Charles,
dressed in moth-eaten British country tweed.

The nanny appears to the other side, staring at Danny
with grave concern.

Behind Danny, the powerful figure of the groundsman
arrives from outside.

He shuts the main doors.

Danny waits, pinned between these four sets of eyes.

A noise: a crack like thunder.

Charles has brought the tip of his walking stick down
hard on the floor as if to cleave this house in two.

Frances is untroubled by her husband's anger, turning to
him, soothing an agitated child:

                FRANCES
        What harm can it do?

Charles speaks. For the first time. Slowly. Like a rusted
machine coming to life.

                CHARLES
        What good can it do?

Frances responds, partly to him, partly to herself.

                FRANCES
        What good? What possible good?
        What good can any of us do? Better
        leave him be? He's just a boy?

Is she even speaking about Danny?

To their surprise Charles begins to laugh. Horribly.

                CHARLES
        Just a *stupid* boy.

Charles disappears into the gloom, taking his horrible
laugh with him. Frances appears shaken.

She looks at the groundsman, some signal given.

The groundsman steps forward and pats Danny down. Car
keys. Wallet. The fake research manuscript.

And the reassembled family photo on the card.

The manuscript and photo are handed to Frances. She's
regained her composure.

> FRANCES
> I take it there's something you
> wish to discuss?
> (studying Danny)
> More than that...
> (amazed)
> You intend to accuse me?

Deliberate resonance, in Danny's mind, with the funeral:

> DANNY
> I have a question.

> FRANCES
> A question.
> (considers)
> I'll permit you a question.
> (beat)
> But just one.

Danny understands that she means to enforce it literally.

She turns, walking towards the Grand Hall.

Danny passes the Nanny. He stares at her.

She observes the intensity of his glance, fearful of
Danny's venture, but unable to intervene.

She turns and leaves, disappearing into the darkness.
Danny watches her go.

The groundsman remains close behind.

INT. MANSION. GRAND HALL. NIGHT

They pass through the plastic sheeting, shadows and
scaffolding into the other half of the room.

The Groundsman has followed them, standing at the back,
intending to stay. Frances dismisses him.

> FRANCES
> That will be all.

He doesn't want to leave. The master-servant power
dynamic becomes ambiguous.

Danny wonders if this man is merely a Groundsman.

Frances holds her stare. On the verge of repeating the
order. A touch of humiliation about the necessity.

Reluctantly the Groundsman retires. Into the shadows.

Yet they do not feel alone.

Danny has the theatre of this space. Frances waits for him to speak. And suddenly Danny's confidence falters.

In a remarkable reversal from their previous encounter, Frances is no longer hostile.

She starts to build a fire in the old fireplace.

Danny watches. She glances back at him.

He walks forward, joining her.

INT. MANSION. GRAND HALL. NIGHT

The two of them building the fire. She observes the way he methodically spirals the fire-starting coils of paper.

                    FRANCES
          I see some of his technique.

They light the fire together from opposite sides. The flames spread quickly.

Frances sits beside it, on a low cushioned stool. Danny does the same. They're close to the fire and each other.

An intimate corner in this vast strange house.

                    FRANCES (CONT'D)
          We both loved him.

                    DANNY
          Yes.

                    FRANCES
          Can't we pretend, for a while,
          that's all we need to say?

But the silence cannot hold.

Danny's eyes rest on her hands. He reaches out for one.

She's surprised. But after consideration she allows him to take it. He concentrates on her palm, not for any literal reason, as if trying to get closer to her.

                    FRANCES (CONT'D)
          You always did have something of
          the mystic about you. Fortune
          teller-soothsayer, a person who
          knows nothing yet sees everything.

                    DANNY
          Alex was the last person to hold
          your hand.

>   FRANCES
>   (with delicate
>   lethality)
>   A question?

>   DANNY
>   A statement.

Frances casts her mind back --

>   FRANCES
>   Yes. Yes he was.

                                        FLASH TO:

EXT. MANSION. GROUNDS. MAZE. DAY (PAST)

Close on Frances's hand around Alex's little hand.

They walk side by side through the maze.

                                   FLASH BACK TO:

INT. MANSION. GRAND HALLWAY. NIGHT (PRESENT)

Still holding Frances's hand Danny moves to his question.

>   DANNY
>   You blame me for his death.

>   FRANCES
>   (with delicate
>   lethality)
>   A question?

>   DANNY
>   A statement.

>   FRANCES
>   Yes. I do.

>   DANNY
>   How can you blame me unless you
>   know why he was killed?

Frances takes back her hand. She's impressed.

>   FRANCES
>   It is... a good question.

Danny picks up the research manuscript as though it were
vital evidence. He hands it to Frances.

Wanting to see what she'll do with it.

Frances takes the manuscript.

And without examining it, tosses the papers into the
fire. The meaningless numbers burn, turning to ash.

They both watch them burn for a moment. *An admission.*

Frances stands and pours herself a measure of brandy. She
looks to Danny to see if he wants one.

Danny stands, slowly - unsure what the implications are.
He joins her but refuses a drink.

> DANNY
> (changing his mind)
> Actually, I will.

She pours him one. They sip.

> FRANCES
> (without anger)
> For all your efforts, all your
> loss, all your grief. And
> sacrifice. You have nothing.

The reference to Scottie is tremendously painful.

> FRANCES (CONT'D)
> You accept that I'm continuing
> this conversation solely for my
> own personal reasons?

> DANNY
> Which are?

> FRANCES
> It's very important to me that you
> understand how much I loved my
> son.

Danny wonders if she's quite sane.

> DANNY
> Show me his room.

Frances doesn't react.

Danny's eyes concentrate on the necklace we glimpsed in
episode two, which Frances would occasionally and
instinctively touch, unaware she was doing so.

Danny reaches out, slowly, carefully towards her neck.

Frances doesn't flinch.

He takes hold of the silver chain around her neck. He
pulls it up, from beneath her shirt, revealing --

An aged silver key.

In a mirroring of the action, Frances reaches out,
slowly, towards Danny's neck.

Danny doesn't flinch.

She lifts the string from around his neck, pulling from
under his shirt the silver cylinder.

The two stand, examining each other's prized possession.
Frances admires the cylinder, proud of its craftsmanship.

Danny's fingers are on the key --

INT. MANSION. HALLWAY. NIGHT

The silver key slots into a lock.

We're at a door we've never seen before. A corridor we've
never seen. In near darkness.

Frances, looks at Danny, offering him a last chance.

> FRANCES
> You've always underestimated the
> task ahead of you. A peculiar
> strength, as it turns out.
> (beat)
> If we go inside I cannot promise
> to know where we'll end up.

The door unlocks. Danny walks through to --

INT. MANSION. SECRET STUDY. NIGHT

A remarkable study.

Across all the walls - floor to ceiling - are
blackboards, covered in chalk equations.

Even more notable there are blackboards across the
ceiling, also covered in equations.

The writing should be precise and small so that the
overall effect is beautiful. Numbers, numbers everywhere.

A desk in the middle of the room - modern, steel,
austere. A steel chair in front of it.

On the desk a glass filled with sharp pencils. A stack of
papers. Each paper filled with more neat numbers.

In this space, this room, nothing soft. Nothing
comfortable. And nothing high tech.

Several ladders, of different lengths, to reach the top
of the blackboards. And the ceiling.

Frances is proud and scared of this room.

                    FRANCES
          Alistair spent more time in this
          room than any other.

Frances walks to the boards, covered with Alex's writing,
his numbers, equations are preserved: we see how precious
they are to her. Many years old. A museum to his mind.

With each footstep chalk dust falls from the numbers on
the ceiling.

Danny tilts his head upwards, watching the dust fall --

                                        FLASH TO:

INT. DANNY'S APARTMENT. BEDROOM. NIGHT (PAST)

At night, Danny and Alex are in bed, on their back,
looking up at the cracked plaster ceiling --

A light white dust falls due to the sex going on in the
room above. Rhythmic vibrations.

Danny finds it ridiculous, embarrassed by the state of
his abode. But Alex seems to react differently --

Solemn, he closes his eyes, allowing the dust to settle
on his face --

                                    FLASH BACK TO:

INT. MANSION. SECRET STUDY. NIGHT (PRESENT)

As the first particles of chalk dust settle on Danny's
face he's hit by grief & anger.

Moving sharply, he picks up one of the board cleaners,
intending to wipe the blackboards clean.

Frances moves swiftly, grabbing his wrist, stopping him.

                    DANNY
          How do you know?

She's not strong enough to hold his arm. The board
cleaner touches the blackboard, Danny begins to wipe, the
precious numbers reducing to chalk dust.

                    DANNY (CONT'D)
          How?

More precious numbers disappearing.

                      FRANCES
                  (desperate)
           Please!

But Danny doesn't stop.

                  FRANCES (CONT'D)
           Because he's my spy!

Danny stops. No more numbers destroyed.

                  FRANCES (CONT'D)
           I made him. A spy.

Frances collects herself. She moves away from Danny. And
then, composed again:

                  FRANCES (CONT'D)
           I told you that my husband was an
           important man. An important man,
           with a second rate mind. We were
           at Cambridge together. The tutors
           who recruited him were as blind to
           my talents as they were to his
           flaws. None-the-less, in the
           gentlemen's club of MI6, Charles
           flourished. While I was relegated
           to hosting dinners and cocktail
           parties for his spies.

                                  FLASH TO:

INT. MANSION. DINING ROOM. NIGHT (PAST)

A grand spy dinner.

From Frances' point of view, looking out, down the full
length of this silver service table.

Servants. Art on the walls. The house in splendour.

At the far end of the table, a distant blur, is Charles.

The men seated either side are discussing, entertaining,
some flirting with other men's wives.

We follow Frances's glance from man to man, from spy to
spy, picking out their gestures, their manner.

One of the men, a heavy drinker, large-set, laughs
raucously. Everyone turns to look.

Except for two men who continue their conversation and do
not react. Frances notices. No one else does.

INT. MANSION. LIBRARY & HALLWAY. NIGHT (PAST)

Frances's retreating point of view as she retires from
the library crowded with the spies smoking cigars.

Backing out, ignored, her hands close the doors, catching
a faint wisp of cigar smoke.

We remain outside these antique doors staring upwards at
the wisp of cigar smoke, listening to the hum of their
confidential chatter.

Cigar smoke and chatter. All that we're privy to.

                                        FLASH BACK TO:

INT. MANSION. SECRET STUDY. NIGHT (PRESENT)

Frances toys with a stick of chalk. She cracks it into
three uneven chunks. And places them on the steel table.

                    FRANCES
          Three spies at the heart of his
          organization. And Charles didn't
          see them. Worse still, he defended
          their reputations when suspicions
          arose. They were men like him,
          dressed like him, spoke like him,
          fucked like him. Well, two did,
          anyway. They were his friends.
          Agents were lost. Operations
          compromised. When the three
          finally defected we were
          disgraced, removed from the
          service, exiled from power, left
          to rot, in this place, guarded
          night and day by agents for fear
          that we too might be traitors.
                    (beat)
          I took to drink. For a while. I
          became promiscuous. For a while.
          Scandal engulfed me. But it
          couldn't go on. Behaving like
          that. You either step into the
          abyss. Or step back from it. You
          cannot walk along its edge for
          long.

Danny reacts. Frances observes him. They've shared this.

                    FRANCES (CONT'D)
          You know this... edge?

                    DANNY
          Yes.

                          FRANCES
          Alex was your step back? He was
          mine too. I decided to have a
          child. He'd be my future. My
          saviour. My second chance. I'd
          make him the spy I should've been.
          My spy. Made by me.
                    (beat, upset)
          It was a mistake.

Danny considers carefully.

                          DANNY
          Not a lie. Not the truth.

                          FRANCES
          For once your intuition lets you
          down.

                          DANNY
                    (musing)
          "You decided to have a child".
                    (beat)
          Fuck old Charles and see what
          happens? Not much of a plan,
          considering how stupid you think
          he is. But luck was on your side.
          Your child was a genius?

                          FRANCES
          Be very careful what you say next.

                          DANNY
          I want to tell you a story.

Frances is off balance. Sensing danger.

                          DANNY (CONT'D)
          About a man.

                                                      FLASH TO:

INT. DANNY'S APARTMENT. BEDROOM. NIGHT (PAST)

Late at night.

Danny and Alex are sitting cross-legged on the floor of
the darkened bedroom, opposite each other.

The apartment's quiet. With the giddy zeal of a new
couple they're sharing stories and secrets.

                          ALEX
          While other people were laughing.
          And drinking. This man would just
          walk.

EXT. THAMES. SOUTHBANK. DAY (PAST)

Dusk on the river. A warm summer evening. Crowds drinking
in bars and restaurants.

Alex walks alone, smartly dressed, as if he were on route
to meet a partner or a date.

He appears confident, assured, content.

Alex weaves through, reaching the railings by the river,
opening the gate leading to the steps down to the water.

                    ALEX (V.O.)
              Until he reached the exact same
              spot --

He descends the steps and sits on the lower level with
the air of someone who has done this before, looking out
at the sunset behind Waterloo Bridge.

Cut off from everyone else. Unapproachable.

                    ALEX (V.O.)
              Where he'd sit, with his back to
              all those people --

Unseen by those on the promenade, Alex's melancholy eyes
concentrate on the fading sunlight.

                    ALEX (V.O.)
              While he did everything to signal
              to the world that he wanted to be
              left alone --

INT. DANNY'S APARTMENT. BEDROOM. NIGHT (PAST)

Danny opposite Alex.

                    ALEX
                 (continuing)
              -- more than anything, he hoped
              someone would understand that what
              he really wanted, was the exact
              opposite, and that this 'someone'
              would sit next to him. And
              strike up a conversation.
                 (beat)
              I was that man. You were that
              someone.

                              FLASH BACK TO:

INT. MANSION. SECRET STUDY. NIGHT (PRESENT)

Danny has finished telling Alex's story.

Both Frances and Danny are upset. For once, Frances is
unable to fully conceal her emotion.

>   DANNY
>   Why was he so lonely?

>   FRANCES
>   (weak)
>   I put too much pressure on him. I
>   made him too important in my life.
>   It was unfair. I realize that now.
>   No child can redeem their parents.

Danny takes out the reassembled family portrait. The
messed up vertical strips - Dad. Mum. Danny. Mingled.

>   DANNY
>   Hard to connect to people. When
>   you're not sure how they're
>   connected to you.

He shows her the family photo. She holds it, perplexed.

>   DANNY (CONT'D)
>   For an hour or two I hoped my real
>   parents were real parents.

Danny studies Frances's reaction. And she understands
what he's talking about but pretends not to.

Danny walks to the door. He leaves the study.

INT. MANSION. CORRIDOR. NIGHT

Danny walking away.

Frances stands in the doorway.

>   FRANCES
>   Daniel!

Danny continues walking. Frances follows.

He reaches the stairway and descends.

INT. MANSION. DECAYING KITCHEN. NIGHT

Danny enters the enormous decaying kitchen.

The room is completely dark. Except for a solitary gas
ring. A blue circle of light in the corner.

The Nanny sits on a wooden stool, her back to Danny, a
pitiful figure, face part illuminated by the blue.

On the gas ring is a saucer: she's warming some milk. She registers Danny in the room. But does not turn around.

Danny walks forward, reaching the stove, looking down at her. She looks up at him.

And she knows that he knows.

She stands, ashamed, unable to hold his look, stirring the milk, diverting her energy into menial tasks.

> NANNY
> I was a state, Danny. I didn't
> deserve to be his mum.

Frances catches up, entering the kitchen. And assesses in an instant that the secret is out.

The nanny finishes the milk. Pours it into a mug. She puts it down, ready for Danny.

And now takes up a subservient position behind Frances.

The master. And the servant. The two mothers.

> FRANCES
> Surely you can't be so
> conventional as to think there's
> only one way to bring up a child?
> We are both his mother. Neither
> one less real nor more real than
> the other. I took care of his
> mind. She took care of his other
> needs.

The Nanny seems content with this insane description.

> DANNY
> He didn't know?

> FRANCES
> Of course not.

> DANNY
> Except he did. Didn't he? He knew.

> FRANCES
> On some level... maybe... He was
> very young when it happened. At
> the time she was working for me.
> And stealing. I went to her house,
> to threaten her with the police if
> she didn't return the items.
> (remembers)
> I've never seen anything like it.

> FLASH TO:

INT. SQUALID HOUSE. LIVING ROOM. DAY (PAST)

From Frances's point of view:

The most wretched conditions. Damp & dirt. Empty booze
bottles. Heroin paraphernalia. Savage poverty.

And then the sound of a child crying --

INT. SQUALID HOUSE. BEDROOM. DAY (PAST)

A cold bedroom, as wretched as the living room.

Little Alex at the back of the room. Three years old.
Eyes red, sniffling, he's no longer crying.

Instead, at the large three panel window, he draws on the
condensation formed because of the cold.

The entire window is filled, not with numbers, but with
patterns and shapes. They're intricate & self taught.

As beautiful as any church stained-glass window.

INT. SQUALID HOUSE. LIVING ROOM. DAY (PAST)

From Frances's point of view:

We open a silly children's colouring book. Instead of
blocks of crude crayon colour, we see more remarkable
lattice patterns. Mathematical precision.

Not the product of education. An expression of raw
genius. Page after page after page.

                                        FLASH BACK TO:

INT. MANSION. KITCHEN. NIGHT (PRESENT)

Frances continues.

                    FRANCES
          If you'd seen him... if you'd seen
          the conditions... No father. No
          mother to speak of. She thought
          the boy disturbed. Damaged by her
          drink. And drugs. I saw how
          precious he really was.
               (beat)
          We came to an arrangement.

                    DANNY
          "An Arrangement?"

                    FRANCES
          I would be the boy's mother.

For the first time Frances turns to the Nanny. She nods
at her and allows her to speak.

                    NANNY
          I'd be his nanny.

Frances turns back to face Danny.

                    FRANCES
          He'd be provided for in every way.
          Every opportunity. Every comfort.

                    DANNY
          Charles agreed?

                    FRANCES
          He resisted, initially.
               (beat)
          He was persuaded.

                    DANNY
          You can persuade anyone. Of
          anything. Can't you?

Danny stares at the Nanny but she does not look him in
the eye, keeping her glance down, at the floor.

No hint of sexual relations between these women.

                    FRANCES
          In this society it's not enough to
          be born brilliant.

                                        FLASH TO:

INT. MANSION. ALEX'S BEDROOM. DAY (PAST)

Little Alex's vast bedroom. With the four poster bed.

He's dressed for boarding school. Blazer. Tie. Cap.

In front of him is the antique boarding school trunk.
Filled with books. Far advanced for his age.

                                    FLASH BACK TO:

INT. MANSION. KITCHEN. NIGHT (PRESENT)

Frances finishes the story.

                    FRANCES
          I opened up a world that would've
          been closed to him.

                    DANNY
        He didn't belong there. He wasn't
        you. He wasn't like you.

                    FRANCES
        A few years, that's all I asked.
        And then he was free to do
        whatever he wanted.

                    DANNY
        Such as end all lies?

                    FRANCES
            (angry)
        A sentimental, ridiculous notion.
            (sad)
        I warned him...

Frances almost talking to herself again. A touch of
madness returning to her speech.

                    FRANCES (CONT'D)
        I tried to save him...

She appears quite sick with grief at the memory.

                    FRANCES (CONT'D)
        I tried...

                                        FLASH TO:

INT/EXT. CAR / ALEX'S APARTMENT BUILDING. NIGHT (PAST)

Frances in the back of a car, watching as --

EXT. ALEX'S APARTMENT BUILDING. NIGHT (PAST)

Danny rings the doorbell one final time. The night Alex
disappeared. No answer.

INT/EXT. CAR / ALEX'S APARTMENT BUILDING. NIGHT (PAST)

Frances in the back of a car, watching. Now we reveal in
the front car are two intelligence officers with her.

EXT. ALEX'S APARTMENT BUILDING. NIGHT (PAST)

Outside, Danny on the steps. Grim-faced. He walks into
the street and looks up at the flat window.

The terrace. The bedroom. No lights. Silent.

He glances around. At the car where Frances is sitting.
The windscreen is tinted. He can't see in.

                        268

INT/EXT. CAR / ALEX'S APARTMENT BUILDING. NIGHT (PAST)

Frances sees Danny. He does not see her. She watches as
he walks away. The intelligence officers turn to Frances.

EXT. ALEX'S APARTMENT BUILDING. NIGHT (PAST)

Frances walks towards the building. Flanked by two
intelligence officers. She reaches the front door.

It opens. An intelligence officer inside.

She enters --

INT. ALEX'S APARTMENT BUILDING. STAIRWAY. NIGHT (PAST)

The door closes behind her.

The building is dark. Silent. And ordinary. No sign of
anything unusual.

Frances follows the agents up to the first floor landing.
The door to the apartment opens.

She enters --

INT. SECURITY SERVICE APARTMENT. NIGHT (PAST)

Bustling activity. A room filled with agents. Diverse -
international. Saudi. American. Israeli.

A bank of video screens showing live footage from Alex's
apartment and attic.

This is the equipment that created the outlines we saw in
the surveillance apartment in the opening scenes.

Frances is directed to the bedroom.

INT. SECURITY SERVICE APARTMENT. BEDROOM. NIGHT (PAST)

A female intelligence agent stands guard as Frances gets
changed. She takes off her shoes.

In front of her are crime-scene-style forensic plastic
over-suits. Gloves. A surgical face mask.

INT. ALEX'S APARTMENT BUILDING. STAIRWAY. NIGHT (PAST)

Wearing the plastic overalls, the gloves, the face mask,
Frances climbs the final set of stairs.

The door to Alex's apartment opens. She enters --

INT. ALEX'S APARTMENT. HALLWAY. NIGHT (PAST)

The agents inside Alex's apartment are wearing forensic overalls just like Frances.

The atmosphere, unlike downstairs, is hushed and precise.

They indicate the ladder up to the attic.

Frances climbs up --

INT. ALEX'S APARTMENT. ATTIC. NIGHT (PAST)

The attic has not yet been staged.

But we see some of the 'props' - the old televisions, the furniture, the sex toys - in a corner, waiting.

The attic is a raw empty space. Not gloomy and dark. Brightly lit. Stark-white-lights.

The boarding school trunk is flat, not on its side. A different position to how Danny discovered it.

Frances walks towards it.

At the trunk, she crouches down, placing her plastic covered hands on the top. About to speak --

The agent overseeing the attic moves forward, showing Frances a stop watch, counting down.

Five minutes left.

Frances waits with her sleeping child.

INT. BOARDING SCHOOL TRUNK. ATTIC. NIGHT (PAST)

Alex folded up inside the trunk, limbs compressed.

The sedatives are wearing off. He opens his eyes.

He's dripping in sweat. The oxygen levels are already low. His breath is shallow.

He has no idea where he is. He explores the texture of the trunk with his fingers.

From confusion to panic.

He attempts to kick but his legs can't stretch out. He tries to punch but his arms can't extend.

He rocks back and forth, turning the trunk on its side, upside down. Nightmarish rotations.

But the case is sturdy. Unbreakable.

He hears --

                    FRANCES (V.O.)
          Alistair!

Alex stops moving, panting with exertion. He listens.

                    FRANCES (V.O.)
          Alistair?

He's relieved.

                    ALEX
          Frances?

INT. ALEX'S APARTMENT. ATTIC. NIGHT (PAST)

Frances places her plastic-gloved-hands on the trunk at
the place where she can see the curve of Alex's body.

                    FRANCES
          Alistair.

INT. BOARDING SCHOOL TRUNK. ATTIC. NIGHT (PAST)

Alex sees her hand through the material. He touches it.
Their hands together yet separated by the trunk.

INT. ALEX'S APARTMENT. ATTIC. NIGHT (PAST)

Frances touching the trunk.

The agent stands over her, watching carefully.

                    FRANCES
          Listen to me carefully. We don't
          have much time. You're in a great
          deal of trouble. But there's a way
          out. Do you understand?

She waits, nervously.

INT. BOARDING SCHOOL TRUNK. ATTIC. NIGHT (PAST)

Alex dripping in sweat. He realizes Frances is working
with the agencies. Sadness comes over him.

                    FRANCES (V.O.)
          Alistair!

                    ALEX
          I understand.

INT. ALEX'S APARTMENT. ATTIC. NIGHT (PAST)

Frances trying to sound calm and collected, but in
reality frantic and fearful.

>   FRANCES
>   It's all been arranged. This is a
>   warning.
>   (voice breaks)
>   You'll go to America, to work, for
>   a few years. A new identity. A new
>   name. A new life. But you must
>   leave everything behind. This
>   project...

A flash of frustration and anger.

>   FRANCES (CONT'D)
>   What were you thinking?

She quickly adjusts, back to the solution.

>   FRANCES (CONT'D)
>   All you have to do is say yes.
>   You'll be flown tonight. No bags.
>   No belongings. All you have to do
>   is agree, Alistair. All you have
>   to do is agree.

INT. BOARDING SCHOOL TRUNK. ATTIC. NIGHT (PAST)

Alex listens. He considers.

>   ALEX
>   I agree.

>   FRANCES (V.O.)
>   Will you go to America?

>   ALEX
>   I'll go.

>   FRANCES (V.O.)
>   You have to say it clearly.

>   ALEX
>   I'll go to America.

>   FRANCES (V.O.)
>   Will you destroy your research?

>   ALEX
>   I'll destroy it.

>   FRANCES (V.O.)
>   And never work on it again?

>   ALEX
>   And never work on it again.

>   FRANCES (V.O.)
>   You'll leave it all behind?

Alex pauses, realizing what she is referring to.

EXT. VAUXHALL BRIDGE. DAWN (PAST)

The moment on the bridge. From Alex's point of view.

Handsome, forlorn, lost, Danny, absorbed in the pantomime of his thoughts.

Alex watching, a few metres away.

Danny eventually realizing he's being watched.

He turns. *That first look.*

INT. ALEX'S APARTMENT. ATTIC. NIGHT (PAST)

Frances nervous, her face close to the trunk.

>   FRANCES
>   (desperate)
>   Alistair, you must never make
>   contact with anyone from this life
>   again?

INT. BOARDING SCHOOL TRUNK. ATTIC. NIGHT (PAST)

Alex contemplates.

>   ALEX
>   (a whisper)
>   His name is Danny.

>   FRANCES (V.O.)
>   Alistair?

>   ALEX
>   I'll never speak to him again.

INT. ALEX'S APARTMENT. ATTIC. NIGHT (PAST)

Frances, by the trunk, crying with relief. About to unlock the trunk when the agent stops her.

He gestures that he'll deal with it. She needs to go downstairs. She nods.

But before Frances goes, she returns to the trunk, and pulls down her surgical mask.

>   FRANCES
>   It will be a new start for us too.
>   You'll hate me. For a while. But I
>   love you very much.

INT. BOARDING SCHOOL TRUNK. ATTIC. NIGHT (PAST)

Alex hears those words.

>   ALEX
>   I love you too.

INT. ALEX'S APARTMENT. ATTIC. NIGHT (PAST)

Frances, at the stairs, glances back --

She descends.

INT. ALEX'S APARMTENT. HALLWAY. NIGHT (PAST)

The waiting agent gestures for Frances to go to the door.

INT. ALEX'S APARTMENT BUILDING. STAIRWAY. NIGHT (PAST)

Frances descends to the first floor apartment. Feeling overwhelming relief. She enters --

INT. SECURITY SERVICE APARTMENT. NIGHT (PAST)

All the equipment has been set up to decipher Alex's responses. They're playing back the exchange.

The computer is analyzing his voice. Tone. Stress.

There's a buttonhole camera inside the trunk: focused on Alex's facial expressions.

It maps the lines in his skin. The direction of his eyes. Pupil dilation. The flutter of his eyelids.

Frances is puzzled by the process, as she watches.

>   ALEX (ON SCREEN)
>   I'll go to America.

>   FRANCES (ON SCREEN)
>   Will you destroy your research?

>   ALEX (ON SCREEN)
>   I'll destroy it.

>   FRANCES (ON SCREEN)
> And never work on it again?

>   ALEX (ON SCREEN)
> And never work on it again.

>   FRANCES (ON SCREEN)
> You'll leave it all behind?

On screen we see Alex pausing, realizing what she's euphemistically referring to.

On screen we see Frances nervous, her face by the trunk, waiting for the answer she desperately wants.

>   FRANCES (ON SCREEN) (CONT'D)
>   (desperate)
> Alistair, you must never make
> contact with anyone from this life
> again?

>   ALEX (ON SCREEN)
>   (a whisper)
> His name is Danny.

>   FRANCES (ON SCREEN)
> Alistair?

>   ALEX (ON SCREEN)
> I'll never speak to him again.

>   FRANCES (ON SCREEN)
> It will be a new start for us too.
> You'll hate me. For a while. But I
> love you very much.

>   ALEX (ON SCREEN)
> I love you too.

The computer continues to process the information. Running Alex's own programme on his responses.

Fear creeps into Frances's expression.

The computer returns a verdict - statement by statement.

Never work on research again. **A lie.**

Leave it all behind. **A lie.**

Never make contact with Danny. **A lie.**

And finally, whether he loves Frances. **A lie.**

>   FRANCES
> It's wrong.

The agents simply look at her. Inscrutable.

FRANCES (CONT'D)
It's wrong!

Making no progress. She changes tack.

FRANCES (CONT'D)
I'll go back up. I'll talk to him.
I'll explain it. He'll listen.

An agent moves behind her, blocking the door.

There are no second chances.

FRANCES (CONT'D)
He didn't understand, that's all.
I can persuade him. He'll listen
to me. He'll listen to me!

Becoming agitated, she turns, to force her way out.

FRANCES (CONT'D)
Let me speak to him!

The agent doesn't move.

FRANCES (CONT'D)
Let me speak to my son!

Another agent secures her.

Frances fights. She fights as if her own life depends on
it. She's strong. And it's hard to contain her.

FRANCES (CONT'D)
My son!

Several agents overwhelm her. One agent readies a needle.

INT/EXT. OFFICIAL CAR / MOTORWAY. NIGHT (PAST)

Frances is on the back seat. She opens her eyes, groggy,
barely able to move. Two agents are driving her home.

EXT. MANSION. GROUNDS. DAWN (PAST)

Frances steps out of the car. Woozy with the journey and
the drugs and grief. She drops to her knees.

Charles is waiting on the steps. He does not comfort her.
He does not speak.

The car drives off.

The groundsman stands watch.

Frances, wretched, left on the ground, on her knees, before the mansion, not staring at Charles.

Staring at the Nanny, in one of the windows.

FLASH BACK TO:

INT. MANSION. SECRET STUDY. NIGHT (PRESENT)

Frances has finished her story. With emotion and grief.

Danny has listened. With emotion and grief.

The nanny, subservient. With emotion and grief.

Frances is expecting fury and anger and outrage from Danny. But he has another idea.

> DANNY
> I know a police officer.

Frances is dismissive in a weary kind of way.

> FRANCES
> You fail to grasp what has been done to you. The fact you know the truth is irrelevant. No one will publish anything you say. No one will investigate your claims.
> (fundamentally)
> *No one will believe you.*

> DANNY
> But they'll believe you.

The idea that she could go to the police has never even crossed Frances's mind.

> DANNY (CONT'D)
> You're his mother.

Danny says that to both of them.

The Nanny looks up, seduced by the idea. She looks at the back of Frances's head, waiting for her decision.

> DANNY (CONT'D)
> What do you owe them?

Frances toys with the notion.

> DANNY (CONT'D)
> You gave them your son?

The prospect flutters through Frances's thoughts with redemptive energy.

> FRANCES
> (intrigued)
> Tell me... Were I to agree... What
> would we do?

> DANNY
> We'd tell the truth.

Frances is tempted. Desperately so. Behind her, the nanny
is also desperate for her to say yes.

But it is as though this oppressive mansion speaks to
her, reminding her of her place. Frances shakes her head.

> FRANCES
> I can't.

Danny directs his attention to the Nanny. It infuriates
Frances. She doesn't turn around, speaking for the Nanny.

> FRANCES (CONT'D)
> She can't.

> DANNY
> (to the nanny)
> I want to hear it from you.

> FRANCES
> You've heard it from me.

Danny doesn't give up, addressing the Nanny.

> DANNY
> His name was Alex. His real name.
> The name you gave him.

> FRANCES
> She won't help you.

> DANNY
> (referring to
> Frances)
> She renamed him. But you let it
> slip, didn't you? Deliberately?

> FRANCES
> She can't help you.

Wracked with grief and powerlessness, tormented, the
nanny can't take any more.

She hurries out, through the door, into the grounds -
outside - into the darkness of the night.

The door remains open, wind gusts through the kitchen,
rattling plates and pots, extinguishing the blue flame.

> FRANCES (CONT'D)
> It's time you left.

Danny goes to the door, looking after the Nanny.

> FRANCES (CONT'D)
> She's gone.

INT. MANSION. STAIRWAY. NIGHT

Danny sadly follows Frances up the stairs. He has everything. He has nothing.

INT. MANSION. CORRIDOR. NIGHT

A dark corridor. Danny follows Frances, trying to think of what he can say, to snatch victory from defeat.

But she flows through this mansion, decision fixed, rigid in her determination. And Danny can only follow.

INT/EXT. MANSION. HALLWAY / GARDEN NIGHT

Danny and Frances turn into a corridor and both come to an immediate stop.

Unlike the previous corridor, which was dark and gloomy, this corridor is bright, with a fierce orange light.

Danny and Frances, surprised, move to the window --

EXT. MANSION. MAZE. NIGHT

From the centre of the maze, geometrically precise lines of fire forming. It's the route out of the maze.

There's a delay. And then a new line of fire is lit.

INT. MANSION. HALLWAY. NIGHT

The geometric lines of fire reflected in the window.

Danny and Frances watch, silent, stunned.

EXT. MANSION. MAZE. NIGHT

The nanny appears at the entrance to the maze, throwing down a petrol can.

She lights the last strip of hedge. And now the complete route out of the maze burns.

INT. MANSION. HALLWAY. NIGHT

As the maze burns in the window, Danny looks to Frances,
watching her expression.

She's engrossed in this fire, as if it were a piece of
theatre, her eyes alive, again, to possibilities.

EXT. MANSION. MAZE. NIGHT

Grief stricken, powerless, the nanny drops to her knees
before this fire memorial to her son.

Ignoring her, the groundsman sets about trying to
extinguish the fire. But it's out of control.

EXT. MANSION. HALLWAY. NIGHT

Geometric lines of fire reflected in the glass. Danny
looking at Frances.

> DANNY
> For her son.

Frances turns to him - her expression faltering.

> DANNY (CONT'D)
> All she could do.

Unsteady, her certainty shattered, it takes a supreme
effort to turn her back on the fire.

Frances continues towards the front doors.

Danny watches her go. Angry & frustrated.

> DANNY (CONT'D)
> It was all she could do!

His voice echoes around the space.

INT. MANSION. GRAND HALLWAY. NIGHT

Frances stands by the door, holding it open. Her stance
is formal. She's recovered her poise. And her decision.

Danny stands before her.

> DANNY
> Just a stupid boy?

Frances looks him the eye. Ice cold. Danny sees nothing
in those eyes. No hope. No chance.

EXT. MANSION. GROUNDS. SUNRISE

Danny walks to his car.

When he looks back, the front door is shut. Without a goodbye. In haste. Just as his own mother did.

INT/EXT. CAR / MANSION GROUNDS. SUNRISE

Danny at the wheel. Exhausted. Emotional.

He leaves with nothing.

Suddenly the car door opens and Frances gets into the passenger seat. She shuts the door.

She seems breathless and excited. She looks in the rear view mirror at the fire and smoke. She looks at Danny.

> FRANCES
> Let's burn them down for real.

Elated, giddy, younger, lighter, happier.

Danny in disbelief. He does nothing.

> FRANCES (CONT'D)
> We should probably 'hurry'.

Danny starts the car.

And he drives, picking at speed, excited, nervous, unsure what is happening or about to happen.

He checks on Frances.

Her expression is of great happiness & warmth.

Danny looking at the mansion in the rear view mirror.

No one seems to be after them.

Frances seems happy, as happy as when Alex held her hand.

Danny looks forward. The path is clear. Escape certain.

And then, the Groundsman steps out, at the end of the drive, holding a hunting shotgun.

The groundsman raises the gun, takes aim.

In an attempt to avoid the shot, Danny swerves.

The groundsman fires, knocking out the front tyre, which explodes in a shower of rubber.

The car loses control, off the drive, through the grass, shuddering to a stop.

Frances has knocked her head on the dashboard. Blood runs down her forehead. A superficial injury.

The Groundsman approaches, reloading.

But he simply stands, and waits.

Charles, dressed for a walk in the country, gets into the back seat of the car, addressing Frances.

> CHARLES
> Frances Mary Taylor.

She touches her head, looking at her bloody fingertip.

> FRANCES
> Yes.
> > (beat)
> Yes.
> > (beat)
> Yes.

Charles gets out.

Frances turns to Danny.

> FRANCES (CONT'D)
> I see why Alistair fell in love
> with you.

She steps out of the car.

After a beat, Danny also steps out.

EXT. MANSION. GROUNDS. DRIVEWAY. NIGHT

The Groundsman stands over them. Clearly he's a security agent, sent to guard the couple.

With blood streaming down her face, Frances addresses this agent, with Lady of the Manor formality, as though he were staff, an illusion he is happy to maintain.

> FRANCES
> You'll change his tyre?

The groundsman nods.

Charles and Frances head back towards the mansion.

Danny watches them go.

EXT. MANSION. GROUNDS. DRIVEWAY. NIGHT

Danny sits on the gravel, watching as the groundsman
replaces the front tyre he shot out. It's surreal.

And then Danny sees smoke - a fire is burning behind the
mansion. Plumes of acrid-dense smoke.

Danny stands. He walks towards it, speed increasing until
he's running, and running fast.

EXT. MANSION. GROUNDS MAZE. NIGHT

Danny runs around the mansion, arriving at the maze.

It's on fire. The desiccated hedgerow bushes burning.

Danny loops round to the entrance.

He enters the burning maze.

EXT. MANSION. MAZE. NIGHT

Danny crouched, through the burning maze.

Cans of petrol deposited like bread-crumbs.

Some of the hedges are completely ablaze, others less so.
Danny follows the trail of fire, until he reaches   --

EXT. MANSION. CENTRE OF MAZE. NIGHT

Danny enters the centre of the maze, seeing the nanny,
seated beside the statue of the limbless male angel.

She's looking at the mansion while the maze burns.

Danny turns to see --

At the window to Alex's bedroom stand both Charles and
Frances, watching the fire.

Danny also watches the maze burn.

Everyone seems quite calm. As though this were normal.

In the end, Danny sits beside the nanny. She takes his
hand, as she must have taken Alex's many times in the
past, and they watch the fire burn.

EXT. MANSION. CENTRE OF MAZE. DAWN

Sunrise.

The blackened bushes smoulder. Danny turns to the nanny.

                    DANNY
        You can't stay here?

She seems surprised by the idea.

                    NANNY
        Why not?

Danny thinks the charred maze is sufficient reply.

                    NANNY (CONT'D)
        I've worked in this house for
        twenty five years.

Danny still isn't convinced.

                    NANNY (CONT'D)
        These people prize loyalty above
        all else.

She stands.

                    NANNY (CONT'D)
        Everything will stay the same.
        We'll go back to how it was
        before. All of us, the same.
        Except for you.

She disappears into the maze.

However, after a moment, she returns.

                    NANNY (CONT'D)
        He's buried at St. Thomas's
        Church. It's not far...

And with that she disappears into the charred maze.

Danny looks up at the faceless anonymous statue.

INT/EXT. SCOTTIE'S CAR / MANSION. DAY

With the car fixed, a new tyre, Danny pulls out of the grass, back onto the gravel drive.

He stops - one last look in the rear view mirror.

Frances and Charles stand at the top of the steps.

Frances takes hold of Charles's hand. And they stand there, a couple.

The groundsman, still with his gun, to one side.

And at the window to the mansion is the Nanny.

Danny drives off.

EXT. ST THOMAS'S CHURCH. GRAVEYARD. DAY

A picturesque rural church.

Danny walks through the tombstones, searching.

He finds Alex's gravestone.

Engraved on it is the name 'Alistair'.

INT. ST. THOMAS'S CHURCH. DAY

Danny enters the church. The information. He finds a
comment card and a pen.

EXT. ST. THOMAS'S CHURCH. GRAVEYARD. DAY

Danny places the note on Alex's grave.

Written on it is:

"Alex - I found you - you found me - *love Danny*"

INT. SCOTTIE'S HOUSE. LIVING ROOM. DAY

Danny throws opens the blinds, sunlight floods in.

INT. SCOTTIE'S HOUSE. STUDY. DAY

Danny gets together pens and notebooks.

EXT. SCOTTIE'S FRONT GARDEN. DAY

Danny takes the bike from the garage. He sets off.

EXT. PRIMROSE HILL. PARK. DAY

Danny cycling down at speed, towards the city.

EXT. LONDON. DAY

Danny cycling through London.

EXT. UCL. MAIN QUAD. DAY

Danny locks up his bike. With his bag he walks towards
the entrance. The quad is crowded with students.

But we hold back. Not following him inside. The many other students weave in and out of frame.

In the distance, one among many, Danny climbs the steps. And enters the building.

He's gone.

We linger for a while, watching the other students on the steps and campus: the energy of hopes and ambitions.

END OF SERIES

Acknowledgements

These scripts wouldn't exist without Polly Hill. She believed in the project from the beginning and supported it through many difficult moments. She is the best friend a writer, or any creative could hope for. I owe her a great deal.

As we neared transmission, I remember discussing whether a story featuring a gay love story would result in us losing some of our potential audience. I didn't know how many, but my sense was that the loss would be significant. Polly was amazed by the notion and refused to accept it. When over three million people tuned in for the first episode, it encouraged me to be more optimistic — the world has changed. It's been a privilege to witness this love story being embraced by so many and I'd like to thank the BBC for making that possible.

On the subject of love, I have to pay special thanks to Ben Whishaw. He is a genius and he championed the show from an early stage, attracting an extraordinary cast who wanted to work with him. The part of Danny was written for him and in return he created the most wonderfully attractive and complex portrayal of a man struggling with the world. I defy anyone to watch his performance and not fall in love with him.

I'd also like to thank Michael Edelstein from NBC Universal. All shows need champions and he was steadfast in his belief that the show could be something special and that it was worth protecting. Without his support, the show as we know it, and this book, wouldn't exist. I will be forever grateful to him.

Working Title Television were behind the making of the show. I remember when I was a child, growing up, struggling with my own sexuality, watching their pioneering movie MY BEAUTIFUL LAUNDERETTE. Since the remote control was broken I sat close to the screen, finger loitering near the off button, ready to turn it off in case anyone should return home and discover what I was watching. It felt like a neat answer to that experience, bringing this show to them — the first ever thriller on British television headed by a gay love story.

Finally, on the production side, I'd like to thank Hilary Salmon, who came on as an executive producer for the BBC. It is rare to find people who care about a project as much as you do and who are able to handle it as delicately as though it were their own. She was brilliant and I owe her a tremendous debt of gratitude.

With regards to the production of this book, it's entirely down to Suzanne Baboneau and Ian Chapman, from S&S UK, both of whom thought we could produce a book that was more than a functional copy of the scripts but a celebration of the show, and everyone who worked so hard on it, which is why we're including some of the beautiful stills, and the fans' remarkable reactions. Suzanne and Ian's enthusiasm is endless and their support is always much appreciated. Thanks also to Laura Nolan at the Kuhn Projects Literary Agency in New York for expertly navigating all the complex rights issues and for championing this book.

The story behind *London Spy*
By Tom Rob Smith

Twenty years ago, when I was seventeen years old, I stood one night on the dangerous and decrepit former incarnation of the Hungerford pedestrian bridge which connects the north and south sides of the river Thames. The old bridge was narrow, grotty and afflicted with crime, in one horrific incident, a law student had been thrown to his death, and it wasn't a place to linger. But that night the bridge matched my state of mind and I looked out over the London skyline and asked, as though London were a wise mentor capable of answering back, whether life got any easier. I don't recall another occasion when I've seriously contemplated suicide but standing there, I realized that death would be the end of everything good, as well as everything bad. What I didn't realize at the time was that had I arrived at a different decision my suicide would've wound up as a statistic, engulfed by a much wider narrative of a society in which many young gay people struggle to cope. My life, which in reality, had been a largely happy one, full of love and potential, would've been rewritten in those troubled hours, as one of perpetual despair leading to that act. I'm very glad I lived to tell a different story but perhaps because of this moment I'm acutely aware of how our deaths can tell a story separate to the story of our lives.

Herein lies the premise for my first television drama series *London Spy*, a thriller which opens with Ben Whishaw's character Danny, standing on Lambeth Bridge, feeling low and wretched, and asking the London skyline whether life gets any easier. London answers him with a chance encounter, an early morning runner who stops to ask if he's okay — a question that can be both trivial and also profoundly human. So begins a love story that promises happiness for both. However, eight months into their relationship his lover is found dead in circumstances that appear to tell a story of a life entirely different to one that Danny has come to share with his partner. Danny's perfect love, which has rejuvenated him, is, in an instant, rewritten. He is no longer this man's partner but merely one of many nameless sexual hook ups, with a preference for extreme bondage, high risk kink fuelled by drugs and an appetite for exploring the outer limits of sensuality. In this death, Danny not only loses his lover, he loses their love story too, and so his battle begins for the truth, to find out what really happened, and to try and recover the story of their love and life together.

The question has been asked of me whether there are any parallels to the Gareth Williams case, the GCHQ operative found dead in his apartment in Pimlico. I should be clear at this point that this series is entirely a work of fiction, none of the characters are real. In addition, it isn't intended as a commentary on the police investigation, the security services, or what might have happened. I haven't sat through the evidence, or heard the testimonies, and I'm in no position to make a judgement. However, it is an indisputable fact that at the heart of the press, the public and indeed my interest in this case, is the question of whether his death told a story of his life, or whether his death was staged to tell a story that would disguise and distract us from his murder.

If it were a murder, the concepts behind its construction are not new. While researching another project some years back, I stumbled across a training manual allegedly drafted by the CIA and distributed to agents and operatives at the time of the Agency's 1954 covert coup in Guatemala, which ousted the democratically elected president Jacobo Arbenz Guzman. I cannot vouch for this document's authenticity, and there is so much misinformation in circulation, if it turned out to be another agency's attempt to smear the CIA, I wouldn't be surprised. Regardless, it remains a striking document for the ideas embedded in it. Here is a direct quote:

> 'For secret assassination ... the contrived accident is the most effective technique. When successfully executed it causes little excitement, and is only casually investigated'

We are now so immersed in paranoia and suspicion that an accident isn't sufficient to divert our attention — fundamentally we don't believe in coincidence, but we do believe in stories, or at least, we believe in stories that are well told. In order to make sure a death doesn't become a murder, the murderer must become a story teller. In a subsection of the manual, under the label "Techniques" it declares: "A subject's personal habits may be exploited to prepare him for a contrived accident of any kind." Which is to say, in order to create a plausible lie, you weave in elements of truth. I would go much further in my analysis of this approach, as with all story telling, it's important to have your audience in mind, which means understanding, or trying to, how they'd react to certain story elements. Prejudices are useful in this context because they're stories people believe without requiring any evidence. For example, the murder of a charity worker would be much less toxic if it was implied that he or she was embezzling money from the charity they worked for, after all, deep down we believe bad people get what they deserve, and people who flirt with the underworld of our society, do so at their peril.

In *London Spy*, Danny argues that storytelling of a different kind is at play. The death of his lover draws on my own very powerful fear that I've experienced throughout my teenage years, and adult life, that the intimacy I crave will ultimately be my destruction. At school I thought my attraction to the same sex would end my career before it had begun. Desire was sublimated, configured in my brain as a threat to my ambitions, my place in this world, and with the arrival of HIV/AIDS as a threat to my life. I reasoned that if I could convince myself that I was straight maybe I could convince other people too, as if sexuality were merely a matter of presentation. My thoughts were distorted by this self-appointed undercover operation to such an extent that it's taken many years to unpick the damage, indeed, perhaps some of the damage is not yet undone. So, in *London Spy*, when Danny finds love and intimacy, on a deeper level he fears it will end badly because that is the narrative lodged in his mind. For this very reason Danny does everything possible to avoid the pitfalls of a relationship ending badly — he promises to tell the truth, he avoids drugs, or excessive drink, he's faithful, committed, he's devoted. He does everything right. That is why Danny must fight, because that narrative of death and despair is from the past. Just as that old Hungerford bridge has been ripped down and replaced with a bridge where many linger and enjoy the view, we are in a new world, with new narratives. But as with anyone trying to tell a new story, a story previously untold, the stories of old have great weight behind them. What is worse, they often have some element of truth, and the battle is not as straightforward as Danny might think.

London Spy
Cast List and Production Credits

Series Directed by Jakob Verbruggen

Ben Whishaw	Danny (5 episodes, 2015)
Edward Holcroft	Alex (5 episodes, 2015)
Jim Broadbent	Scottie (5 episodes, 2015)
Zrinka Cvitesic	Sara (4 episodes, 2015)
Samantha Spiro	Detective Taylor (4 episodes, 2015)
Harriet Walter	Claire (3 episodes, 2015)
Josef Altin	Pavel (2 episodes, 2015)
Richard Cunningham	Danny's Lawyer (2 episodes, 2015)
Adrian Lester	Professor Marcus Shaw (2 episodes, 2015)
David Hayman	Mr. Turner (2 episodes, 2015)
Charlotte Rampling	Frances (2 episodes, 2015)

Lorraine Ashbourne	Mrs. Turner (2 episodes, 2015)
Nicolas Chagrin	Charles (2 episodes, 2015)
Priyanga Burford	Clinician (2 episodes, 2015)
Kate Dickie	Editor (1 episode, 2015)
Riccardo Scamarcio	Doppelganger (1 episode, 2015)
Michaela Coel	Journalist (1 episode, 2015)
Henry Goodman	Silversmith (1 episode, 2015)
James Copestake	Lead Party Guy (1 episode, 2015)
Sean McKee	Dealer (1 episode, 2015)
Tatsujiro Oto	Geisha (1 episode, 2015)
Grant Stimpson	Danny's Boss (1 episode, 2015)
Mark Gatiss	Rich (1 episode, 2015)
Lizzy McInnerny	Danny's Mother (1 episode, 2015)
David Meyer	Danny's Father (1 episode, 2015)
Antonia Campbell-Hughes	Magician (1 episode, 2015)
Steffan Donnelly	Raphael (1 episode, 2015)
Sam Kenyon	HIV Group Chair (1 episode, 2015)
Jay Benedict	Phone Voice (1 episode, 2015)
Deon Lee-Williams	Ryan (1 episode, 2015)
George Hewer	Restaurant Diner (1 episode, 2015)
Clarke Peters	The American (1 episode, 2015)
Heronimo Sehmi	Club Staff (1 episode, 2015)

James Fox	James (1 episode, 2015)
Matthew Stagg	Young Alex (1 episode, 2015)
Nicola Grier	Agent in the Attic (1 episode, 2015)
Oliver Messenger	Front of House Manager (1 episode, 2015)
Neil Alexander Smith	Nightclub Doorman (1 episode, 2015)
Richard Clark	Warehouse Worker (uncredited) (1 episode, 2015)
Svyatoslav Ketchin	Doctor (uncredited) (1 episode, 2015)

Series Produced by:

Tim Bevan	executive producer (5 episodes, 2015)
Charlotte Bloxham	line producer (5 episodes, 2015)
Eric Fellner	executive producer (5 episodes, 2015)
Guy Heeley	producer (5 episodes, 2015)
Polly Hill	executive producer (5 episodes, 2015)
Juliette Howell	executive producer (5 episodes, 2015)
Hilary Salmon	executive producer (5 episodes, 2015)
Tom Rob Smith	executive producer (5 episodes, 2015)